THE
VANISHED
MESSENGER

E. Phillips Oppenheim

The Vanished Messenger

E. Phillips Oppenheim

© 1st World Library – Literary Society, 2004
PO Box 2211
Fairfield, IA 52556
www.1stworldlibrary.org
First Edition

LCCN: 2005906463

Softcover ISBN: 1-4218-1521-4
Hardcover ISBN: 1-4218-1421-8
eBook ISBN: 1-4218-1621-0

Purchase *"The Vanished Messenger"*
as a traditional bound book at:
www.1stWorldLibrary.org/purchase.asp?ISBN=1-4218-1521-4

1st World Library Literary Society is a nonprofit organization dedicated to promoting literacy by:

- Creating a free internet library accessible from any computer worldwide.
- Hosting writing competitions and offering book publishing scholarships.

Readers interested in supporting literacy through sponsorship, donations or membership please contact:
literacy@1stworldlibrary.org
Check us out at: www.1stworldlibrary.ORG
and start downloading free ebooks today.

The Vanished Messenger
contributed by Tim, Ed & Rodney
in support of
1st World Library Literary Society

CHAPTER I

There were very few people upon Platform Number Twenty-one of Liverpool Street Station at a quarter to nine on the evening of April 2 - possibly because the platform in question is one of the most remote and least used in the great terminus. The station-master, however, was there himself, with an inspector in attendance. A dark, thick-set man, wearing a long travelling ulster and a Homburg hat, and carrying in his hand a brown leather dressing-case, across which was painted in black letters the name MR. JOHN P. DUNSTER, was standing a few yards away, smoking a long cigar, and, to all appearance absorbed in studying the advertisements which decorated the grimy wall on the other side of the single track. A couple of porters were seated upon a barrow which contained one solitary portmanteau. There were no signs of other passengers, no other luggage. As a matter of fact, according to the time-table, no train was due to leave the station or to arrive at it, on this particular platform, for several hours.

Down at the other end of the platform the wooden barrier was thrust back, and a porter with some luggage upon a barrow made his noisy approach. He was followed by a tall young man in a grey tweed suit and a straw hat on which were the colours of a famous cricket club.

The inspector watched them curiously. "Lost his way, I should think," he observed.

The station-master nodded. "It looks like the young man who missed the boat train," he remarked. "Perhaps he has come to beg a lift."

The young man in question made steady progress up the platform. His hands were thrust deep into the pockets of his coat, and his forehead was contracted in a frown. As he approached more closely, he singled out Mr. John P. Dunster, and motioning his porter to wait, crossed to the edge of the track and addressed him.

"Can I speak to you for a moment, sir?"

Mr. John P. Dunster turned at once and faced his questioner. He did so without haste - with a certain deliberation, in fact - yet his eyes were suddenly bright and keen. He was neatly dressed, with the quiet precision which seems as a rule to characterise the travelling American. He was apparently of a little less than middle-age, clean-shaven, broad-shouldered, with every appearance of physical strength. He seemed like a man on wires, a man on the alert, likely to miss nothing.

"Are you Mr. John P. Dunster?" the youth asked.

"I carry my visiting-card in my hand, sir," the other replied, swinging his dressing-case around. "My name is John P. Dunster."

The young man's expression was scarcely ingratiating. To a natural sullenness was added now the nervous

E. Phillips Oppenheim

distaste of one who approaches a disagreeable task.

"I want, if I may, to ask you a favour," he continued. "If you don't feel like granting it, please say no and I'll be off at once. I am on my way to The Hague. I was to have gone by the boat train which left half an hour ago. I had taken a seat, and they assured me that the train would not leave for at least ten minutes, as the mails weren't in. I went down the platform to buy some papers and stood talking for a moment or two with a man whom I know. I suppose I must have been longer than I thought, or they must have been quicker than they expected with the mailbags. Anyhow, when I came back the train was moving. They would not let me jump in. I could have done it easily, but that fool of an inspector over there held me."

"They are very strict in this country, I know."

Mr. Dunster agreed, without change of expression. "Please go on."

"I saw you arrive - just too late for the train. While I was swearing at the inspector, I heard you speak to the station-master. Since then I have made inquiries. I understand that you have ordered a special train to Harwich."

Mr. John P. Dunster said nothing, only his keen, clear eyes seemed all the time to be questioning this gloomy-looking but apparently harmless young man.

"I went to the station-master's office," the latter continued, "and tried to persuade them to let me ride in the guard's van of your special, but he made a stupid fuss about it, so I thought I'd better come to you. Can I beg a seat in your compartment, or anywhere in the train, as far as Harwich?"

Mr. Dunster avoided, for the moment, a direct reply. He had the air of a man who, whether reasonably or unreasonably, disliked the request which had been made to him.

"You are particularly anxious to cross to-night?" he asked.

"I am," the youth admitted emphatically. "I never ought to have risked missing the train. I am due at The Hague to-morrow."

Mr. John P. Dunster moved his position a little. The light from a rain-splashed gas lamp shone now full upon the face of his suppliant: a boy's face, which would have been pleasant and even handsome but for the discontented mouth, the lowering forehead, and a shadow in the eyes, as though, boy though he certainly was in years, he had already, at some time or another, looked upon the serious things of life. His nervousness, too, was almost grotesque. He had the air of disliking immensely this asking a favour from a stranger. Mr. Dunster appreciated all these things, but there were reasons which made him slow in granting the young man's request.

"What is the nature of your pressing business at The Hague?" he asked.

The youth hesitated.

"I am afraid," he said grimly, "that you will not think it of much importance. I am on my way to play in a golf tournament there."

"A golf tournament at The Hague!" Mr. Dunster repeated, in a slightly altered tone. "What is your name?"

"Gerald Fentolin."

Mr. Dunster stood quite still for a moment. He was possessed of a wonderful memory, and he was conscious at that moment of a subtle appeal to it. Fentolin! There was something in the name which seemed to him somehow associated with the things against which he was on guard. He stood with puzzled frown, reminiscent for several minutes, unsuccessful. Then he suddenly smiled, and moving underneath the gas lamp, shook open an evening paper which he had been carrying. He turned over the pages until he arrived at the sporting items. Here, in almost the first paragraph, he saw the name which had happened to catch his eye a moment or two before:

GOLF AT THE HAGUE

Among the entrants for the tournament which commences to-morrow, are several well-known English players, including Mr. Barwin, Mr. Parrott, Mr. Hillard and Mr. Gerald Fentolin.

Mr. Dunster folded up the newspaper and replaced it in his pocket. He turned towards the young man.

"So you're a golfer, are you?"

"I play a bit," was the somewhat indifferent reply.

Mr. Dunster turned to another part of the paper and pointed to the great black head-lines.

"Seems a queer thing for a young fellow like you to be worrying about games," he remarked. "I haven't been in this country more than a few hours, but I expected to find all the young men getting ready."

"Getting ready for what?"

"Why, to fight, of course," Mr. Dunster replied. "Seems pretty clear that there's an expeditionary force being fitted out, according to this evening's paper, somewhere up in the North Sea. The only Englishman I've spoken to on this side was willing to lay me odds that war would be declared within a week."

The young man's lack of interest was curious.

"I am not in the army," he said. "It really doesn't affect me."

Mr. Dunster stared at him.

"You'll forgive my curiosity," he said, "but say, is there nothing you could get into and fight if this thing came along?"

"Nothing at all, that I know of," the youth replied coolly. "War is an affair which concerns only the military and naval part of two countries. The civil population -"

"Plays golf, I suppose," Mr. Dunster interrupted. "Young man, I haven't been in England for some years, and you rather take my breath away. All the same, you can come along with me as far as Harwich."

The young man showed signs of some satisfaction. "I am very much obliged to you, sir," he declared. "I promise you I won't be in the way."

The station-master, who had been looking through a little pile of telegrams brought to him by a clerk from his office, now turned towards them. His expression was a little grave.

"Your special will be backing down directly, sir," he announced, "but I am sorry to say that we hear very bad accounts of the line. They say that this is only the fag-end of the storm that we are getting here, and that it's been raging for nearly twenty-four hours on the east coast. I doubt whether the Harwich boat will be able to put off."

"We must take our chance about that," Dunster remarked. "If the mail boat doesn't run, I presume there will be something else we can charter."

The station-master looked the curiosity which he did not actually express in words.

"Money will buy most things, nowadays, sir," he observed, "but if it isn't fit for our mail boat, it certainly isn't fit for anything else that can come into Harwich Harbour. However, you'll hear what they say when you get there."

Mr. Dunster nodded and relapsed into a taciturnity which was obviously one of his peculiarities. The young man strolled down the platform, and catching up with the inspector, touched him on the shoulder.

"Do you know who the fellow is?" he asked curiously. "It's awfully decent of him to let me go with him, but he didn't seem very keen about it."

The inspector shook his head.

"No idea, sir," he replied. "He drove up just two minutes after the train had gone, came straight into the office and ordered a special. Paid for it, too, in Bank of England notes before he went out. I fancy he's an American, and he gave his name as John P. Dunster."

The young man paused to light a cigarette.

"If he's an American, I suppose that accounts for it," he observed. "He must be in a precious hurry to get somewhere, though."

"A night like this, too!" the inspector remarked, with a shiver. "I wouldn't leave London myself unless I had to. They say there's a tremendous storm blowing on the east coast. Here comes the train, sir - just one saloon and the guard's van."

The little train backed slowly along the platform side. The engine was splashed with mud and soaking wet. The faces of the engine-driver and his companion shone from the dripping rain. The station-master held open the door of the saloon.

"You've a rough journey before you, sir," he said. "You'll catch the boat all right, though - if it goes. The mail train was very heavy to-night. You should catch her up this side of Colchester."

Mr. Dunster nodded.

E. Phillips Oppenheim

"I am taking this young gentleman with me," he announced shortly. "It seems that he, too, missed the train. I am much obliged to you, station-master, for your attention. Good night!"

They were about to start when Mr. Dunster once more let down the window.

"By the way," he said, "as it is such a wild night, you will oblige me very much if you will tell the engine-driver that there will be a five pound note for himself and his companion if we catch the mail. Inspector!"

The inspector touched his hat. The station-master had turned discreetly away. He had been an inspector himself once, and sovereigns had been useful to him, too. Then the train glided from the platform side, plunged with a scream through a succession of black tunnels, and with rapidly increasing speed faced the storm.

CHAPTER II

The young man sat on one side of the saloon and Mr. John P. Dunster on the other. Although both of them were provided with a certain amount of railway literature, neither of them made any pretence at reading. The older man, with his feet upon the opposite seat and his arms folded, was looking pensively through the rain-splashed window-pane into the impenetrable darkness. The young man, although he could not ignore his companion's unsociable instincts, was fidgety.

"There will be some floods out to-morrow," he remarked.

Mr. Dunster turned his head and looked across the saloon. There was something in the deliberate manner of his doing so, and his hesitation before he spoke, which seemed intended to further impress upon the young man the fact that he was not disposed for conversation.

"Very likely," was his sole reply.

Gerald Fentolin sighed as though he regretted his companion's taciturnity and a few minutes later strolled to the farther end of the saloon. He spent some time trying to peer through the streaming window into

E. Phillips Oppenheim

the darkness. He chatted for a few minutes with the guard, who was, however, in a bad temper at having had to turn out and who found little to say. Then he took one of his golf clubs from the bag and indulged in several half swings. Finally he stretched himself out upon one of the seats and closed his eyes.

"May as well try to get a nap," he yawned. "There won't be much chance on the steamer, if it blows like this."

Mr. Dunster said nothing. His face was set, his eyes were looking somewhere beyond the confines of the saloon in which he was seated. So they travelled for over an hour. The young man seemed to be dozing in earnest when, with a succession of jerks, the train rapidly slackened speed. Mr. Dunster let down the window. The interior of the carriage was at once thrown into confusion. A couple of newspapers were caught up and whirled around, a torrent of rain beat in. Mr. Dunster rapidly closed the window and rang the bell. The guard came in after a moment or two. His clothes were shiny from the wet; raindrops hung from his beard.

"What is the matter?" Mr. Dunster demanded. "Why are we waiting here?"

"There's a block on the line somewhere," the man replied. "Can't tell where exactly. The signals are against us; that's all we know at present."

They crawled on again in about ten minutes, stopped, and resumed their progress at an even slower rate. Mr. Dunster once more summoned the guard.

"Why are we travelling like this?" he asked impatiently. "We shall never catch the boat."

"We shall catch the boat all right if it runs, sir," the man assured him. "The mail is only a mile or two ahead of us; that's one reason why we have to go so slowly. Then the water is right over the line where we are now, and we can't get any news at all from the other side of Ipswich. If it goes on like this, some of the bridges will be down; that's what I'm afraid of."

Mr. Dunster frowned. For the first time he showed some signs of uneasiness.

"Perhaps," he muttered, half to himself, "a motor-car would have been better."

"Not on your life," his young companion intervened. "All the roads to the coast here cross no end of small bridges - much weaker affairs than the railway bridges. I bet there are some of those down already. Besides, you wouldn't be able to see where you were going, on a night like this."

"There appears to be a chance," Mr. Dunster remarked drily, "that you will have to scratch for your competition to-morrow."

"Also," the young man observed, "that you will have taken this special train for nothing. I can't fancy the Harwich boat going out a night like this."

Mr. Dunster relapsed into stony but anxious silence. The train continued its erratic progress, sometimes stopping altogether for a time, with whistle blowing repeatedly; sometimes creeping along the metals as though feeling its way to safety. At last, after a somewhat prolonged wait, the guard, whose hoarse voice they had heard on the platform of the small station in which they were standing, entered the carriage. With him came a gust of wind, once more sending the papers flying around the compartment. The rain dripped from his clothes on to the carpet. He had lost his hat, his hair was tossed with the wind, his face was bleeding from a slight wound on the temple.

"The boat train's just ahead of us, sir," he announced. "She can't get on any better than we can. We've just heard that there's a bridge down on the line between Ipswich and Harwich."

"What are we going to do, then?" Mr. Dunster demanded.

"That's just what I've come to ask you, sir," the guard replied. "The mail's going slowly on as far as Ipswich. I fancy they'll lie by there until the morning. The best thing that I can see is, if you're agreeable, to take you back to London. We can very likely do that all right, if we start at once."

Mr. Dunster, ignoring the man's suggestion, drew from one of the voluminous pockets of his ulster a small map. He spread it open upon the table before him and studied it attentively.

"If I cannot get to Harwich," he asked, "is there any possibility of keeping straight on and reaching Yarmouth?"

The guard hesitated.

"We haven't heard anything about the line from Ipswich to Norwich, sir," he replied, "but we can't very well change our course without definite instructions."

"Your definite instructions," Mr. Dunster reminded him drily, "were to take me to Harwich. You have been forced to depart from them. I see no harm in your adopting any suggestions I may have to make concerning our altered destination. I will pay the extra mileage, naturally."

"How far did you wish to go, sir?" the guard enquired.

"To Yarmouth," Mr. Dunster replied firmly. "If there are bridges down, and communication with Harwich is blocked, Yarmouth would suit me better than anywhere."

The guard shook his head.

"I couldn't go on that way, sir, without instructions."

"Is there a telegraph office at this station?" Mr. Dunster inquired.

"We can speak anywhere on the line," the guard replied.

"Then wire to the station-master at Liverpool Street," Mr. Dunster instructed. "You can get a reply from him in the course of a few minutes. Explain the situation and tell him what my wishes are."

The guard hesitated.

"It's a goodish way from here to Norwich," he

observed, "and for all we know -"

"When we left Liverpool Street Station," Mr. Dunster interrupted, "I promised five pounds each to you, the engine-driver, and his mate. That five pounds shall be made twenty-five if you succeed in getting me to the coast. Do your best for me."

The guard raised his hat and departed without another word.

"It will probably suit you better," Mr. Dunster continued, turning to his companion, "to leave me at Ipswich and join the mail."

The latter shook his head.

"I don't see that there's any chance, anyway, of my getting over in time now," he remarked. "If you'll take me on with you as far as Norwich, I can go quietly home from there!"

"You live in this part of the world, then?" Mr. Dunster asked.

The young man assented. Again there was a certain amount of hesitation in his manner.

"I live some distance the other side of Norwich," he said. "I don't want to sponge on you too much," he went on, "but if you're really going to stick it out and try and get there, I'd like to go on, too. I am afraid I can't offer to share the expense, but I'd work my passage if there was anything to be done."

Mr. Dunster drummed for a moment upon the table

with his fingers. All the time the young man had been speaking, his eyes had been studying his face. He turned now once more to his map.

"It was my idea," he said, "to hire a steam trawler from Yarmouth. If I do so, you can, if you wish, accompany me so far as the port at which we may land in Holland. On the other hand, to be perfectly frank with you, I should prefer to go alone. There will be, no doubt, a certain amount of risk in crossing to-night. My own business is of importance. A golf tournament, how-ever, is scarcely worth risking your life for, is it?"

"Oh, I don't know about that!" the young man replied grimly. "I fancy I should rather like it. Let's see whether we can get on to Norwich, anyhow, shall we? We may find that there are bridges down on that line."

They relapsed once more into silence. Presently the guard reappeared.

"Instructions to take you on to Yarmouth, if possible, sir," he announced, "and to collect the mileage at our destination."

"That will be quite satisfactory," Mr. Dunster agreed. "Let us be off, then, as soon as possible." Presently they crawled on. They passed the boat train in Ipswich Station, where they stayed for a few moments. Mr. Dunster bought wine and sandwiches, and his companion followed his example. Then they continued their journey. An hour or more passed; the storm showed no signs of abatement. Their speed now rarely exceeded ten or fifteen miles an hour. Mr. Dunster smoked all the time, occasionally rubbing the window-pane and trying to look out. Gerald Fentolin slept fitfully.

"Have you any idea where we are?" Mr. Dunster asked once.

The boy cautiously let down the window a little way. With the noise of the storm came another sound, to which he listened for a moment with puzzled face: a dull, rumbling sound like the falling of water. He closed the window, breathless.

"I don't think we are far from Norwich. We passed Forncett, anyhow, some time ago."

"Still raining?"

"In torrents! I can't see a yard ahead of me. I bet we get some floods after this. I expect they are out now, if one could only see."

They crept on. Suddenly, above the storm, they heard what sounded at first like the booming of a gun, and then a shrill whistle from some distance ahead. They felt the jerk as their brakes were hastily applied, the swaying of the little train, and then the crunching of earth beneath them, the roar of escaping steam as their engine ploughed its way on into the road bed.

"Off the rails!" the boy cried, springing to his feet. "Hold on tightly, sir. I'd keep away from the window."

The carriage swayed and rocked. Suddenly a telegraph post seemed to come crashing through the window and the polished mahogany panels. The young man escaped it by leaping to one side. It caught Mr. Dunster, who had just risen to his feet, upon the forehead. There was a crash all around of splitting glass, a further shock. They were both thrown off their feet. The light was suddenly extinguished. With the crashing of glass, the splitting of timber - a hideous, tearing sound - the wrecked saloon, dragging the engine half-way over with it, slipped down a low embankment and lay on its side, what remained of it, in a field of turnips.

E. Phillips Oppenheim

CHAPTER III

As the young man staggered to his feet, he had somehow a sense of detachment, as though he were commencing a new life, or had suddenly come into a new existence. Yet his immediate surroundings were charged with ugly reminiscences. Through a great gap in the ruined side of the saloon the rain was tearing in. As he stood up, his head caught the fragments of the roof. He was able to push back the wreckage with ease and step out. For a moment he reeled, as he met the violence of the storm. Then, clutching hold of the side of the wreck, he steadied himself. A light was moving back and forth, close at hand. He cried out weakly: "Hullo!"

A man carrying a lantern, bent double as he made his way against the wind, crawled up to them. He was a porter from the station close at hand.

"My God!" he exclaimed. "Any one alive here?"

"I'm all right," Gerald muttered, "at least, I suppose I am. What's it all - what's it all about? We've had an accident."

The porter caught hold of a piece of the wreckage with which to steady himself.

"Your train ran right into three feet of water," he answered. "The rails had gone - torn up. The telegraph line's down."

"Why didn't you stop the train?"

"We were doing all we could," the man retorted gloomily. "We weren't expecting anything else through to-night. We'd a man along the line with a lantern, but he's just been found blown over the embankment, with his head in a pool of water. Any one else in your carriage?"

"One gentleman travelling with me," Gerald answered. "We'd better try to get him out. What about the guard and engine-driver?"

"The engine-driver and stoker are both alive," the porter told him. "I came across them before I saw you. They're both knocked sort of sillylike, but they aren't much hurt. The guard's stone dead."

"Where are we?"

"A few hundred yards from Wymondham. Let's have a look for the other gentleman."

Mr. John P. Dunster was lying quite still, his right leg doubled up, and a huge block of telegraph post, which the saloon had carried with it in its fall, still pressing against his forehead. He groaned as they dragged him out and laid him down upon a cushion in the shelter of the wreckage.

"He's alive all right," the porter remarked. "There's a doctor on the way. Let's cover him up quick and wait."

E. Phillips Oppenheim

"Can't we carry him to shelter of some sort?" Gerald proposed.

The man shook his head. Speech of any sort was difficult. Even with his lips close to the other's ears, he had almost to shout.

"Couldn't be done," he replied. "It's all one can do to walk alone when you get out in the middle of the field, away from the shelter of the embankment here. There's bits of trees flying all down the lane. Never was such a night! Folks is fair afraid of the morning to see what's happened. There's a mill blown right over on its side in the next field, and the man in charge of it lying dead. This poor chap's bad enough."

Gerald, on all fours, had crept back into the compartment. The bottle of wine was smashed into atoms. He came out, dragging the small dressing-case which his companion had kept on the table before him. One side of it was dented in, but the lock, which was of great strength, still held.

"Perhaps there's a flask somewhere in this dressing-case," Gerald said. "Lend me a knife."

Strong though it had been, the lock was already almost torn out from its foundation. They forced the spring and opened it. The porter turned his lantern on the widening space. Just as Gerald was raising the lid very slowly to save the contents from being scattered by the wind, the man turned his head to answer an approaching hail. Gerald raised the lid a little higher and suddenly closed it with a bang.

"There's folks coming at last!" the porter exclaimed,

turning around excitedly. "They've been a time and no mistake. The village isn't a quarter of a mile away. Did you find a flask, sir?"

Gerald made no answer. The dressing-case once more was closed, and his hand pressed upon the lid. The porter turned the light upon his face and whistled softly.

"You're about done yourself, sir," he remarked. "Hold up."

He caught the young man in his arms. There was another roar in Gerald's ears besides the roar of the wind. He had never fainted in his life, but the feeling was upon him now - a deadly sickness, a swaying of the earth. The porter suddenly gave a little cry.

"If I'm not a born idiot!" he exclaimed, drawing a bottle from the pocket of his coat with his disengaged hand. "There's whisky here. I was taking it home to the missis for her rheumatism. Now, then."

He drew the cork from the bottle with his teeth and forced some of the liquid between the lips of the young man. The voices now were coming nearer and nearer. Gerald made a desperate effort.

"I am all right," he declared. "Let's look after him."

They groped their way towards the unconscious man, Gerald still gripping the dressing-case with both hands. There were no signs of any change in his condition, but he was still breathing heavily. Then they heard a shout behind, almost in their ears. The porter staggered to his feet.

"It's all right now, sir!" he exclaimed. "They've brought blankets and a stretcher and brandy. Here's a doctor, sir."

A powerful-looking man, hatless, and wrapped in a great ulster, moved towards them.

"How many are there of you?" he asked, as he bent over Mr. Dunster.

"Only we two," Gerald replied. "Is my friend badly hurt?"

"Concussion," the doctor announced. "We'll take him to the village. What about you, young man? Your face is bleeding, I see."

"Just a cut," Gerald faltered; "nothing else."

"Lucky chap," the doctor remarked. "Let's get him to shelter of some sort. Come along. There's an inn at the corner of the lane there."

They all staggered along, Gerald still clutching the dressing-case, and supported on the other side by an excited and somewhat incoherent villager.

"Such a storm as never was," the latter volunteered. "The telegraph wires are all down for miles and miles. There won't be no trains running along this line come many a week, and as for trees - why, it's as though some one had been playing ninepins in Squire Fellowes's park. When the morning do come, for sure there will be things to be seen. This way, sir. Be careful of the gate."

They staggered along down the lane, climbing once over a tree which lay across the lane and far into the adjoining field. Soon they were joined by more of the villagers, roused from their beds by rumours of terrible happenings. The little, single-storey, ivy-covered inn was all lit up and the door held firmly open. They passed through the narrow entrance and into the stone-flagged barroom, where the men laid down their stretcher. As many of the villagers as could crowd in filled the passage. Gerald sank into a chair. The sudden absence of wind was almost disconcerting. He felt himself once more in danger of fainting. He was only vaguely conscious of drinking hot milk, poured from a jug by a red-faced and sympathetic woman. Its restorative effect, however, was immediate and wonderful. The mist cleared from before his eyes, his brain began to work. Always in the background the horror and the shame were there, the shame which kept his hand pressed with unnatural strength upon the broken lock of that dressing-case. He sat a little apart from the others and listened. Above the confused murmur of voices he could hear the doctor's comment and brief orders, as he rose to his feet after examining the unconscious man.

"An ordinary concussion," he declared. "I must get round and see the engine-driver now. They have got him in a shed by the embankment. I'll call in again later on. Let's have one more look at you, young man."

He glanced at the cut on Gerald's forehead, noted the access of colour in his cheeks, and nodded.

"Born to be hanged, you were," he pronounced. "You've had a marvellous escape. I'll be in again presently. No need to worry about your friend. He

E. Phillips Oppenheim

looks as though he'd got a mighty constitution. Light my lantern, Brown. Two of you had better come with me to the shed. It's no night for a man to be wandering about alone."

He departed, and many of the villagers with him. The landlady sat down and began to weep.

"Such a night! Such a night!" she exclaimed, wringing her hands. "And there's the doctor talks about putting the poor gentleman to bed! Why, the roof's off the back part of the house, and not a bedroom in the place but mine and John's, and the rain coming in there in torrents. Such a night! It's the judgment of the Lord upon us! That's what it is - the judgment of the Lord!"

"Judgment of the fiddlesticks!" her husband growled. "Can't you light the fire, woman? What's the good of sitting there whining?"

"Light the fire," she repeated bitterly, "and the chimney lying out in the road! Do you want to suffocate us all, or is the beer still in your head? It's your evil doings, Richard Budden, and others like you, that have brought this upon us. If Mr. Wembley would but come in and pray!"

Her husband scoffed. He was dressed only in his shirt and trousers, his hair rough, his braces hanging down behind.

"Come in and pray!" he repeated. "Not he! Not Mr. Wembley! He's safe tucked up in his bed, shivering with fear, I'll bet you. He's not getting his feet wet to save a body or lend a hand here. Souls are his job. You let the preacher alone, mother, and tell us what we're going to do with this gentleman."

"The Lord only knows!" she cried, wringing her hands.

"Can I hire a motor-car from anywhere near?" Gerald asked.

"There's motor-cars, right enough," the innkeeper replied, "but not many as would be fools enough to take one out. You couldn't see the road, and I doubt if one of them plaguey things would stir in this storm."

"Such nonsense as you talk, Richard Budden!" his wife exclaimed sharply. "It's twenty minutes past three of the clock, and there's light coming on us fast. If so be as the young gentleman knows folks round about here, or happens to live nigh, why shouldn't he take one of them motor-cars and get away to some decent place? It'll be better for the poor gentleman than lying here in a house smitten by the Lord."

Gerald rose stiffly to his feet. An idea was forming in his brain. His eyes were bright. He looked at the body of John Dunster upon the floor, and felt once more in his pocket.

"How far off is the garage?" he asked.

"It's right across the way," the innkeeper replied, "a speculation of Neighbour Martin's, and a foolish one it do seem to me. He's two cars there, and one he lets to the Government for delivering the mails."

Gerald felt in his pocket and produced a sovereign.

"Give this," he said, "to any man you can find who will

go across there and bring me a car - the most powerful they've got, if there's any difference. Tell them I'll pay well. This - my friend will be much better at home with me than in a strange place when he comes to his senses."

"It's sound common sense," the woman declared. "Be off with you, Richard."

The man was looking at the coin covetously, but his wife pushed him away.

"It's not a sovereign you'll be taking from the gentleman for a little errand like that," she insisted sharply. "He shall pay us for what he's had when he goes, and welcome, and if so be that he's willing to make it a sovereign, to include the milk and the brandy and the confusion we've been put to this night, well and good. It's a heavy reckoning, maybe, but the night calls for it. We'll see about that afterwards. Get along with you, I say, Richard."

"I'll be wet through," the man muttered.

"And serve you right!" the woman exclaimed. "If there's a man in this village to-night whose clothes are dry, it's a thing for him to be ashamed of."

The innkeeper reluctantly departed. They heard the roar of the wind as the door was opened and closed. The woman poured out another glass of milk and brought it to Gerald.

"A godless man, mine," she said grimly. "If so happen as Mr. Wembley had come to these parts years ago, I'd have seen myself in my grave before I'd have married a publican. But it's too late now. We're mostly too late about the things that count in this world. So it's your friend that's been stricken down, young man. A well-living man, I hope?"

Gerald shivered ever so slightly. He drank the milk, however. He felt that he might need his strength.

"What train might you have been on?" the woman continued. "There's none due on this line that we knew of. David Bass, the station-master, was here but two hours ago and said he'd finished for the night, and praised the Lord for that. The goods trains had all been stopped at Ipswich, and the first passenger train was not due till six o'clock."

Gerald shook his head with an affectation of weariness.

"I don't know," he replied. "I don't remember anything about it. We were hours late, I think."

The woman was looking down at the unconscious man. Gerald rose slowly to his feet and stood by her side. The face of Mr. John P. Dunster, even in unconsciousness, had something in it of strength and purpose. The shape of his head, the squareness of his jaws, the straightness of his thick lips, all seemed to speak of a hard and inflexible disposition. His hair was coal black, coarse, and without the slightest sprinkling of grey. He had the neck and throat of a fighter. But for that single, livid, blue mark across his forehead, he carried with him no signs of his accident. He was a little inclined to be stout. There was a heavy gold chain stretched across his waist-coat. From where he lay, the shining handle of his revolver protruded from his hip, pocket.

E. Phillips Oppenheim

"Sakes alive!" the woman muttered, as she looked down. "What does he carry a thing like that for - in a peaceful country, too!"

"It was just an idea of his," Gerald answered. "We were going abroad in a day or two. He was always nervous. If you like, I'll take it away."

He stooped down and withdrew it from the unconscious man's pocket. He started as he discovered that it was loaded in every chamber.

"I can't bear the sight of them things," the woman declared. "It's the men of evil ways, who've no trust in the Lord, who need that sort of protection."

They heard the door pushed open, the howl of wind down the passage, and the beating of rain upon the stone flags. Then it was softly closed again. The landlord staggered into the room, followed by a young man.

"This 'ere is Mr. Martin's chaffer," he announced. "You can tell him what you want yerself."

Gerald turned almost eagerly towards the newcomer.

"I want to go to the other side of Holt," he said, "and get my friend - get this gentleman away from here - get him home, if possible. Can you take me?"

The chauffeur looked doubtful.

"I'm afraid of the roads, sir," he replied. "There's talk about many bridges down, and trees, and there's floods out everywhere. There's half a foot of water, even, across the village street now. I'm afraid we shouldn't get very far."

"Look here," Gerald begged eagerly, "let's make a shot at it. I'll pay you double the hire of the car, and I'll be responsible for any damage. I want to get out of this beastly place. Let's get somewhere, at any rate, towards a civilised country. I'll see you don't lose anything. I'll give you a five pound note for yourself if we get as far as Holt."

"I'm on," the young man agreed shortly. "It's an open car, you know."

"It doesn't matter," Gerald replied. "I can stick it in front with you, and we can cover - him up in the tonneau."

"You'll wait until the doctor comes back?" the landlord asked.

"And why should they?" his wife interposed sharply. "Them doctors are all the same. He'll try and keep the poor gentleman here for the sake of a few extra guineas, and a miserable place for him to open his eyes upon, even if the rest of the roof holds, which for my part I'm beginning to doubt. They'd have to move him from here with the daylight, anyhow. He can't lie in the bar parlour all day, can he?"

"It don't seem right, somehow," the man com plained doggedly. "The doctor didn't say anything about having him moved."

"You get the car," Gerald ordered the young man. "I'll take the whole responsibility."

E. Phillips Oppenheim

The chauffeur silently left the room. Gerald put a couple of sovereigns upon the mantelpiece.

"My friend is a man of somewhat peculiar temperament," he said quietly. "If he finds himself at home in a comfortable room when he comes to his senses, I am quite sure that he will have a better chance of recovery. He cannot possibly be made comfortable here, and he will feel the shock of what has happened all the more if he finds himself still in the neighbourhood when he opens his eyes. If there is any change in his condition, we can easily stop somewhere on the way."

The woman pocketed the two sovereigns.

"That's common sense, sir," she agreed heartily, "and I'm sure we are very much obliged to you. If we had a decent room, and a roof above it, you'd be heartily welcome, but as it is, this is no place for a sick man, and those that say different don't know what they are talking about. That's a real careful young man who's going to take you along in the motor-car. He'll get you there safe, if any one will."

"What I say is," her husband protested sullenly, "that we ought to wait for the doctor's orders. I'm against seeing a poor body like that jolted across the country in an open motor-car, in his state. I'm not sure that it's for his good."

"And what business is it of yours, I should like to know?" the woman demanded sharply. "You get upstairs and begin moving the furniture from where the rain's coming sopping in. And if so be you can remember while you do it that this is a judgment that's come upon us, why, so much the better. We are evil-doers, all of us, though them as likes the easy ways generally manage to forget it."

The man retreated silently. The woman sat down upon a stool and waited. Gerald sat opposite to her, the battered dressing-case upon his knees. Between them was stretched the body of the unconscious man.

"Are you used to prayer, young sir?" the woman asked.

Gerald shook his head, and the woman did not pursue the subject. Only once her eyes were half closed and her words drifted across the room.

"The Lord have mercy on this man, a sinner!"

CHAPTER IV

"My advice to you, sir, is to chuck it!"

Gerald turned towards the chauffeur by whose side he was seated a little stiffly, for his limbs were numbed with the cold and exhaustion. The morning had broken with a grey and uncertain light. A vaporous veil of mist seemed to have taken the place of the darkness. Even from the top of the hill where the car had come to a standstill, there was little to be seen.

"We must have come forty miles already," the chauffeur continued, "what with going out of our way all the time because of the broken bridges. I'm pretty well frozen through, and as for him," he added, jerking his thumb across his shoulder, "it seems to me you're taking a bit of a risk."

"The doctor said he would remain in exactly the same condition for twenty-four hours," Gerald declared.

"Yes, but he didn't say anything about shaking him up over forty miles of rough road," the other protested. "You'll excuse me, sir," he continued, in a slightly changed tone; "it isn't my business, of course, but I'm fairly done. It don't seem reasonable to stick at it like this. There's Holt village not a mile away, and a comfortable inn and a fire waiting. I thought that was as far as you wanted to come. We might lie up there for a few hours, at any rate."

His passenger slipped down from his place, and, lifting the rug, peered into the tonneau of the car, over which they had tied a hood. To all appearance, the condition of the man who lay there was unchanged. There was a slightly added blueness about the lips but his breathing was still perceptible. It seemed even a little stronger. Gerald resumed his seat.

"It isn't worth while to stay at Holt," he said quietly. "We are scarcely seven miles from home now. Sit still for a few minutes and get your wind."

"Only seven miles," the chauffeur repeated more cheerfully. "That's something, anyway."

"And all downhill."

"Towards the sea, then?"

"Straight to the sea," Gerald told him. "The place we are making for is St. David's Hall, near Salthouse."

The chauffeur seemed a little startled.

"Why, that's Squire Fentolin's house!"

Gerald nodded.

"That is where we are going. You follow this road almost straight ahead."

The chauffeur slipped in the clutch.

"Oh, I know the way now, sir, right enough!" he exclaimed. "There's Salthouse marsh to cross, though. I don't know about that."

"We shall manage that all right," Gerald declared. "We've more light now, too."

They both looked around. During the last few minutes the late morning seemed to have forced its way through the clouds. They had a dim, phantasmagoric view of the stricken country: a watery plain, with here and there great patches of fields, submerged to the hedges, and houses standing out amidst the waste of waters like toy dwellings. There were whole plantations of uprooted trees. Close to the road, on their left, was a roofless house, and a family of children crying underneath a tarpaulin shelter. As they crept on, the wind came to them with a brackish flavour, salt with the sea. The chauffeur was gazing ahead doubtfully.

"I don't like the look of the marsh," he grumbled. "Can't see the road at all. However, here goes."

"Another half-hour," Gerald assured him encouragingly, "and we shall be at St. David's Hall. You can have as much rest as you like then."

They were facing the wind now, and conversation became impossible. Twice they had to pull up sharp and make a considerable detour, once on account of a fallen tree which blocked the road, and another time because of the yawning gap where a bridge had fallen away. Gerald, however, knew every inch of the country they were in and was able to give the necessary directions. They began to meet farm wagons now, full of people who had been driven from their homes. Warnings and information as to the state of the roads were shouted to them continually. Presently they came to the last steep descent, and emerged from the devastated fragment of a wood almost on to the sea level. The chauffeur clapped on his brakes and stopped short.

"My God!" he exclaimed. "Here's more trouble!"

Gerald for a moment was speechless. They seemed to have come suddenly upon a huge plain of waters, an immense lake reaching as far as they could see on either side. The road before them stretched like a ribbon for the next three miles. Here and there it disappeared and reappeared again. In many places it was lapped by little waves. Everywhere the hedges were either altogether or half under water. In the distance was one farmhouse, only the roof of which was visible, and from which the inhabitants were clambering into a boat. And beyond, with scarcely a break save for the rising of one strangely-shaped hill, was the sea. Gerald pointed with his finger.

"There's St. David's Hall," he said, "on the other side of the hill. The road seems all right."

"Does it!" the chauffeur grunted. "It's under water more than half the way, and Heaven knows how deep it is at the sides! I'm not going to risk my life along there. I am going to take the car back to Holt."

His hand was already upon the reverse lever, but Gerald gripped it.

"Look here," he protested, "we haven't come all this

way to turn back. You don't look like a coward."

"I am not a coward, sir," was the quiet answer.
"Neither am I a fool. I don't see any use in risking our
lives and my master's motor-car, because you want to
get home."

"Naturally," Gerald answered calmly, "but remember
this. I am responsible for your car - not you. Mr.
Fentolin is my uncle."

The chauffeur nodded shortly.

"You're Mr. Gerald Fentolin, aren't you, sir?" he
remarked. "I thought I recognised you."

"I am," Gerald admitted. "We've had a rough journey,
but it doesn't seem sense to turn back now, does it,
with the house in sight?"

"That's all very well, sir," the chauffeur objected
doubtfully, "but I don't believe the road's even
passable, and the floods seem to me to be rising."

"Try it," the young man begged. "Look here, I don't
want to bribe you, or anything of that sort. You know
you're coming out of this well. It's a serious matter for
me, and I shan't be likely to forget it. I want to take this
gentleman to St. David's Hall and not to a hospital.
You've brought me here so far like a man. Let's go
through with it. If the worst comes to the worst, we can
both swim, I suppose, and we are not likely to get out
of our depth."

The chauffeur moved his head backwards.

"How about him?"

"He must take his chance," Gerald replied. "He's all right where he is. The car won't upset and there are plenty of people who'll see if we get into trouble. Come, let's make a dash for it."

The chauffeur thrust in his clutch and settled himself down. They glided off along that winding stretch of road. To its very edge, on either side of them, so close that they could almost touch it, came the water, water which stretched as far as they could see, swaying, waveless, sinister-looking. Even Gerald, after his first impulse of wonder, kept his eyes averted and fixed upon the road ahead. Soon they reached a place where the water met in front. There were only the rows of white palings on either side to guide them. The chauffeur muttered to himself as he changed to his first speed.

"If the engine gets stopped," he said, "I don't know how we shall get out of this."

They emerged on the other side. For some time they had a clear run. Then suddenly the driver clapped on his brakes.

"My God!" he cried. "We can't get through that!"

In front of them for more than a hundred yards the water seemed suddenly to have flowed across the road. Still a mile distant, perched on a ridge of that strangely-placed hill, was their destination.

"It can't be done, sir!" the man groaned. "There isn't a car ever built could get through that. See, it's nearly up to the top of those posts. I must put her in the reverse and get back, even if we have to wait on the higher part of the road for a boat."

He glanced behind, and a second cry broke from his lips. Gerald stood up in his place. Already the road which had been clear a few minutes before was hidden. The water was washing almost over the tops of the white posts behind them. Little waves were breaking against the summit of the raised bank.

"We're cut off!" the chauffeur exclaimed. "What a fool I was to try this! There's the tide coming in as well!"

Gerald sat down in his place.

"Look here," he said, "we can't go back, whether we want to or not. It's much worse behind there than it is in front. There's only one chance. Go for it straight ahead in your first speed. It may not stop the engine. In any case, it will be worse presently. There's no use funking it. If the worst happens, we can sit in the car. The water won't be above our heads and there are some boats about. Blow your horn well first, in case there's any one within hearing, and then go for it."

The chauffeur obeyed. They hissed and spluttered into the water. Soon all trace of the road was completely lost. They steered only by the tops of the white posts.

"It's getting deeper," the man declared. "It's within an inch or two of the bonnet now. Hold on."

A wave broke almost over them but the engine continued its beat.

"If we stop now," he gasped, "we're done!"

The engine began to knock.

"Stick at it," Gerald cried, rising in his place a little. "Look, there's only one post lower than the last one that we passed. They get higher all the time, ahead. You can almost see the road in front there. Now, in with your gear again, and stick at it."

Another wave broke, this time completely over them. They listened with strained ears - the engine continued to beat. They still moved slowly. Then there was a shock. The wheel had struck something in the road - a great stone or rock. The chauffeur thrust the car out of gear. The engine still beat. Gerald leaped from the car. The water was over his knees. He crossed in front of the bonnet and stooped down.

"I've got it!" he exclaimed, tugging hard. "It's a stone."

He moved it, rolled it on one side, and pushed at the wheel of the car as his companion put in the speed. They started again. He jumped back his place.

"We've done it, all right!" he cried. "Don't you see? It's getting lower all the time."

The chauffeur had lost his nerve. His cheeks were pale, his teeth were chattering. The engine, however, was still beating. Gradually the pressure of the water grew less. In front of them they caught a glimpse of the road. They drew up at the top of a little bridge over one of the dikes. Gerald uttered a brief exclamation of triumph.

"We're safe!" he almost sobbed. "There's the road, straight ahead and round to the right. There's no more water anywhere near."

They had left the main part of the flood behind them. There were still great pools in the side of the road, and huge masses of seaweed had been carried up and were lying in their track. There was no more water, however. At every moment they drew nearer to the strangely-shaped hill with its crown of trees.

"The house is on the other side," Gerald pointed out. "We can go through the lodge gates at the back here. The ascent isn't so steep."

They turned sharply to the right, along another stretch of straight road set with white posts, ending before a red brick lodge and a closed gate. They blew the horn and a gardener came out. He gazed at them in amazement.

"It's all right," Gerald cried. "Let us through quickly, Foulds. We've a gentleman in behind who's ill."

The man swung open the gate with a respectful salute. They made their way up a winding drive of considerable length, and at last they came to a broad, open space almost like a platform. On their left were the marshes, and beyond, the sea. Along their right stretched the long front of an Elizabethan mansion. They drew up in front of the hail door. Their coming had been observed, and servants were already waiting. Gerald sprang to the ground.

"There's a gentleman in behind who's ill," he explained to the butler. "He has met with an accident on the way.

Three or four of you had better carry him up to a bedroom - any one that is ready. And you, George," he added, turning to a boy, "get into the car and show this man the way round to the garage, and then take him to the servants' hall."

Several of the servants hastened to do his bidding, and Gerald did his best to answer the eager but respectful stream of questions. And then, just as they were in the act of lifting the still unconscious man on to the floor of the hall, came a queer sound - a shrill, reverberating whistle. They all looked up the stairs.

"The master is awake," Henderson, the butler, remarked, dropping his voice a little.

Gerald nodded.

"I will go to him at once," he said.

CHAPTER V

Accustomed though he was to the sight which he was about to face, Gerald shivered slightly as he opened the door of Mr. Fentolin's room. A strange sort of fear seemed to have crept into his bearing and expression, a fear of which there had been no traces whatever during those terrible hours through which he had passed - not even during that last reckless journey across the marshes. He walked with hesitating footsteps across the spacious and lofty room. He had the air of some frightened creature approaching his master. Yet all that was visible of the despot who ruled his whole household in deadly fear was the kindly and beautiful face of an elderly man, whose stunted limbs and body were mercifully concealed. He sat in a little carriage, with a rug drawn closely across his chest and up to his armpits. His beautifully shaped hands were exposed, and his face; nothing else. His hair was a silvery white; his complexion parchment-like, pallid, entirely colourless. His eyes were a soft shade of blue. His features were so finely cut and chiselled that they resembled some exquisite piece of statuary. He smiled as his nephew came slowly towards him. One might almost have fancied that the young man's abject state was a source of pleasure to him.

"So you are back again, my dear Gerald. A pleasant surprise, indeed, but what is the meaning of it? And what of my little commission, eh?"

The young man's face was dark and sullen. He spoke quickly but without any sign of eagerness or interest in the information he vouchsafed.

"The storm has stopped all the trains," he said. "The boat did not cross last night, and in any case I couldn't have reached Harwich. As for your commission, I travelled down from London alone with the man you told me to spy upon. I could have stolen anything he had if I had been used to the work. As it was - I brought the man himself."

Mr. Fentolin's delicate fingers played with the handle of his chair. The smile had passed from his lips. He looked at his nephew in gentle bewilderment.

"My dear boy," he protested, "come, come, be careful what you are saying. You have brought the man himself! So far as my information goes, Mr. John P. Dunster is charged with a very important diplomatic commission. He is on his way to Cologne, and from what I know about the man, I think that it would require more than your persuasions to induce him to break off his journey. You do not really wish me to believe that you have brought him here as a guest?"

"I was at Liverpool Street Station last night," Gerald declared. "I had no idea how to accost him, and as to stealing any of his belongings, I couldn't have done it. You must hear how fortune helped me, though. Mr. Dunster missed the train; so did I - purposely. He ordered a special. I asked permission to travel with him. I told him a lie as to how I had missed the train. I hated it, but it was necessary."

Mr. Fentolin nodded approvingly.

"My dear boy," he said, "to trifle with the truth is always unpleasant. Besides, you are a Fentolin, and our love of truth is proverbial. But there are times, you know, when for the good of others we must sacrifice our scruples. So you told Mr. Dunster a falsehood."

"He let me travel with him," Gerald continued. "We were all night getting about half-way here. Then - you know about the storm, I suppose?"

Mr. Fentolin spread out his hands.

"Could one avoid the knowledge of it?" he asked. "Such a sight has never been seen."

"We found we couldn't get to Harwich," Gerald went on. "They telegraphed to London and got permission to bring us to Yarmouth. We were on our way to Norwich, and the train ran off the line."

"An accident?" Mr. Fentolin exclaimed.

Gerald nodded.

"Our train ran off the line and pitched down an embankment. Mr. Dunster has concussion of the brain. He and I were taken to a miserable little inn near Wymondham. From there I hired a motor-car and brought him here."

"You hired a motor-car and brought him here," Mr. Fentolin repeated softly. "My dear boy - forgive me if I find this a little hard to understand. You say that you have brought him here. Had he nothing to say about it?"

"He was unconscious when we picked him up," Gerald explained. "He is unconscious now. The doctor said he would remain so for at least twenty-four hours, and it didn't seem to me that the journey would do him any particular harm. The roof had been stripped off the inn where we were, and the place was quite uninhabitable, so we should have had to have moved him somewhere. We put him in the tonneau of the car and covered him up. They have carried him now into a bedroom, and Sarson is looking after him."

Mr. Fentolin sat quite silent. His eyes blinked once or twice, and there was a curious curve about his lips.

"You have done well, my boy," he pronounced slowly. "Your scheme of bringing him here sounds a little primitive, but success justifies everything."

Mr. Fentolin raised to his lips and blew softly a little gold whistle which hung from a chain attached to his waistcoat. Almost immediately the door opened. A man entered, dressed somberly in black, whose bearing and demeanour alike denoted the servant, but whose physique was the physique of a prize-fighter. He was scarcely more than five feet six in height, but his shoulders were extraordinarily broad. He had a short, bull neck and long, mighty arms. His face, with the heavy jaw and small eyes, was the face of the typical fighting man, yet his features seemed to have become disposed by habit into an expression of gentle, almost servile civility.

"Meekins," Mr. Fentolin said, "a visitor has arrived. Do you happen to have noticed what luggage

E. Phillips Oppenheim

he brought?"

"There is one small dressing-case, sir," the man replied; "nothing else that I have seen."

"That is all we brought," Gerald interposed.

"You will bring the dressing-case here at once," Mr. Fentolin directed, "and also my compliments to Doctor Sarson, and any pocket-book or papers which may help us to send a message to the gentleman's friends."

Meekins closed the door and departed. Mr. Fentolin turned back towards his nephew.

"My dear boy," he said, "tell me why you look as though there were ghosts flitting about the room? You are not ill, I trust?"

"Tired, perhaps," Gerald answered shortly. "We were many hours in the car. I have had no sleep."

Mr. Fentolin's face was full of kindly sympathy.

"My dear fellow," he exclaimed, "I am selfish, indeed! I should not have kept you here for a moment. You had better go and lie down."

"I'll go directly," Gerald promised. "Can I speak to you for one moment first?"

"Speak to me," Mr. Fentolin repeated, a little wonderingly. "My dear Gerald, is there ever a moment when I am not wholly at your service?"

"That fellow Dunster, on the platform, the first

moment I spoke to him, made me feel like a cur," the boy said, with a sudden access of vigour in his tone. "I told him I was on my way to a golf tournament, and he pointed to the news about the war. Is it true, uncle, that we may be at war at any moment?"

Mr. Fentolin sighed.

"A terrible reflection, my dear boy," he admitted softly, "but, alas! the finger of probability points that way."

"Then what about me?" Gerald exclaimed. "I don't want to complain, but listen. You dragged me home from a public school before I could even join my cadet corps. You've kept me banging around here with a tutor. You wouldn't let me go to the university. You've stopped my entering either of the services. I am nineteen years old and useless. Do you know what I should do to-morrow if war broke out? Enlist! It's the only thing left for me."

Mr. Fentolin was shocked.

"My dear boy!" he exclaimed. "You must not talk like that! I am quite sure that it would break your mother's heart. Enlist, indeed! Nothing of the sort. You are part of the civilian population of the country."

"Civilian population be d-d!" the boy suddenly cried, white with rage. "Uncle, forgive me, I have stood all I can bear. If you won't let me go in for the army - I could pass my exams to-morrow - I'm off. I'll enlist without waiting for the war. I can't bear this idle life any longer."

E. Phillips Oppenheim

Mr. Fentolin leaned a little forward in his chair.

"Gerald!" he said softly.

The boy turned his head, turned it unwillingly. He had the air of a caged animal obeying the word of his keeper. A certain savage uncouthness seemed to have fallen upon him during the last few minutes. There was something almost like a snarl in his expression.

"Gerald!" Mr. Fentolin repeated.

Then it was obvious that there was something between those two, some memory or some living thing, seldom, if ever, to be spoken of, and yet always present. The boy began to tremble.

"You're a little overwrought, Gerald," Mr. Fentolin declared. "Sit quietly in my easy-chair for a few moments. Walt until I have examined Mr. Dunster's belongings. Ah! Meekins has been prompt, indeed."

There was a stealthy tap at the door. Meekins entered with the small dressing-case in his hand. He brought it over to his master's chair. Mr. Fentolin pointed to the floor.

"Open it there, Meekins," he directed. "I fancy that the pocket-book you are carrying will prove more interesting. We will just glance through the dressing-case first. Thank you. Yes, you can lay the things upon the floor. A man of Spartan-like life, I should imagine Mr. Dunster. A spare toothbrush, though, I am glad to see. Pyjamas of most unattractive pattern. And what a taste in shirts! Nothing but wearing apparel and singularly little of that, I fancy."

The dressing-case was empty, its contents upon the floor. Mr. Fentolin held out his hand and took the pocket-book which Meekins had been carrying. It was an ordinary morocco affair, similar to those issued by American banking houses to enclose letters of credit. One side of it was filled with notes. Mr. Fentolin withdrew them and glanced them through.

"Dear me!" he murmured. "No wonder our friend engages special trains! He travels like a prince, indeed. Two thousand pounds, or near it, in this little compartment. And here, I see, a letter, a sealed letter with no address."

He held it out in front of him. It was a long commercial envelope of ordinary type, and although the flap was secured with a blob of sealing wax, there was no particular impression upon it.

"We can match this envelope, I think," Mr. Fentolin said softly. "The seal we can copy. I think that, for the sake of others, we must discover the cause for this hurried journey on the part of Mr. John P. Dunster."

With his long, delicate forefinger Mr. Fentolin slit the envelope and withdrew the single sheet of paper which it contained. There were a dozen lines of written matter, and what appeared to be a dozen signatures appended. Mr. Fentolin read it, at first with ordinary interest. Then a change came. The look of a man drawn out of himself, drawn out of all knowledge of his surroundings or his present state, stole into his face. Literally he became transfixed. The delicate fingers of his, left hand gripped the sides of his little carriage. His eyes shone as though those few written lines upon which they were riveted were indeed some message from an unknown, an unimagined world. Yet no word ever passed his lips. There came a time when the tension seemed a little relaxed. With fingers which still trembled, he folded up the sheet and replaced it in the envelope. He guarded it with both his hands and sat quite still. Neither Gerald nor his servant moved. Somehow, the sense of Mr. Fentolin's suppressed excitement seemed to have become communicated to them. It was a little tableau, broken at last by Mr. Fentolin himself.

"I should like," he said, turning to Gerald, "to be alone. It may interest you to know that this document which Mr. Dunster has brought across the seas, and which I hold in my hands, is the most amazing message of modern times."

Gerald rose to his feet.

"What are you going to do about it?" he asked abruptly. "Do you want any one in from the telegraph room?"

Mr. Fentolin shook his head slowly.

"At present," he announced, "I am going to reflect. Meekins, my chair to the north window - so. I am going to sit here," he went on, "and I am going to look across the sea and reflect. A very fortunate storm, after all, I think, which kept Mr. John P. Dunster from the Harwich boat last night. Leave me, Gerald, for a time. Stand behind my chair, Meekins, and see that no one enters."

Mr. Fentolin sat in his chair, his hands still gripping the wonderful document, his eyes travelling over the ocean now flecked with sunlight. His eyes were fixed upon the horizon. He looked steadily eastward.

E. Phillips Oppenheim

CHAPTER VI

Mr. John P. Dunster opened his eyes upon strange surroundings. He found himself lying upon a bed deliciously soft, with lace-edged sheets and lavender-perfumed bed hangings. Through the discreetly opened upper window came a pleasant and ozone-laden breeze. The furniture in the room was mostly of an old-fashioned type, some of it of oak, curiously carved, and most of it surmounted with a coat of arms. The apartment was lofty and of almost palatial proportions. The whole atmosphere of the place breathed comfort and refinement. The only thing of which he did not wholly approve was the face of the nurse who rose silently to her feet at his murmured question:

"Where am I?"

She felt his forehead, altered a bandage for a moment, and took his wrist between her fingers.

"You have been ill," she said. "There was a railway accident. You are to lie quite still and not say a word. I am going to fetch the doctor now. He wished to see you directly you spoke."

Mr. Dunster dozed again for several moments. When he reopened his eyes, a man was standing by his bedside, a short man with a black beard and gold-rimmed glasses. Mr. Dunster, in this first stage of his convalescence, was perhaps difficult to please, for he did not like the look of the doctor, either.

"Please tell me where I am?" he begged.

"You have been in a railway accident," the doctor told him, "and you were brought here afterwards."

"In a railway accident," Mr. Dunster repeated. "Ah, yes, I remember! I took a special to Harwich - I remember now. Where is my dressing-bag?"

"It is here by the side of your bed."

"And my pocket-book?"

"It is on your dressing-table."

"Have any of my things been looked at?"

"Only so far as was necessary to discover your identity," the doctor assured him. "Don't talk too much. The nurse is bringing you some beef tea."

"When," Mr. Dunster enquired, "shall I be able to continue my journey?"

"That depends upon many things," the doctor replied.

Mr. Dunster drank his beef tea and felt considerably stronger. His head still ached, but his memory was returning.

"There was a young man in the carriage with me," he asked presently. "Mr. Gerald something or other I think he said his name was?"

"Fentolin," the doctor said. "He is unhurt. This is his relative's house to which you have been brought."

Mr. Dunster lay for a time with knitted brows. Once more the name of Fentolin seemed somehow familiar to him, seemed somehow to bring with it to his memory a note of warning. He looked around the room fretfully. He looked into the nurse's face, which he disliked exceedingly, and he looked at the doctor, whom he was beginning to detest.

"Whose house exactly is this?" he demanded.

"This is St. David's Hall - the home of Mr. Miles Fentolin," the doctor told him. "The young gentleman with whom you were travelling is his nephew."

"Can I send a telegram?" Mr. Dunster asked, a little abruptly.

"Without a doubt," the doctor replied. "Mr. Fentolin desired me to ask you if there was any one whom you would like to apprise of your safety."

Again the man upon the bed lay quite still, with knitted brows. There was surely something familiar about that name. Was it his fevered fancy or was there also something a little sinister?

The nurse, who had glided from the room, came back presently with some telegraph forms. Mr. Dunster held out his hand for them and then hesitated.

"Can you tell me any date, Doctor, upon which I can

rely upon leaving here?"

"You will probably be well enough to travel on the third day from now," the doctor assured him.

"The third day," Mr. Dunster muttered. "Very well."

He wrote out three telegrams and passed them over.

"One," he said, "is to New York, one to The Hague, and one to London. There was plenty of money in my pocket. Perhaps you will find it and pay for these."

"Is there anything more," the doctor asked, "that can be done for your comfort?"

"Nothing at present," Mr. Dunster replied. "My head aches now, but I think that I shall want to leave before three days are up. Are you the doctor in the neighbourhood?"

Sarson shook his head.

"I am physician to Mr. Fentolin's household," he answered quietly. "I live here. Mr. Fentolin is himself somewhat of an invalid and requires constant medical attention."

Mr. Dunster contemplated the speaker steadfastly.

"You will forgive me," he said. "I am an American and I am used to plain speech. I am quite unused to being attended by strange doctors. I understand that you are not in general practice now. Might I ask if you are fully qualified?"

"I am an M.D. of London," the doctor replied. "You can make yourself quite easy as to my qualifications. It would not suit Mr. Fentolin's purpose to entrust himself to the care of any one without a reputation."

He left the room, and Mr. Dunster closed his eyes. His slumbers, however, were not altogether peaceful ones. All the time there seemed to be a hammering inside his head, and from somewhere back in his obscured memory the name of Fentolin seemed to be continually asserting itself. From somewhere or other, the amazing sense which sometimes gives warning of danger to men of adventure, seemed to have opened its feelers. He rested because he was exhausted, but even in his sleep he was ill at ease.

The doctor, with the telegrams in his hand, made his way down a splendid staircase, past the long picture gallery where masterpieces of Van Dyck and Rubens frowned and leered down upon him; descended the final stretch of broad oak stairs, crossed the hail, and entered his master's rooms. Mr. Fentolin was sitting before the open window, an easel in front of him, a palette in his left hand, painting with deft, swift touches.

"Ah!" he exclaimed, without looking around, "it is my friend the doctor, my friend Sarson, M.D. of London, L.R.C.P. and all the rest of it. He brings with him the odour of the sick room. For a moment or two, just for a moment, dear friend, do not disturb me. Do not bring any alien thoughts into my brain. I am absorbed, you see - absorbed. It is a strange problem of colour, this."

He was silent for several moments, glancing repeatedly out of the window and back to his canvas, painting all the time with swift and delicate precision.

"Meekins, who stands behind my chair," Mr. Fentolin continued, "even Meekins is entranced. He has a soul, my friend Sarson, although you might not think it. He, too, sees sometimes the colour in the skies, the glitter upon the sands, the clear, sweet purity of those long stretches of virgin water. Meekins, I believe, has a soul, only he likes better to see these things grow under his master's touch than to wander about and solve their riddles for himself."

The man remained perfectly immovable. Not a feature twitched. Yet it was a fact that, although he stood where Mr. Fentolin could not possibly observe him, he never removed his gaze from the canvas.

"You see, my medical friend, that there has been a great tide in the night, following upon the flood? Even our small landmarks are shifted. Soon, in my little carriage, I shall ride down to the Tower. I shall sit there, and I shall watch the sea. I think that this evening, with the turn of the tide, the spray may reach even to my windows there. I shall paint again. There is always something fresh in the sea, you know - always something fresh in the sea. Like a human face - angry or pleased, sullen or joyful. Some people like to paint the sea at its calmest and most beautiful. Some people like to see happy faces around them. It is not every one who appreciates the other things. It is not quite like that with me, eh, Sarson?"

His hand fell to his side. Momentarily he had finished his work. He turned around and eyed the doctor, who stood in taciturn silence.

　　　　　E. Phillips Oppenheim

"Answer. Answer me," he insisted.

The doctor's gloomy face seemed darker still.

"You have spoken the truth, Mr. Fentolin," he admitted. "You are not one of the vulgar herd who love to consort with pleasure and happiness. You are one of those who understand the beauty of unhappiness - in others," he added, with faint emphasis.

Mr. Fentolin smiled. His face became almost like the face of one of those angels of the great Italian master.

"How well you know me!" he murmured. "My humble effort, Doctor - how do you like it?"

The doctor bent over the canvas.

"I know nothing about art," he said, a little roughly. "Your work seems to me clever - a little grotesque, perhaps; a little straining after the hard, plain things which threaten. Nothing of the idealist in your work, Mr. Fentolin."

Mr. Fentolin studied the canvas himself for a moment.

"A clever man, Sarson," he remarked coolly, "but no courtier. Never mind, my work pleases me. It gives me a passing sensation of happiness. Now, what about our patient?"

"He recovers," the doctor pronounced. "From my short examination, I should say that he had the constitution of an ox. I have told him that he will be up in three days. As a matter of fact, he will be able, if he wants to, to walk out of the house to-morrow."

Mr. Fentolin shook his head.

"We cannot spare him quite so soon," he declared. "We must avail ourselves of this wonderful chance afforded us by my brilliant young nephew. We must keep him with us for a little time. What is it that you have in your hands, Doctor? Telegrams, I think. Let me look at them."

The doctor held them out. Mr. Fentolin took them eagerly between his thin, delicate fingers. Suddenly his face darkened, and became like the face of a spoilt and angry child.

"Cipher!" he exclaimed furiously. "A cipher which he knows so well as to remember it, too! Never mind, it will be easy to decode. It will amuse me during the afternoon. Very good, Sarson. I will take charge of these."

"You do not wish anything dispatched?"

"Nothing at present," Mr. Fentolin sighed. "It will be well, I think, for the poor man to remain undisturbed by any communications from his friends. Is he restless at all?"

"He wants to get on with his journey."

"We shall see," Mr. Fentolin remarked. "Now feel my pulse, Sarson. How am I this morning?"

The doctor held the thin wrist for a moment between his fingers, and let it go.

"In perfect health, as usual," he announced grimly.

"Ah, but you cannot be sure!" Mr. Fentolin protested. "My tongue, if you please."

He put it out.

"Excellent!"

"We must make quite certain," Mr. Fentolin continued. "There are so many people who would miss me. My place in the world would not be easily filed. Undo my waistcoat, Sarson. Feel my heart, please. Feel carefully. I can see the end of your stethoscope in your pocket. Don't scamp it. I fancied this morning, when I was lying here alone, that there was something almost like a palpitation - a quicker beat. Be very careful, Sarson. Now."

The doctor made his examination with impassive face. Then he stepped back.

"There is no change in your condition, Mr. Fentolin," he announced. "The palpitation you spoke of is a mistake. You are in perfect health."

Mr. Fentolin sighed gently.

"Then," he said, "I will now amuse myself by a gentle ride down to the Tower. You are entirely satisfied, Sarson? You are keeping nothing back from me?"

The doctor looked at him with grim, impassive face. "There is nothing to keep back," he declared. "You have the constitution of a cowboy. There is no reason why you should not live for another thirty years."

Mr. Fentolin sighed, as though a weight had been

removed from his heart.

"I will now," he decided, reaching forward for the handle of his carriage, "go down to the Tower. It is just possible that a few days' seclusion might be good for our guest."

The doctor turned silently away. There was no one there to see his expression as he walked towards the door.

E. Phillips Oppenheim

CHAPTER VII

The two men who were supping together in the grillroom at the Café Milan were talking with a seriousness which seemed a little out of keeping with the rose-shaded lamps and the swaying music of the band from the distant restaurant. Their conversation had started some hours before in the club smoking-room and had continued intermittently throughout the evening. It had received a further stimulus when Richard Hamel, who had bought an Evening Standard on their way from the theatre a few minutes ago, came across a certain paragraph in it which he read aloud.

"Hanged if I understand things over here, nowadays, Reggie!" he declared, laying the paper down. "Here's another Englishman imprisoned in Germany - this time at a place no one ever heard of before. I won't try to pronounce it. What does it all mean? It's all very well to shrug your shoulders, but when there are eighteen arrests within one week on a charge of espionage, there must be something up."

For the first time Reginald Kinsley seemed inclined to discuss the subject seriously. He drew the paper towards him and read the little paragraph, word by word. Then he gave some further order to an attentive maitre d'hotel and glanced around to be sure that they were not overheard.

"Look here, Dick, old chap," he said, "you are just back from abroad and you are not quite in the hang of things yet. Let me ask you a plain question. What do you think of us all?"

"Think of you?" Hamel repeated, a little doubtfully. "Do you mean personally?"

"Take it any way you like," Kinsley replied. "Look at me. Nine years ago we played cricket in the same eleven. I don't look much like cricket now, do I?"

Hamel looked at his companion thoughtfully. For a man who was doubtless still young, Kinsley had certainly an aged appearance. The hair about his temples was grey; there were lines about his mouth and forehead. He had the air of one who lived in an atmosphere of anxiety.

"To me," Hamel declared frankly, "you look worried. If I hadn't heard so much of the success of your political career and all the rest of it, I should have thought that things were going badly with you."

"They've gone well enough with me personally," Kinsley admitted, "but I'm only one of many. Politics isn't the game it was. The Foreign Office especially is ageing its men fast these few years. We've been going through hell, Hamel, and we are up against it now, hard up against it."

The slight smile passed from the lips of Hamel's sunburnt, good-natured face. He himself seemed to become infected with something of his companion's anxiety.

"There's nothing seriously wrong, is there, Reggie?" he asked.

"Dick," said Kinsley, with a sigh, "I am afraid there is. It's very seldom I talk as plainly as this to any, one but you are just the person one can unburden oneself to a little; and to tell you the truth, it's rather a relief. As you say, these eighteen arrests in one week do mean something. Half of the Englishmen who have been arrested are, to my certain knowledge, connected with our Secret Service, and they have been arrested, in many cases, where there are no fortifications worth speaking of within fifty miles, on one pretext or another. The fact of the matter is that things are going on in Germany, just at the present moment, the knowledge of which is of vital interest to us."

"Then these arrests," Hamel remarked, "are really bona fide?"

"Without a doubt," his companion agreed. "I only wonder there have not been more. I am telling you what is a pretty open secret when I tell you that there is a conference due to be held this week at some place or another on the continent - I don't know where, myself - which will have a very important bearing upon our future. We know just as much as that and not much more."

"A conference between whom?" Hamel asked.

Kinsley dropped his voice almost to a whisper.

"We know," he replied, "that a very great man from Russia, a greater still from France, a minister from Austria, a statesman from Italy, and an envoy from

Japan, have been invited to meet a German minister whose name I will not mention, even to you. The subject of their proposed discussion has never been breathed. One can only suspect. When I tell you that no one from this country was invited to the conference, I think you will be able, broadly speaking, to divine its purpose. The clouds have been gathering for a good many years, and we have only buried our heads a little deeper in the sands. We have had our chances and wilfully chucked them away. National Service or three more army corps four years ago would have brought us an alliance which would have meant absolute safety for twenty-one years. You know what happened. We have lived through many rumours and escaped, more narrowly than most people realise, a great many dangers, but there is every indication this time that the end is really coming."

"And what will the end be?" Hamel enquired eagerly.

Kinsley shrugged his shoulders and paused while their glasses were filled with wine.

"It will be in the nature of a diplomatic coup," he said presently. "Of that much I feel sure. England will be forced into such a position that she will have no alternative left but to declare war. That, of course, will be the end of us. With our ridiculously small army and absolutely no sane scheme for home defence, we shall lose all that we have worth fighting for - our colonies - without being able to strike a blow. The thing is so ridiculously obvious. It has been admitted time after time by every sea lord and every commander-in-chief. We have listened to it, and that's all. Our fleet is needed under present conditions to protect our own shores. There isn't a single battleship which could be safely spared. Canada, Australia, New Zealand, Egypt, India, must take care of themselves. I wonder when a nation of the world ever played fast and loose with great possessions as we have done!"

"This is a nice sort of thing to hear almost one's first night in England," Hamel remarked a little gloomily. "Tell me some more about this conference. Are you sure that your information is reliable?"

"Our information is miserably scanty," Kinsley admitted. "Curiously enough, the man who must know most about the whole thing is an Englishman, one of the most curious mortals in the British Empire. A spy of his succeeded in learning more than any of our people, and without being arrested, too."

"And who is this singular person?" Hamel asked.

"A man of whom you, I suppose, never heard," Kinsley replied. " His name is Fentolin - Miles Fentolin - and he lives somewhere down in Norfolk. He is one of the strangest characters that ever lived, stranger than any effort of fiction I ever met with. He was in the Foreign Office once, and every one was predicting for him a brilliant career. Then there was an accident - let me see, it must have been some six or seven years ago - and he had to have both his legs amputated. No one knows exactly how the accident happened, and there was always a certain amount of mystery connected with it. Since then he has buried himself in the country. I don't think, in fact, that he ever moves outside his place; but somehow or other he has managed to keep in touch with all the political movements of the day."

"Fentolin," Hamel repeated softly to himself. "Tell me, whereabouts does he live?"

"Quite a wonderful place in Norfolk, I believe, somewhere near the sea. I've forgotten the name, for the moment. He has had wireless telegraphy installed; he has a telegraph office in the house, half-a-dozen private wires, and they say that he spends an immense amount of money keeping in touch with foreign politics. His excuse is that he speculates largely, as I dare say he does; but just lately," Kinsley went on more slowly, "he has been an object of anxiety to all of us. It was he who sent the first agent out to Germany, to try and discover at least where this conference was to be held. His man returned in safety, and he has one over there now who has not been arrested. We seem to have lost nearly all of ours."

"Do you mean to say that this man Fentolin actually possesses information which the Government hasn't as to the intentions of foreign Powers?" Hamel asked.

Kinsley nodded. There was a slight flush upon his pallid cheeks.

"He not only has it, but he doesn't mean to part with it. A few hundred years ago, when the rulers of this country were men with blood in their veins, he'd have been given just one chance to tell all he knew, and hung as a traitor if he hesitated. We don't do that sort of thing nowadays. We rather go in for preserving traitors. We permit them even in our own House of Commons. However, I don't want to depress you and play the alarmist so soon after your return to London. I dare say the old country'll muddle along through our time."

"Don't be foolish," Hamel begged. "There's no other subject of conversation could interest me half as much. Have you formed any idea yourself as to the nature of this conference?"

"We all have an idea," Kinsley replied grimly; "India for Russia; a large slice of China for Japan, with probably Australia thrown in; Alsace-Lorraine for France's neutrality. There's bribery for you. What's to become of poor England then? Our friends are only human, after all, and it's merely a question of handing over to them sufficient spoil. They must consider themselves first: that's the first duty of their politicians towards their country."

"You mean to say," Hamel asked, "that you seriously believe that a conference is on the point of being held at which France and Russia are to be invited to consider suggestions like this?"

"I am afraid there's no doubt about it," Kinsley declared. "Their ambassadors in London profess to know nothing. That, of course, is their reasonable attitude, but there's no doubt whatever that the conference has been planned. I should say that to-night we are nearer war, if we can summon enough spirit to fight, than we have been since Fashoda."

"Queer if I have returned just in time for the scrap," Hamel remarked thoughtfully. "I was in the Militia once, so I expect I can get a job, if there's any fighting."

"I can get you a better job than fighting - one you can start on to-morrow, too," Kinsley announced abruptly, "that is if you really want to help?"

"Of course I do," Hamel insisted. "I'm on for anything."

"You say that you are entirely your own master for the next six months?"

"Or as much longer as I like," Hamel assented. "No plans at all, except that I might drift round to the Norfolk coast and look up some of the places where the governor used to paint. There's a queer little house - St. David's Tower, I believe they call it - which really belongs to me. It was given to my father, or rather he bought it, from a man who I think must have been some relative of your friend. I feel sure the name was Fentolin."

Reginald Kinsley set down his wine-glass.

"Is your St. David's Tower anywhere near a place called Salthouse?" he asked reflectively.

"That's the name of the village," Hamel admitted. "My father used to spend quite a lot of time in those parts, and painted at least a dozen pictures down there."

"This is a coincidence," Reginald Kinsley declared, lighting a cigarette. "I think, if I were you, Dick, I'd go down and claim my property."

"Tired of me already?" Hamel asked, smiling.

Reginald Kinsley knocked the ash from his cigarette.

"It isn't that. The fact is, that job I was speaking to you about was simply this. We want some one to go down to Salthouse - not exactly as a spy, you know, but some one who has his wits about him. We are all of us very curious about this man Fentolin. There are no end of rumours which I won't mention to you, for they might only put you off the scent. But the man seems to be always intriguing. It wouldn't matter so much if he were our friend, or if he were simply a financier, but to tell you the truth, we have cause to suspect him."

"But he's an Englishman, surely?" Hamel asked. "The Fentolin who was my father's friend was just a very wealthy Norfolk squire - one of the best, from all I have heard."

"Miles Fentolin is an Englishman," Kinsley admitted. "It is true, too, that he comes of a very ancient Norfolk family. It doesn't do, however, to build too much upon that. From all I can learn of him, he is a sort of Puck, a professional mischief-maker. I don't suppose there's anything an outsider could find out which would be really useful to us, but all the same, if I had the time, I should certainly go down to Norfolk myself."

The conversation drifted away for a while. Mutual acquaintances entered, there were several intro-ductions, and it was not until the two found themselves together in Kinsley's rooms for a few minutes before parting that they were alone again. Hamel returned then once more to the subject.

"Reggie," he said, "if you think it would be of the slightest use, I'll go down to Salthouse to-morrow. I am rather keen on going there, anyway. I am absolutely fed up with life here already."

"It's just what I want you to do," Kinsley said. "I am afraid Fentolin is a little too clever for you to get on the right side of him, but if you could only get an idea as to what his game is down there, it would be a great help. You see, the fellow can't have gone into all this sort of thing blindfold. We've lost several very useful agents abroad and two from New York who've gone into his pay. There must be a method in it somewhere. If it really ends with his financial operations - why, all right. That's very likely what it'll come to, but we should like to know. The merest hint would be useful."

"I'll do my best," Hamel promised. "In any case, it will be just the few days' holiday I was looking forward to."

Kinsley helped himself to whisky and soda and turned towards his friend.

"Here's luck to you, Dick! Take care of yourself. All sorts of things may happen, you know. Old man Fentolin may take a fancy to you and tell you secrets that any statesman in Europe would be glad to hear. He may tell you why this conference is being held and what the result will be. You may be the first to hear of our coming fall. Well, here's to you, anyway! Drop me a line, if you've anything to report."

"Cheero!" Hamel answered, as he set down his empty tumbler. "Astonishing how keen I feel about this little adventure. I'm perfectly sick of the humdrum life I have been leading the last week, and you do sort of take one back to the Arabian Nights, you know, Reggie. I am never quite sure whether to take you seriously or not."

Kinsley smiled as he held his friend's hand for a moment.

E. Phillips Oppenheim

"Dick," he said earnestly, "if only you'd believe it, the adventures in the Arabian Nights were as nothing compared with the present-day drama of foreign politics. You see, we've learned to conceal things nowadays - to smooth them over, to play the part of ordinary citizens to the world while we tug at the underhand levers in our secret moments. Good night! Good luck!"

CHAPTER VIII

Richard Hamel, although he certainly had not the appearance of a person afflicted with nerves, gave a slight start. For the last half-hour, during which time the train had made no stop, he had been alone in his compartment. Yet, to his surprise, he was suddenly aware that the seat opposite to him had been noiselessly taken by a girl whose eyes, also, were fixed with curious intentness upon the broad expanse of marshland and sands across which the train was slowly making its way. Hamel had spent a great many years abroad, and his first impulse was to speak with the unexpected stranger. He forgot for a moment that he was in England, travelling in a first-class carriage, and pointed with his left hand towards the sea.

"Queer country this, isn't it?" he remarked pleasantly. "Do you know, I never heard you come in. It gave me quite a start when I found that I had a fellow-passenger."

She looked at him with a certain amount of still surprise, a look which he returned just as steadfastly, because even in those few seconds he was conscious of that strange selective interest, certainly unaccounted for by his own impressions of her appearance. She seemed to him, at that first glance, very far indeed from being good-looking, according to any of the

E. Phillips Oppenheim

standards by which he had measured good looks. She was thin, too thin for his taste, and she carried herself with an aloofness to which he was unaccustomed. Her cheeks were quite pale, her hair of a soft shade of brown, her eyes grey and sad. She gave him altogether an impression of colourlessness, and he had been living in a land where colour and vitality meant much. Her speech, too, in its very restraint, fell strangely upon his ears.

"I have been travelling in an uncomfortable compartment," she observed. "I happened to notice, when passing along the corridor, that yours was empty. In any case, I am getting out at the next station."

"So am I," he replied, still cheerfully. "I suppose the next station is St. David's?"

She made no answer, but so far as her expression counted for anything at all, she was a little surprised. Her eyes considered him for a moment. Hamel was tall, well over six feet, powerfully made, with good features, clear eyes, and complexion unusually sunburnt. He wore a flannel collar of unfamiliar shape, and his clothes, although they were neat enough, were of a pattern and cut obviously designed to afford the maximum of ease and comfort with the minimum regard to appearance. He wore, too, very thick boots, and his hands gave one the impression that they were seldom gloved. His voice was pleasant, and he had the easy self-confidence of a person sure of himself in the world. She put him down as a colonial - perhaps an American - but his rank in life mystified her.

"This seems the queerest stretch of country," he went on; "long spits of sand jutting right out into the sea, dikes and creeks - miles and miles of them. Now, I wonder, is it low tide or high? Low, I should think, because of the sea-shine on the sand there."

She glanced out of the window.

"The tide," she told him, "is almost at its lowest."

"You live in this neighbourhood, perhaps?" he enquired.

"I do," she assented.

"Sort of country one might get very fond of," he ventured.

She glanced at him from the depths of her grey eyes.

"Do you think so?" she rejoined coldly. "For my part, I hate it."

He was surprised at the unexpected emphasis of her tone - the first time, indeed, that she had shown any signs of interest in the conversation.

"Kind of dull I suppose you find it," he remarked pensively, looking out across the waste of lavender-grown marshes, sand hummocks piled with seaweed, and a far distant line of pebbled shore. "And yet, I don't know. I have lived by the sea a good deal, and however monotonous it may seem at first, there's always plenty of change, really. Tide and wind do such wonderful work."

She, too, was looking out now towards the sea.

"Oh, it isn't exactly that," she said quietly. "I am quite willing to admit what all the tourists and chance visitors call the fascination of these places. I happen to dislike them, that is all. Perhaps it is because I live here, because I see them day by day; perhaps because the sight of them and the thought of them have become woven into my life."

She was talking half to herself. For a moment, even the knowledge of his presence had escaped her. Hamel, however, did not realise that fact. He welcomed her confidence as a sign of relaxation from the frigidity of her earlier demeanour.

"That seems hard," he observed sympathetically. "It seems odd to hear you talk like that, too. Your life, surely, ought to be pleasant enough."

She looked away from the sea into his face. Although the genuine interest which she saw there and the kindly expression of his eyes disarmed annoyance, she still stiffened slightly.

"Why ought it?"

The question was a little bewildering.

"Why, because you are young and a girl," he replied. "It's natural to be cheerful, isn't it?"

"Is it?" she answered listlessly. "I cannot tell. I have not had much experience."

"How old are you?" he asked bluntly.

This time it certainly seemed as though her reply

would contain some rebuke for his curiosity. She glanced once more into his face, however, and the instinctive desire to administer that well-deserved snub passed away. He was so obviously interested, his question was asked so naturally, that its spice of impertinence was as though it had not existed.

"I am twenty-one," she told him.

"And how long have you lived here?"

"Since I left boarding-school, four years ago."

"Anywhere near where I am going to bury myself for a time, I wonder?" he went on.

"That depends," she replied. "Our only neighbours are the Lorneybrookes of Market Burnham. Are you going there?"

He shook his head.

"I've got a little shanty of my own," he explained, "quite close to St. David's Station. I've never even seen it yet."

She vouchsafed some slight show of curiosity.

"Where is this shanty, as you call it?" she asked him.

"I really haven't the faintest idea," he replied. "I am looking for it now. All I can tell you is that it stands just out of reach of the full tides, on a piece of rock, dead on the beach and about a mile from the station. It was built originally for a coastguard station and meant to hold a lifeboat, but they found they could never

E. Phillips Oppenheim

launch the lifeboat when they had it, so the man to whom all the foreshore and most of the land around here belongs - a Mr. Fentolin, I believe - sold it to my father. I expect the place has tumbled to pieces by this time, but I thought I'd have a look at it."

She was gazing at him steadfastly now, with parted lips.

"What is your name?" she demanded.

"Richard Hamel."

"Hamel."

She repeated it lingeringly. It seemed quite unfamiliar.

"Was your father a great friend of Mr. Fentolin's, then?" she asked.

"I believe so, in a sort of way," he answered. "My father was Hamel the artist, you know. They made him an R.A. some time before he died. He used to come out here and live in a tent. Then Mr. Fentolin let him use this place and finally sold it to him. My father used often to speak to me about it before he died."

"Tell me," she enquired, "I do not know much about these matters, but have you any papers to prove that it was sold to your father and that you have the right to occupy it now when you choose?"

He smiled.

"Of course I have," he assured her. "As a matter of fact, as none of us have been here for so long, I thought I'd better bring the title-deed, or whatever they call it, along with me. It's with the rest of my traps at Norwich. Oh, the place belongs to me, right enough!" he went on, smiling. "Don't tell me that any one's pulled it down, or that it's disappeared from the face of the earth?"

"No," she said, "it still remains there. When we are round the next curve, I think I can show it to you. But every one has forgotten, I think, that it doesn't belong to Mr. Fentolin still. He uses it himself very often."

"What for?"

She looked at her questioner quite steadfastly, quite quietly, speechlessly. A curious uneasiness crept into his thoughts. There were mysterious things in her face. He knew from that moment that she, too, directly or indirectly, was concerned with those strange happenings at which Kinsley had hinted. He knew that there were things which she was keeping from him now.

"Mr. Fentolin uses one of the rooms as a studio. He likes to paint there and be near the sea," she explained. "But for the rest, I do not know. I never go near the place."

"I am afraid," he remarked, after a few moments of silence, "that I shall be a little unpopular with Mr. Fentolin. Perhaps I ought to have written first, but then, of course, I had no idea that any one was making use of the place."

"I do not understand," she said, "how you can possibly expect to come down like this and live there, without any preparation."

"Why not?"

"You haven't any servants nor any furniture nor things to cook with."

He laughed.

"Oh! I am an old campaigner," he assured her. "I meant to pick up a few oddments in the village. I don't suppose I shall stay very long, anyhow, but I thought I'd like to have a look at the place. By-the-by, what sort of a man is Mr. Fentolin?"

Again there was that curious expression in her eyes, an expression almost of secret terror, this time not wholly concealed. He could have sworn that her hands were cold.

"He met with an accident many years ago," she said slowly. "Both his legs were amputated. He spends his life in a little carriage which he wheels about himself."

"Poor fellow!" Hamel exclaimed, with a strong man's ready sympathy for suffering. "That is just as much as I have heard about him. Is he a decent sort of fellow in other ways? I suppose, anyhow, if he has really taken a fancy to my little shanty, I shall have to give it up."

Then, as it seemed to him, for the first time real life leaped into her face. She leaned towards him. Her tone was half commanding, half imploring, her manner entirely confidential.

"Don't!" she begged. "It is yours. Claim it. Live in it. Do anything you like with it, but take it away from Mr. Fentolin!"

Hamel was speechless. He sat a little forward, a hand on either knee, his mouth ungracefully open, an expression of blank and utter bewilderment in his face. For the first time he began to have vague doubts concerning this young lady. Everything about her had been so strange: her quiet entrance into the carriage, her unusual manner of talking, and finally this last passionate, inexplicable appeal.

"I am afraid," he said at last, "I don't quite understand. You say the poor fellow has taken a fancy to the place and likes being there. Well, it isn't much of a catch for me, anyway. I'm rather a wanderer, and I dare say I shan't be back in these parts again for years. Why shouldn't I let him have it if he wants it? It's no loss to me. I'm not a painter, you know, like my father."

She seemed on the point of making a further appeal. Her lips, even, were parted, her head a little thrown back. And then she stopped. She said nothing. The silence lasted so long that he became almost embarrassed.

"You will forgive me if I am a little dense, won't you?" he begged. "To tell you the truth," he went on, smiling, "I've got a sort of feeling that I'd like to do anything you ask me. Now won't you just explain a little more clearly what you mean, and I'll blow up the old place sky high, if it's any pleasure to you."

She seemed suddenly to have reverted to her former self - the cold and colourless young woman who had first taken the seat opposite to his.

"Mine was a very foolish request," she admitted quietly. "I am sorry that I ever made it. It was just an impulse, because the little building we were speaking of has been connected with one or two very disagreeable episodes. Nevertheless, it was foolish of me. How long did you think of staying there - that is," she added, with a faint smile, "providing that you find it possible to prove your claim and take up possession?"

"Oh, just for a week or so," he answered lightly, "and as to regaining possession of it," he went on, a slightly pugnacious instinct stirring him, "I don't imagine that there'll be any difficulty about that."

"Really!" she murmured.

"Not that I want to make myself disagreeable," he continued, "but the Tower is mine, right enough, even if I have let it remain unoccupied for some time."

She let down the window - a task in which he hastened to assist her. A rush of salt, cold air swept into the compartment. He sniffed it eagerly.

"Wonderful!" he exclaimed.

She stretched out a long arm and pointed. Away in the distance, on the summit of a line of pebbled shore, standing, as it seemed, sheer over the sea, was a little black speck.

"That," she said, "is the Tower."

He changed his position and leaned out of the window.

"Well, it's a queer little place," he remarked. "It doesn't look worth quarrelling over, does it?"

"And that," she went on, directing his attention to the hill, "is Mr. Fentolin's home, St. David's Hall."

For several moments he made no remark at all. There was something curiously impressive in that sudden sweep up from the sea-line; the strange, miniature mountain standing in the middle of the marshes, with its tree-crowned background; and the long, weather-beaten front of the house turned bravely to the sea.

"I never saw anything like it," he declared. "Why, it's barely a quarter of a mile from the sea, isn't it?"

"A little more than that. It is a strangely situated abode, isn't it?"

"Wonderful!" he agreed, with emphasis. "I must study the geological formation of that hill," he continued, with interest. "Why, it looks almost like an island now."

"That is because of the floods," she told him. "Even at high tide the creeks never reach so far as the back there. All the water you see stretching away inland is flood water - the result of the storm, I suppose. This is where you get out," she concluded, rising to her feet.

She turned away with the slightest nod. A maid was already awaiting her at the door of the compartment. Hamel was suddenly conscious of the fact that he disliked her going immensely.

"We shall, perhaps, meet again during the next few days," he remarked.

She half turned her head. Her expression was

E. Phillips Oppenheim

scarcely encouraging.

"I hope," she said, "that you will not be disappointed in your quarters."

Hamel followed her slowly on to the platform, saw her escorted to a very handsome motor-car by an obsequious station-master, and watched the former disappear down the stretch of straight road which led to the hill. Then, with a stick in one hand, and the handbag which was his sole luggage in the other, he left the station and turned seaward.

CHAPTER IX

Mr. Fentolin, surrounded by his satellites, was seated in his chair before the writing-table. There were present in the room most of the people important to him in his somewhat singular life. A few feet away, in characteristic attitude, stood Meekins. Doctor Sarson, with his hands behind him, was looking out of the window. At the further end of the table stood a confidential telegraph clerk, who was just departing with a little sheaf of messages. By his side, with a notebook in her hand, stood Mr. Fentolin's private secretary - a white-haired woman, with a strangely transparent skin and light brown eyes, dressed in somber black, a woman who might have been of any age from thirty to fifty. Behind her was a middle-aged man whose position in the household no one was quite sure about - a clean-shaven man whose name was Ryan, and who might very well have been once an actor or a clergyman. In the background stood Henderson, the perfect butler.

"It is perhaps opportune," Mr. Fentolin said quietly, "that you all whom I trust should be present here together. I wish you to understand one thing. You have, I believe, in my employ learned the gift of silence. It is to be exercised with regard to a certain visitor brought here by my nephew, a visitor whom I regret to say is now lying seriously ill."

E. Phillips Oppenheim

There was absolute silence. Doctor Sarson alone turned from the window as though about to speak, but met Mr. Fentolin's eye and at once resumed his position.

"I rely upon you all," Mr. Fentolin continued softly. "Henderson, you, perhaps, have the most difficult task, for you have the servants to control. Nevertheless, I rely upon you, also. If one word of this visitor's presence here leaks out even so far as the village, out they go, every one of them. I will not have a servant in the place who does not respect my wishes. You can give any reason you like for my orders. It is a whim. I have whims, and I choose to pay for them. You are all better paid than any man breathing could pay you. In return I ask only for your implicit obedience."

He stretched out his hand and took a cigarette from a curiously carved ivory box which stood by his side. He tapped it gently upon the table and looked up.

"I think, sir," Henderson said respectfully, "that I can answer for the servants. Being mostly foreigners, they see little or nothing of the village people."

No one else made any remark. It was strange to see how dominated they all were by that queer little fragment of humanity, whose head scarcely reached a foot above the table before which he sat. They departed silently, almost abjectly, dismissed with a single wave of the hand. Mr. Fentolin beckoned his secretary to remain. She came a little nearer.

"Sit down, Lucy," he ordered.

She seated herself a few feet away from him. Mr.

Fentolin watched her for several moments. He himself had his back to the light. The woman, on the other hand, was facing it. The windows were high, and the curtains were drawn back to their fullest extent. A cold stream of northern light fell upon her face. Mr. Fentolin gazed at her and nodded her head slightly.

"My dear Lucy," he declared, "you are wonderful - a perfect cameo, a gem. To look at you now, with your delightful white hair and your flawless skin, one would never believe that you had ever spoken a single angry word, that you had ever felt the blood flow through your veins, or that your eyes had ever looked upon the gentle things of life."

She looked at him, still without speech. The immobility of her face was indeed a marvellous thing. Mr. Fentolin's expression darkened.

"Sometimes," he murmured softly, "I think that if I had strong fingers - really strong fingers, you know, Lucy - I should want to take you by the throat and hold you tighter and tighter, until your breath came fast, and your eyes came out from their shadows."

She turned over a few pages of her notebook. To all appearance she had not heard a word.

"To-day," she announced, "is the fourth of April. Shall I send out the various checks to those men in Paris, New York, Frankfort, St. Petersburg, and Tokio?"

"You can send the checks," he told her. "Be sure that you draw them, as usual, upon the Credit Lyonaise and in the name you know of. Say to Lebonaitre of Paris that you consider his last reports faulty. No mention was made of Monsieur C's visit to the Russian Embassy, or of the supper party given to the Baron von Erlstein by a certain Russian gentleman. Warn him, if you please, that reports with such omissions are useless to me."

She wrote a few words in her book.

"You made a note of that?"

She raised her head.

"I do not make mistakes," she said.

His eyebrows were drawn together. This was his work, he told himself, this magnificent physical subjection. Yet his inability to stir her sometimes maddened him.

"You know who is in this house?" he asked. "You know the name of my unknown guest?"

"I know nothing," she replied. "His presence does not interest me."

"Supposing I desire you to know?" he persisted, leaning a little forward. "Supposing I tell you that it is your duty to know?"

"Then," she said, "I should tell you that I believe him to be the special envoy from New York to The Hague, or whatever place on the Continent this coming conference is to be held at."

"Right, woman!" Mr. Fentolin answered sharply. "Right! It is the special envoy. He has his mandate with him. I have them both - the man and his mandate.

Can you guess what I am going to do with them?"

"It is not difficult," she replied. "Your methods are scarcely original. His mandate to the flames, and his body to the sea!"

She raised her eyes as she spoke and looked over Mr. Fentolin's shoulder, across the marshland to the grey stretch of ocean. Her eyes became fixed. It was not possible to say that they held any expression, and yet one felt that she saw beneath the grey waves, even to the rocks and caverns below.

"It does not terrify you, then," he asked curiously, "to think that a man under this roof is about to die?"

"Why should it?" she retorted. "Death does not frighten me - my own or anybody else's. Does it frighten you?"

His face was suddenly livid, his eyes full of fierce anger. His lips twitched. He struck the table before him.

"Beast of a woman!" he shouted. "You ghoul! How dare you! How dare you -"

He stopped short. He passed his hand across his forehead. All the time the woman remained unmoved.

"Do you know," he muttered, his voice still shaking a little, "that I believe sometimes I am afraid of you? How would you like to see me there, eh, down at the bottom of that hungry sea? You watch sometimes so fixedly. You'd miss me, wouldn't you? I am a good master, you know. I pay well. You've been with me a good many years. You were a different sort of woman when you first came."

"Yes," she admitted, "I was a different sort of woman."

"You don't remember those days, I suppose," he went on, "the days when you had brown hair, when you used to carry roses about and sing to yourself while you beat your work out of that wretched typewriter?"

"No," she answered, "I do not remember those days. They do not belong to me. It is some other woman you are thinking of."

Their eyes met. Mr. Fentolin turned away first. He struck the bell at his elbow. She rose at once.

"Be off!" he ordered. "When you look at me like that, you send shivers through me! You'll have to go; I can see you'll have to go. I can't keep you any longer. You are the only person on the face of the earth who dares to say things to me which make me think, the only person who doesn't shrink at the sound of my voice. You'll have to go. Send Sarson to me at once. You've upset me!"

She listened to his words in expressionless silence. When he had finished, carrying her book in her hand, she very quietly moved towards the door. He watched her, leaning a little forward in his chair, his lips parted, his eyes threatening. She walked with steady, even footsteps. She carried herself with almost machine-like erectness; her skirts were noiseless. She had the trick of turning the handle of the door in perfect silence. He heard her calm voice in the hall.

"Doctor Sarson is to go to Mr. Fentolin."

Mr. Fentolin sat quite still, feeling his own pulse.

"That woman," he muttered to himself, "that - woman - some day I shouldn't be surprised if she really -"

He paused. The doctor had entered the room.

"I am upset, Sarson," he declared. "Come and feel my pulse quickly. That woman has upset me."

"Miss Price?"

"Miss Price, d-n it! Lucy - yes!"

"It seems unlike her," the doctor remarked. "I have never heard her utter a useless syllable in my life."

Mr. Fentolin held out his wrist.

"It's what she doesn't say," he muttered.

The doctor produced his watch. In less than a minute he put it away.

"This is quite unnecessary," he pronounced. "Your pulse is wonderful."

"Not hurried? No signs of palpitation?"

"You have seven or eight footmen, all young men," Doctor Sarson replied drily. "I will wager that there isn't one of them has a pulse so vigorous as yours."

Mr. Fentolin leaned a little back in his chair. An

expression of satisfaction crept over his face.

"You reassure me, my dear Sarson. That is excellent. What of our patient?"

"There is no change."

"I am afraid," Mr. Fentolin sighed, "that we shall have trouble with him. These strong people always give trouble."

"It will be just the same in the long run," the doctor remarked, shrugging his shoulders.

Mr. Fentolin held up his finger.

"Listen! A motor-car, I believe?"

"It is Miss Fentolin who is just arriving," the doctor announced. "I saw the car coming as I crossed the hall."

Mr. Fentolin nodded gently.

"Indeed?" he replied. "Indeed? So my dear niece has returned. Open the door, friend Sarson. Open the door, if you please. She will be anxious to see me. We must summon her."

CHAPTER X

Mr. Fentolin raised to his lips the little gold whistle which hung from his neck and blew it. He seemed to devote very little effort to the operation, yet the strength of the note was wonderful. As the echoes died away, he let it fall by his side and waited with a pleased smile upon his lips. In a few seconds there was the hurried flutter of skirts and the sound of footsteps. The girl who had just completed her railway journey entered, followed by her brother. They were both a little out of breath, they both approached the chair without a smile, the girl in advance, with a certain expression of apprehension in her eyes. Mr. Fentolin sighed. He appeared to notice these things and regret them.

"My child," he said, holding out his hands, "my dear Esther, welcome home again! I heard the car outside. I am grieved that you did not at once hurry to my side."

"I have not been in the house two minutes," Esther replied, "and I haven't seen mother yet. Forgive me."

She had come to a standstill a few yards away. She moved now very slowly towards the chair, with the air of one fulfilling a hateful task. The fingers which accepted his hands were extended almost hesitatingly. He drew her closer to him and held her there.

E. Phillips Oppenheim

"Your mother, my dear Esther, is, I regret to say, suffering from a slight indisposition," he remarked. "She has been confined to her room for the last few days. Just a trifling affair of the nerves; nothing more, Doctor Sarson assures me. But my dear child," he went on, "your fingers are as cold as ice. You look at me so strangely, too. Alas! you have not the affectionate disposition of your dear mother. One would scarcely believe that we have been parted for more than a week."

"For more than a week," she repeated, under her breath.

"Stoop down, my dear. I must kiss your forehead - there! Now bring up a chair to my side. You seem frightened - alarmed. Have you ill news for me?"

"I have no news," she answered, gradually recovering herself.

"The gaieties of London, I fear," he protested gently, "have proved a little unsettling."

"There were no gaieties for me," the girl replied bitterly. "Mrs. Sargent obeyed your orders very faithfully. I was not allowed to move out except with her."

"My dear child, you would not go about London unchaperoned!"

"There is a difference," she retorted, "between a chaperon and a jailer."

Mr. Fentolin sighed. He shook his head slowly. He

seemed pained.

"I am not sure that you repay my care as it deserves, Esther," he declared. "There is something in your deportment which disappoints me. Never mind, your brother has made some atonement. I entrusted him with a little mission in which I am glad to say that he has been brilliantly successful."

"I cannot say that I am glad to hear it," Esther replied quietly.

Mr. Fentolin sat back in his chair. His long fingers played nervously together, he looked at her gravely.

"My dear child," he exclaimed, in a tone of pained surprise, "your attitude distresses me!"

"I cannot help it. I have told you what I think about Gerald and the life he is compelled to live here. I don't mind so much for myself, but for him I think it is abominable."

"The same as ever," Mr. Fentolin sighed. "I fear that this little change has done you no good, dear niece."

"Change!" she echoed. "It was only a change of prisons."

Mr. Fentolin shook his head slowly - a distressful gesture. Yet all the time he had somehow the air of a man secretly gratified.

"You are beginning to depress me," he announced. "I think that you can go away. No, stop for just one moment. Stand there in the light. Dear me, how unfortunate! Who would have thought that so beautiful a mother could have so plain a daughter!"

She stood quite still before him, her hands crossed in front of her, something of the look of the nun from whom the power of suffering has gone in her still, cold face and steadfast eyes.

"Not a touch of colour," he continued meditatively, "a figure straight as my walking-stick. What a pity! And all the taste, nowadays, they tell me, is in the other direction. The lank damsels have gone completely out. We buried them with Oscar Wilde. Run along, my dear child. You do not amuse me. You can take Gerald with you, if you will. I have nothing to say to Gerald just now. He is in my good books. Is there anything I can do for you, Gerald? Your allowance, for instance - a trifling increase or an advance? I am in a generous humour."

"Then grant me what I begged for the other day," the boy answered quickly. "Let me go to Sandhurst. I could enter my name next week for the examinations, and I could pass to-morrow."

Mr. Fentolin tapped the table thoughtfully with his forefinger.

"A little ungrateful, my dear boy," he declared, "a little ungrateful that, I think. Your confidence in yourself pleases me, though. You think you could pass your examinations?"

"I did a set of papers last week," the boy replied. "On the given percentages I came out twelfth or better. Mr. Brown assured me that I could go in for them at any moment. He promised to write you about it before he left."

Mr. Fentolin nodded gently.

"Now I come to think of it, I did have a letter from Mr. Brown," he remarked. "Rather an impertinence for a tutor, I thought it. He devoted three pages towards impressing upon me the necessity of your adopting some sort of a career."

"He wrote because he thought it was his duty," the boy said doggedly.

"So you want to be a soldier," Mr. Fentolin continued musingly. "Well, well, why not? Our picture galleries are full of them. There has been a Fentolin in every great battle for the last five hundred years. Sailors, too - plenty of them - and just a few diplomatists. Brave fellows! Not one, I fancy," he added, "like me - not one condemned to pass their days in a perambulator. You are a fine fellow, Gerald - a regular Fentolin. Getting on for six feet, aren't you?"

"Six feet two, sir."

"A very fine fellow," Mr. Fentolin repeated. "I am not so sure about the army, Gerald. You see, there are some people who say, like your American friend, that we are even now almost on the brink of war."

"All the more reason for me to hurry," the boy begged.

Mr. Fentolin closed his eyes.

"Don't!" he insisted. "Have you ever stopped to think

what war means - the war you speak of so lightly? The suffering, the misery of it! All the pageantry and music and heroism in front; and behind, a blackened world, a trail of writhing corpses, a world of weeping women for whom the sun shall never rise again. Ugh! An ugly thing war, Gerald. I am not sure that you are not better at home here. Why not practise golf a little more assiduously? I see from the local paper that you are still playing at two handicap. Now with your physique, I should have thought you would have been a scratch player long before now."

"I play cricket, sir," the boy reminded him, a little impatiently, "and, after all, there are other things in the world besides games."

Mr. Fentolin's long finger shot suddenly out. He was leaning a little from his chair. His expression of gentle immobility had passed away. His face was stern, almost stony.

"You have spoken the truth, Gerald," he said. "There are other things in the world besides games. There is the real, the tragical side of life, the duties one takes up, the obligations of honour. You have not forgotten, young man, the burden you carry?"

The boy was paler, but he had drawn himself to his full height.

"I have not forgotten, sir," he answered bitterly. "Do I show any signs of forgetting? Haven't I done your bidding year by year? Aren't I here now to do it?"

"Then do it!" Mr. Fentolin retorted sharply. "When I am ready for you to leave here, you shall leave. Until then, you are mine. Remember that. Ah! this is Doctor Sarson who comes, I believe. That must mean that it is five o'clock. Come in, Doctor. I am not engaged. You see, I am alone with my dear niece and nephew. We have been having a little pleasant conversation."

Doctor Sarson bowed to Esther, who scarcely glanced at him. He remained in the background, quietly waiting.

"A very delightful little conversation," Mr. Fentolin concluded. "I have been congratulating my nephew, Doctor, upon his wisdom in preferring the quiet country life down here to the wearisome routine of a profession. He escapes the embarrassing choice of a career by preferring to devote his life to my comfort. I shall not forget it. I shall not be ungrateful. I may have my faults, but I am not ungrateful. Run away now, both of you. Dear children you are, but one wearies, you know, of everything. I am going out. You see, the twilight is coming. The tide is changing. I am going down to meet the sea."

His little carriage moved towards the door. The brother and sister passed out. Esther led Gerald into the great dining-room, and from there, through the open windows, out on to the terrace. She gripped his shoulder and pointed down to the Tower.

"Something," she whispered in his ear, "is going to happen there."

CHAPTER XI

The little station at which Hamel alighted was like an oasis in the middle of a flat stretch of sand and marsh. It consisted only of a few raised planks and a rude shelter - built, indeed, for the convenience of St. David's Hall alone, for the nearest village was two miles away. The station-master, on his return from escorting the young lady to her car, stared at this other passenger in some surprise.

"Which way to the sea?" Hamel asked.

The man pointed to the white gates of the crossing.

"You can take any of those paths you like, sir," he said. "If you want to get to Salthouse, though, you should have got out at the next station."

"This will do for me," Hamel replied cheerfully.

"Be careful of the dikes," the station-master advised him. "Some of them are pretty deep."

Hamel nodded, and passing through the white gates, made his way by a raised cattle track towards the sea. On either side of him flowed a narrow dike filled with salt-water. Beyond stretched the flat marshland, its mossy turf leavened with cracks and creeks of all widths, filled also with sea-slime and sea-water. A slight grey mist rested upon the more distant parts of the wilderness which he was crossing, a mist which seemed to be blown in from the sea in little puffs, resting for a time upon the earth, and then drifting up and fading away like soap bubbles.

More than once where the dikes had overflown he was compelled to change his course, but he arrived at last at the little ridge of pebbled beach bordering the sea. Straight ahead of him now was that strange-looking building towards which he had all the time been directing his footsteps. As he approached it, his forehead slightly contracted. There was ample confirmation before him of the truth of his fellow-passenger's words. The place, left to itself for so many years, without any attention from its actual owner, was neither deserted nor in ruins. Its solid grey stone walls were sea-stained and a trifle worn, but the arched wooden doors leading into the lifeboat shelter, which occupied one side of the building, had been newly painted, and in the front the window was hung with a curtain, now closely drawn, of some dark red material. The lock from the door had been removed altogether, and in its place was the aperture for a Yale latch-key. The last note of modernity was supplied by the telephone wire attached to the roof of the lifeboat shelter. He walked all round the building, seeking in vain for some other means of ingress. Then he stood for a few moments in front of the curtained window. He was a man of somewhat determined disposition, and he found himself vaguely irritated by the liberties which had been taken with his property. He hammered gently upon the framework with his fist, and the windows opened readily inwards, pushing back the curtain with them. He drew himself up on to the sill,

E. Phillips Oppenheim

and, squeezing himself through the opening, landed on his feet and looked around him, a little breathless.

He found himself in a simply furnished man's sitting-room. An easel was standing close to the window. There were reams of drawing paper and several unfinished sketches leaning against the wall. There was a small oak table in the middle of the room; against the wall stood an exquisite chiffonier, on which were resting some cut-glass decanters and goblets. There was a Turkey carpet upon the floor which matched the curtains, but to his surprise there was not a single chair of any sort to be seen. The walls had been distempered and were hung with one or two engravings which, although he was no judge, he was quite sure were good. He wandered into the back room, where he found a stove, a tea-service upon a deal table, and several other cooking utensils, all spotlessly clean and of the most expensive description. The walls here were plainly whitewashed, and the floor was of hard stone. He then tried the door on the left, which led into the larger portion of the building - the shed in which the lifeboat had once been kept. Not only was the door locked, but he saw at once that the lock was modern, and the door itself was secured with heavy iron clamps. He returned to the sitting-room.

"The girl with the grey eyes was right enough," he remarked to himself. "Mr. Fentolin has been making himself very much at home with my property."

He withdrew the curtains, noticing, to his surprise, the heavy shutters which their folds had partly concealed. Then he made his way out along the passage to the front door, which from the inside he was able to open easily enough. Leaving it carefully ajar, he went out with the intention of making an examination of the outside of the place. Instead, however, he paused at the corner of the building with his face turned landwards. Exactly fronting him now, about three-quarters of a mile away, on the summit of that strange hill which stood out like a gigantic rock in the wilderness, was St. David's Hall. He looked at it steadily and with increasing admiration. Its long, red brick front with its masses of clustering chimneys, a little bare and weather-beaten, impressed him with a sense of dignity due as much to the purity of its architecture as the singularity of its situation. Behind - a wonderfully effective background - were the steep gardens from which, even in this uncertain light, he caught faint glimpses of colouring subdued from brilliancy by the twilight. These were encircled by a brick wall of great height, the whole of the southern portion of which was enclosed with glass. From the fragment of rock upon which he had seated himself, to the raised stone terrace in front of the house, was an absolutely straight path, beautifully kept like an avenue, with white posts on either side, and built up to a considerable height above the broad tidal way which ran for some distance by its side. It had almost the appearance of a racing track, and its state of preservation in the midst of the wilderness was little short of remarkable.

"This," Hamel said to himself, as he slowly produced a pipe from his pocket and began to fill it with tobacco from a battered silver box, "is a queer fix. Looks rather like the inn for me!"

"And who might you be, gentleman?"

He turned abruptly around towards his unseen questioner. A woman was standing by the side of the rock upon which he was sitting, a woman from the village, apparently, who must have come with noiseless footsteps along the sandy way. She was dressed in rusty black, and in place of a hat she wore a black woolen scarf tied around her head and underneath her chin. Her face was lined, her hair of a deep brown plentifully besprinkled with grey. She had a curious habit of moving her lips, even when she was not speaking. She stood there smiling at him, but there was something about that smile and about her look which puzzled him.

"I am just a visitor," he replied. "Who are you?"

She shook her head.

"I saw you come out of the Tower," she said, speaking with a strong local accent and yet with a certain unusual correctness, "in at the window and out of the door. You're a brave man."

"Why brave?" he asked.

She turned her head very slowly towards St. David's Hall. A gleam of sunshine had caught one of the windows, which shone like fire. She pointed toward it with her head.

"He's looking at you," she muttered. "He don't like strangers poking around here, that I can tell you."

"And who is he?" Hamel enquired.

"Squire Fentolin," she answered, dropping her voice a little. "He's a very kind-hearted gentleman, Squire Fentolin, but he don't like strangers hanging around."

"Well, I am not exactly a stranger, you see," Hamel remarked. "My father used to stay for months at a time in that little shanty there and paint pictures. It's a good many years ago."

"I mind him," the woman said slowly. "His name was Hamel."

"I am his son," Hamel announced.

She pointed to the Hall. "Does he know that you are here?"

Hamel shook his head. "Not yet. I have been abroad for so long."

She suddenly relapsed into her curious habit. Her lips moved, but no words came. She had turned her head a little and was facing the sea.

"Tell me," Hamel asked gently, "why do you come out here alone, so far from the village?"

She pointed with her finger to where the waves were breaking in a thin line of white, about fifty yards from the beach.

"It's the cemetery, that," she said, "the village cemetery, you know. I have three buried there: George, the eldest; James, the middle one; and David, the youngest. Three of them - that's why I come. I can't put flowers on their graves, but I can sit and watch and look through the sea, down among the rocks where their bodies are, and wonder."

Hamel looked at her curiously. Her voice had grown

lower and lower.

"It's what you land folks don't believe, perhaps," she went on, "but it's true. It's only us who live near the sea who understand it. I am not an ignorant body, either. I was schoolmistress here before I married David Cox. They thought I'd done wrong to marry a fisherman, but I bore him brave sons, and I lived the life a woman craves for. No, I am not ignorant. I have fancies, perhaps - the Lord be praised for them! - and I tell you it's true. You look at a spot in the sea and you see nothing - a gleam of blue, a fleck of white foam, one day; a gleam of green with a black line, another; and a grey little sob, the next, perhaps. But you go on looking. You look day by day and hour by hour, and the chasms of the sea will open, and their voices will come to you. Listen!"

She clutched his arm.

"Couldn't you hear that?" she half whispered.

"'The light!' It was David's voice! 'The light!'" Hamel was speechless. The woman's face was suddenly strangely transformed. Her mood, however, swiftly changed. She turned once more towards the hall.

"You'll know him soon," she went on, "the kindest man in these parts, they say. It's not much that he gives away, but he's a kind heart. You see that great post at the entrance to the river there?" she went on, pointing to it. "He had that set up and a lamp hung from there. Fentolin's light, they call it. It was to save men's lives. It was burning, they say, the night I lost my lads. Fentolin's light!"

"They were wrecked?" he asked her gently.

"Wrecked," she answered. "Bad steering it must have been. James would steer, and they say that he drank a bit. Bad steering! Yes, you'll meet Squire Fentolin before long. He's queer to look at - a small body but a great, kind heart. A miserable life, his, but it will be made up to him. It will be made up to him!"

She turned away. Her lips were moving all the time. She walked about a dozen steps, and then she returned.

"You're Hamel's son, the painter," she said. "You'll be welcome down here. He'll have you to stay at the Hall - a brave place. Don't let him be too kind to you. Sometimes kindness hurts."

She passed on, walking with a curious, shambling gait, and soon she disappeared on her way to the village. Hamel watched her for a moment and then turned his head towards St. David's Hall. He felt somehow that her abrupt departure was due to something which she had seen in that direction. He rose to his feet. His instinct had been a true one.

CHAPTER XII

From where Hamel stood a queer object came strangely into sight. Below the terrace of St. David's Hall - from a spot, in fact, at the base of the solid wall - it seemed as though a gate had been opened, and there came towards him what he at first took to be a tricycle. As it came nearer, it presented even a weirder appearance. Mr. Fentolin, in a black cape and black skull cap, sat a little forward in his electric carriage, with his hand upon the guiding lever. His head came scarcely above the back of the little vehicle, his hands and body were motionless. He seemed to be progressing without the slightest effort, personal or mechanical, as though he rode, in deed, in some ghostly vehicle. From the same place in the wall had issued, a moment or two later, a man upon a bicycle, who was also coming towards him. Hamel was scarcely conscious of this secondary figure. His eyes were fixed upon the strange personage now rapidly approaching him. There was something which seemed scarcely human in that shrunken fragment of body, the pale face with its waving white hair, the strange expression with which he was being regarded. The little vehicle came to a standstill only a few feet away. Mr. Fentolin leaned forward. His features had lost their delicately benevolent aspect; his words were minatory.

"I am under the impression, sir," he said, "that I saw

you with my glasses from the window attempting to force an entrance into that building."

Hamel nodded.

"I not only tried but I succeeded," he remarked. "I got in through the window."

Mr. Fentolin's eyes glittered for a moment. Hamel, who had resumed his place upon the rock close at hand, had been mixed up during his lifetime in many wild escapades. Yet at that moment he had a sudden feeling that there were dangers in life which as yet he had not faced.

"May I ask for your explanation or your excuse?"

"You can call it an explanation or an excuse, whichever you like," Hamel replied steadily, "but the fact is that this little building, which some one else seems to have appropriated, is mine. If I had not been a good-natured person, I should be engaged, at the present moment, in turning out its furniture on to the beach."

"What is your name?" Mr. Fentolin asked suddenly.

"My name is Hamel - Richard Hamel."

For several moments there was silence. Mr. Fentolin was still leaning forward in his strange little vehicle. The colour seemed to have left even his lips. The hard glitter in his eyes had given place to an expression almost like fear. He looked at Richard Hamel as though he were some strange sea-monster come up from underneath the sands.

"Richard Hamel," he repeated. "Do you mean that you are the son of Hamel, the R.A., who used to be in these parts so often? He was my brother's friend."

"I am his son."

"But his son was killed in the San Francisco earthquake. I saw his name in all the lists. It was copied into the local papers here."

Hamel knocked the ashes from his pipe.

"I take a lot of killing," he observed. "I was in that earthquake, right enough, and in the hospital afterwards, but it was a man named Hamel of Philadelphia who died."

Mr. Fentolin sat quite motionless for several moments. He seemed, if possible, to have shrunken into something smaller still. A few yards behind, Meekins had alighted from his bicycle and was standing waiting.

"So you are Richard Hamel," Mr. Fentolin said at last very softly. "Welcome back to England, Richard Hamel! I knew your father slightly, although we were never very friendly."

He stretched out his hand from underneath the coverlet of his little vehicle - a hand with long, white fingers, slim and white and shapely as a woman's. A single ring with a dull green stone was on his fourth finger. Hamel shook hands with him as he would have shaken hands with a woman. Afterwards he rubbed his fingers slowly together. There was something about the touch which worried him.

"You have been making use of this little shanty, haven't you?" he asked bluntly.

Mr. Fentolin nodded. He was apparently beginning to recover himself.

"You must remember," he explained suavely, "that it was built by my grandfather, and that we have had rights over the whole of the foreshore here from time immemorial. I know quite well that my brother gave it to your father - or rather he sold it to him for a nominal sum. I must tell you that it was a most complicated transaction. He had the greatest difficulty in getting any lawyer to draft the deed of sale. There were so many ancient rights and privileges which it was impossible to deal with. Even now there are grave doubts as to the validity of the transaction. When nothing was heard of you, and we all concluded that you were dead, I ventured to take back what I honestly believed to be my own. Owing," he continued slowly, "to my unfortunate affliction, I am obliged to depend for interest in my life upon various hobbies. This little place, queerly enough, has become one of them. I have furnished it, in a way; installed the telephone to the house, connected it with my electric plant, and I come down here when I want to be quite alone, and paint. I watch the sea - such a sea sometimes, such storms, such colour! You notice that ridge of sand out yonder? It forms a sort of natural breakwater. Even on the calmest day you can trace that white line of foam."

"It is a strange coast," Hamel admitted.

Mr. Fentolin pointed with his forefinger northwards.

"Somewhere about there , " he indicated, "is the

E. Phillips Oppenheim

entrance to the tidal river which flows up to the village of St. David's yonder. You see?"

His finger traced its course until it came to a certain point near the beach, where a tall black pillar stood, surmounted by a globe.

"I have had a light fixed there for the benefit or the fishermen," he said, "a light which I work from my own dynamo. Between where we are sitting now and there - only a little way out to sea - is a jagged cluster of cruel rocks. You can see them if you care to swim out in calm weather. Fishermen who tried to come in by night were often trapped there and, in a rough sea, drowned. That is why I had that pillar of light built. On stormy nights it shows the exact entrance to the water causeway."

"Very kind of you indeed," Hamel remarked, "very benevolent."

Mr. Fentolin sighed.

"So few people have any real feeling for sailors," he continued. "The fishermen around here are certainly rather a casual class. Do you know that there is scarcely one of them who can swim? There isn't one of them who isn't too lazy to learn even the simplest stroke. My brother used to say - dear Gerald - that it served them right if they were drowned. I have never been able to feel like that, Mr. Hamel. Life is such a wonderful thing. One night," he went on, dropping his voice and leaning a little forward in his carriage - "it was just before, or was it just after I had fixed that light - I was down here one dark winter night. There was a great north wind and a huge sea running. It was as black as pitch, but I heard a boat making for St. David's causeway strike on those rocks just hidden in front there. I heard those fishermen shriek as they went under. I heard their shouts for help, I heard their death cries. Very terrible, Mr. Hamel! Very terrible!"

Hamel looked at the speaker curiously. Mr. Fentolin seemed absorbed in his subject. He had spoken with relish, as one who loves the things he speaks about. Quite unaccountably, Hamel found himself shivering.

"It was their mother," Mr. Fentolin continued, leaning again a little forward in his chair, "their mother whom I saw pass along the beach just now - a widow, too, poor thing. She comes here often - a morbid taste. She spoke to you, I think?"

"She spoke to me strangely," Hamel admitted. "She gave me the impression of a woman whose brain had been turned with grief."

"Too true," Mr. Fentolin sighed. "The poor creature! I offered her a small pension, but she would have none of it. A superior woman in her way once, filled now with queer fancies," he went on, eyeing Hamel steadily, - "the very strangest fancies. She spends her life prowling about here. No one in the village even knows how she lives. Did she speak of me, by-the-by?"

"She spoke of you as being a very kind-hearted man."

Mr. Fentolin sighed.

"The poor creature! Well, well, let us revert to the object of your coming here. Do you really wish to occupy this little shanty, Mr. Hamel?"

"That was my idea," Hamel confessed. "I only came back from Mexico last month, and I very soon got fed up with life in town. I am going abroad again next year. Till then, I am rather at a loose end. My father was always very keen indeed about this place, and very anxious that I should come and stay here for a little time, so I made up my mind to run down. I've got some things waiting at Norwich. I thought I might hire a woman to look after me and spend a few weeks here. They tell me that the early spring is almost the best time for this coast."

Mr. Fentolin nodded slowly. He moistened his lips for a moment. One might have imagined that he was anxious.

"Mr. Hamel," he said softly, "you are quite right. It is the best time to visit this coast. But why make a hermit of yourself? You are a family friend. Come and stay with us at the Hall for as long as you like. It will give me the utmost pleasure to welcome you there," he went on earnestly, "and as for this little place, of what use is it to you? Let me buy it from you. You are a man of the world, I can see. You may be rich, yet money has a definite value. To me it has none. That little place, as it stands, is probably worth - say a hundred pounds. Your father gave, if I remember rightly, a five pound note for it. I will give you a thousand for it sooner than be disturbed."

Hamel frowned slightly.

"I could not possibly think," he said, "of selling what was practically a gift to my father. You are welcome to occupy the place during my absence in any way you wish. On the other hand, I do not think that I care to part with it altogether, and I should really like to spend just a day or so here. I am used to roughing it under all sorts of conditions - much more used to roughing it than I am to staying at country houses."

Mr. Fentolin leaned a little out of his carriage. He reached the younger man's shoulder with his hand.

"Ah! Mr. Hamel," he pleaded, "don't make up your mind too suddenly. Am I a little spoilt, I wonder? Well, you see what sort of a creature I am. I have to go through life as best I may, and people are kind to me. It is very seldom I am crossed. It is quite astonishing how often people let me have my own way. Do not make up your mind too suddenly. I have a niece and a nephew whom you must meet. There are some treasures, too, at St. David's Hall. Look at it. There isn't another house quite like it in England. It is worth looking over."

"It is most impressive," Hamel agreed, "and wonderfully beautiful. It seems odd," he added, with a laugh, "that you should care about this little shanty here, with all the beautiful rooms you must have of your own."

"It's Naboth's vineyard," Mr. Fentolin groaned. "Now, Mr. Hamel, you are going to be gracious, aren't you? Let us leave the question of your little habitation here alone for the present. Come back with me. My niece shall give you some tea, and you shall choose your room from forty. You can sleep in a haunted chamber, or a historical chamber, in Queen Elizabeth's room, a Victorian chamber, or a Louis Quinze room. All my people have spent their substance in furniture. Don't look at your bag. Clothes are unnecessary. I can supply you with everything. Or, if you prefer it, I can send a fast car into Norwich for your own things. Come and be my guest, please."

Hamel hesitated. He had not the slightest desire to go to St. David's Hall, and though he strove to ignore it, he was conscious of an aversion of which he was heartily ashamed for this strange fragment of humanity. On the other hand, his mission, the actual mission which had brought him down to these parts, could certainly best be served by an entree into the Hall itself - and there was the girl, whom he felt sure belonged there. He had never for a moment been able to dismiss her from his thoughts. Her still, cold face, the delicate perfection of her clothes and figure, the grey eyes which had rested upon his so curiously, haunted him. He was desperately anxious to see her again. If he refused this invitation, if he rejected Mr. Fentolin's proffered friendship, it would be all the more difficult.

"You are really very kind," he began hesitatingly - .

"It is settled," Mr. Fentolin interrupted, "settled. Meekins, you can ride back again. I shall not paint to-day. Mr. Hamel, you will walk by my side, will you not? I can run my little machine quite slowly. You see, I have an electric battery. It needs charging often, but I have a dynamo of my own. You never saw a vehicle like this in all your travellings, did you?"

Hamel shook his head.

"An electrical bath-chair," Mr. Fentolin continued. "Practice has made me remarkably skilful in its manipulation. You see, I can steer to an inch."

He was already turning around. Hamel rose to his feet.

"You are really very kind," he said. "I should like to come up and see the Hall, at any rate, but in the meantime, as we are here, could I just look over the inside of this little place? I found the large shed where the lifeboat used to be kept, locked up."

Mr. Fentolin was manoeuvring his carriage. His back was towards Hamel.

"By all means," he declared. "We will go in together. I have had the entrance widened so that I can ride straight into the sitting-room. But wait."

He paused suddenly. He felt in all his pockets.

"Dear me," he exclaimed, "I find that I have left the keys! We will come down a little later, if you do not mind, Mr. Hamel. Or to-morrow, perhaps. You will not mind? It is very careless of me, but seeing you about the place and imagining that you were an intruder, made me angry, and I started off in a hurry. Now walk by my side up to the house, please, and talk to me. It is so interesting for me to meet men," he went on, as they started along the straight path, "who do things in life; who go to foreign countries, meet strange people, and have new experiences. I have been a good many years like this, you know."

"It is a great affliction," Hamel murmured sympathetically.

"In my youth I was an athlete," Mr. Fentolin continued. "I played cricket for the Varsity and for my county. I hunted, too, and shot. I did all the things a

E. Phillips Oppenheim

man loves to do. I might still shoot, they tell me, but my strength has ebbed away. I am too weak to lift a gun, too weak even to handle a fishing-rod. I have just a few hobbies in life which keep me alive. Are you a politician, Mr. Hamel?"

"Not in the least," Hamel replied. "I have been out of England too long to keep in touch with politics."

"Naturally," Mr. Fentolin agreed. "It amuses me to follow the course of events. I have a good many friends in London and abroad who are kind to me, who keep me informed, send me odd bits of information not available for every one, and it amuses me to put these things together in my mind and to try and play the prophet. I was in the Foreign Office once, you know. I take up my paper every morning, and it is one of my chief interests to see how near my own speculations come to the truth. Just now for example, there are strange things doing on the Continent."

"In America," Hamel remarked, "they affect to look upon England as a doomed Power."

"Not altogether supine yet," Mr. Fentolin observed, "yet even this last generation has seen weakening. We have lost so much self-reliance. Perhaps it is having these grown-up children who we think can take care of us - Canada and Australia, and the others. However, we will not talk of politics. It bores you, I can see. We will try and find some other subject. Now tell me, don't you think this is ingenious?"

They had reached the foot of the hill upon which the Hall was situated. In front of them, underneath the terrace, was a little iron gate, held open now by

Meekins, who had gone on ahead and dismounted from his bicycle.

"I have a subterranean way from here into the Hall," Mr. Fentolin explained. "Come with me. You will only have to stoop a little, and it may amuse you. You need not be afraid. There are electric lights every ten yards. I turn them on with this switch - see."

Mr. Fentolin touched a button in the wall, and the place was at once brilliantly illuminated. A little row of lights from the ceiling and the walls stretched away as far as one could see. They passed through the iron gates, which shut behind them with a click. Stooping a little, Hamel was still able to walk by the side of the man in the chair. They traversed about a hundred yards of subterranean way. Here and there a fungus hung down from the wall, otherwise it was beautifully kept and dry. By and by, with a little turn, they came to an incline and another iron gate, held open for them by a footman. Mr. Fentolin sped up the last few feet into the great hail, which seemed more imposing than ever by reason of this unexpected entrance. Hamel, blinking a little, stepped to his side.

"Welcome!" Mr. Fentolin cried gaily. "Welcome, my friend Mr. Hamel, to St. David's Hall!"

E. Phillips Oppenheim

CHAPTER XIII

During the next half-hour, Hamel was introduced to luxuries to which, in a general way, he was entirely unaccustomed. One man-servant was busy preparing his bath in a room leading out of his sleeping apartment, while another brought him a choice of evening clothes and superintended his disrobing. Hamel, always observant, studied his surroundings with keen interest. He found himself in a queerly mixed atmosphere of luxurious modernity and stately antiquity. His four-poster, the huge couch at the foot of his bed, and all the furniture about the room, was of the Queen Anne period. The bathroom which communicated with his apartment was the latest triumph of the plumber's art - a room with floor and walls of white tiles, the bath itself a little sunken and twice the ordinary size. He dispensed so far as he could with the services of the men and descended, as soon as he was dressed, into the hall. Meekins was waiting at the bottom of the stairs, dressed now in somber black.

"Mr. Fentolin will be glad if you will step into his room, sir," he announced, leading the way.

Mr. Fentolin was seated in his chair, reading the Times in a corner of his library. Shaped blocks had been placed behind and in front of the wheels of his little vehicle , to prevent it from moving. A shaded reading-lamp stood on the table by his side. He did not at once look up, and Hamel glanced around with genuine admiration. The shelves which lined the walls and the winged cases which protruded into the room were filled with books. There was a large oak table with beautifully carved legs, piled with all sorts of modern reviews and magazines. A log fire was burning in the big oaken grate. The perfume from a great bowl of lavender seemed to mingle curiously yet pleasantly with the half musty odour of the old leather-bound volumes. The massive chimneypiece was of black oak, and above it were carved the arms of the House of Fentolin. The walls were oak-panelled to the ceiling.

"Refreshed, I hope, by your bath and change, my dear visitor?" the head of the house remarked, as he laid down his paper. "Draw a chair up here and join me in a glass of vermouth. You need not be afraid of it. It comes to me from the maker as a special favour."

Hamel accepted a quaintly-cut wine-glass full of the amber liquid. Mr. Fentolin sipped his with the air of a connoisseur.

"This," he continued, "is one of our informal days. There is no one in the house save my sister-in-law, niece, and nephew, and a poor invalid gentleman who, I am sorry to say, is confined to his bed. My sister-in-law is also, I regret to say, indisposed. She desired me to present her excuses to you and say how greatly she is looking forward to making your acquaintance during the next few days."

Hamel bowed.

"It is very kind of Mrs. Fentolin," he murmured.

"On these occasions," Mr. Fentolin continued, "we do not make use of a drawing-room. My niece will come in here presently. You are looking at my books, I see. Are you, by any chance, a bibliophile? I have a case of manuscripts here which might interest you."

Hamel shook his head.

"Only in the abstract, I fear," he answered. "I have scarcely opened a serious book since I was at Oxford."

"What was your year?" Mr. Fentolin asked.

"Fourteen years ago I left Magdalen," Hamel replied. "I had made up my mind to be an engineer, and I went over to the Boston Institute of Technology."

Mr. Fentolin nodded appreciatively.

"A magnificent profession," he murmured. "A healthy one, too, I should judge from your appearance. You are a strong man, Mr. Hamel."

"I have had reason to be," Hamel rejoined. "During nearly the whole of the time I have been abroad, I have been practically pioneering. Building railways in the far West, with gangs of Chinese and Italians and Hungarians and scarcely a foreman who isn't terrified of his job, isn't exactly drawing-room work."

"You are going back there?" Mr. Fentolin asked, with interest.

Hamel shook his head.

"I have no plans," he declared. "I have been fortunate

enough, or shall I some day say unfortunate enough, I wonder, to have inherited a large legacy."

Mr. Fentolin smiled.

"Don't ever doubt your good fortune," he said earnestly. "The longer I live - and in my limited way I do see a good deal of life - the more I appreciate the fact that there isn't anything in this world that compares with the power of money. I distrust a poor man. He may mean to be honest, but he is at all times subject to temptation. Ah! here is my niece."

Mr. Fentolin turned towards the door. Hamel rose at once to his feet. His surmise, then, had been correct. She was coming towards them very quietly. In her soft grey dinner-gown, her brown hair smoothly brushed back, a pearl necklace around her long, delicate neck, she seemed to him a very exquisite embodiment of those memories which he had been carrying about throughout the afternoon.

"Here, Mr. Hamel," his host said, "is a member of my family who has been a deserter for a short time. This is Mr. Richard Hamel, Esther; my niece, Miss Esther Fentolin."

She held out her hand with the faintest possible smile, which might have been of greeting or recognition.

"I travelled for some distance in the train with Mr. Hamel this afternoon, I think," she remarked.

"Indeed?" Mr. Fentolin exclaimed. "Dear me, that is very interesting - very interesting, indeed! Mr. Hamel, I am sure, did not tell you of his destination?"

He watched them keenly. Hamel, though he scarcely understood, was quick to appreciate the possible significance of that tentative question.

"We did not exchange confidences," he observed. "Miss Fentolin only changed into my carriage during the last few minutes of her journey. Besides," he continued, "to tell you the truth, my ideas as to my destination were a little hazy. To come and look for some queer sort of building by the side of the sea, which has been unoccupied for a dozen years or so, scarcely seems a reasonable quest, does it?"

"Scarcely, indeed," Mr. Fentolin assented. "You may thank me, Mr. Hamel, for the fact that the place is not in ruins. My blatant trespassing has saved you from that, at least. After dinner we must talk further about the Tower. To tell you the truth, I have grown accustomed to the use of the little place."

The sound of the dinner gong boomed through the house. A moment later Gerald entered, followed by a butler announcing dinner.

"The only remaining member of my family," Mr. Fentolin remarked, indicating his nephew. "Gerald, you will be pleased, I know, to meet Mr. Hamel. Mr. Hamel has been a great traveller. Long before you can remember, his father used to paint wonderful pictures of this coast."

Gerald shook hands with his visitor. His face, for a moment, lighted up. He was looking pale, though, and singularly sullen and dejected.

"There are two of your father's pictures in the modern

side of the gallery up-stairs," he remarked, a little diffidently. "They are great favourites with everybody here."

They all went in to dinner together. Meekins, who had appeared silently, had glided unnoticed behind his master's chair and wheeled it across the hall.

"A partie carree to-night," Mr. Fentolin declared. "I have a resident doctor here, a very delightful person, who often dines with us, but to-night I thought not. Five is an awkward number. I want to get to know you better, Mr. Hamel, and quickly. I want you, too, to make friends with my niece and nephew. Mr. Hamel's father," he went on, addressing the two latter, "and your father were great friends. By-the-by, have I told you both exactly why Mr. Hamel is a guest here to-night - why he came to these parts at all? No? Listen, then. He came to take possession of the Tower. The worst of it is that it belongs to him, too. His father bought it from your father more years ago than we should care to talk about. I have really been a trespasser all this time."

They took their places at a small round table in the middle of the dining-room. The shaded lights thrown downwards upon the table seemed to leave most of the rest of the apartment in semi-darkness. The gloomy faces of the men and women whose pictures hung upon the walls were almost invisible. The servants themselves, standing a little outside the halo of light, were like shadows passing swiftly and noiselessly back and forth. At the far end of the room was an organ, and to the left a little balcony, built out as though for an orchestra. Hamel looked about him almost in wonderment. There was something curiously

E. Phillips Oppenheim

impressive in the size of the apartment and its emptiness.

"A trespasser," Mr. Fentolin continued, as he took up the menu and criticised it through his horn-rimmed eyeglass, "that is what I have been, without a doubt."

"But for your interest and consequent trespass," Hamel remarked, "I should probably have found the roof off and the whole place in ruins."

"Instead of which you found the door locked against you," Mr. Fentolin pointed out. "Well, we shall see. I might, at any rate, have lost the opportunity of entertaining you here this evening. I am particularly glad to have an opportunity of making you known to my niece and nephew. I think you will agree with me that here are two young people who are highly to be commended. I cannot offer them a cheerful life here. There is little society, no gaiety, no sort of excitement. Yet they never leave me. They seem to have no other interest in life but to be always at my beck and call. A case, Mr. Hamel, of really touching devotion. If anything could reconcile me to my miserable condition, it would be the kindness and consideration of those by whom I am surrounded."

Hamel murmured a few words of cordial agreement. Yet he found himself, in a sense, embarrassed. Gerald was looking down upon his plate and his face was hidden. Esther's features had suddenly become stony and expressionless. Hamel felt instinctively that something was wrong.

"There are compensations," Mr. Fentolin continued, with the air of one enjoying speech, "which find their way into even the gloomiest of lives. As I lie on my back, hour after hour, I feel all the more conscious of this. The world is a school of compensations, Mr. Hamel. The interests - the mental interests, I mean - of unfortunate people like myself, come to possess in time a peculiar significance and to yield a peculiar pleasure. I have hobbies, Mr. Hamel. I frankly admit it. Without my hobbies, I shudder to think what might become of me. I might become a selfish, cruel, misanthropical person. Hobbies are indeed a great thing."

The brother and sister sat still in stony silence. Hamel, looking across the little table with its glittering load of cut glass and silver and scarlet flowers, caught something in Esther's eyes, so rarely expressive of any emotion whatever, which puzzled him. He looked swiftly back at his host. Mr. Fentolin's face, at that moment, was like a beautiful cameo. His expression was one of gentle benevolence.

"Let me be quite frank with you," Mr. Fentolin murmured. "My occupation of the Tower is one of these hobbies. I love to sit there within a few yards of the sea and watch the tide come in. I catch something of the spirit, I think, which caught your father, Mr. Hamel, and kept him a prisoner here. In my small way I, too, paint while I am down there, paint and dream. These things may not appeal to you, but you must remember that there are few things left to me in life, and that those, therefore, which I can make use of, are dear to me. Gerald, you are silent to-night. How is it that you say nothing?"

"I am tired, sir," the boy answered quietly.

Mr. Fentolin nodded gravely.

"It is inexcusable of me," he declared smoothly, "to have forgotten even for a moment. My nephew, Mr. Hamel," he went on, "had quite an exciting experience last night - or rather a series of experiences. He was first of all in a railway accident, and then, for the sake of a poor fellow who was with him and who was badly hurt, he motored back here in the grey hours of the morning and ran, they tell me, considerable risk of being drowned on the marshes. A very wonderful and praiseworthy adventure, I consider it. I trust that our friend up-stairs, when he recovers, will be properly grateful."

Gerald rose to his feet precipitately. The service of dinner was almost concluded, and he muttered something which sounded like an excuse. Mr. Fentolin, however, stretched out his hand and motioned him to resume his seat.

"My dear Gerald!" he exclaimed reprovingly. "You would leave us so abruptly? Before your sister, too! What will Mr. Hamel think of our country ways? Pray resume your seat."

For a moment the boy stood quite still, then he slowly subsided into his chair. Mr. Fentolin passed around a decanter of wine which had been placed upon the table by the butler. The servants had now left the room.

"You must excuse my nephew, if you please, Mr. Hamel," he begged. "Gerald has a boy's curious aversion to praise in any form. I am looking forward to hearing your verdict upon my port. The collection of wine and pictures was a hobby of my grandfather's, for which we, his descendants, can never be sufficiently grateful."

Hamel praised his wine, as indeed he had every reason to, but for a few moments the smooth conversation of his host fell upon deaf ears. He looked from the boy's face, pale and wrinkled as though with some sort of suppressed pain, to the girl's still, stony expression. This was indeed a house of mysteries! There was something here incomprehensible, some thing about the relations of these three and their knowledge of one another, utterly baffling. It was the queerest household, surely, into which any stranger had ever been precipitated.

"The planting of trees and the laying down of port are two virtues in our ancestors which have never been properly appreciated," Mr. Fentolin continued. "Let us, at any rate, free ourselves from the reproach of ingratitude so far as regards my grandfather - Gerald Fentolin - to whom I believe we are indebted for this wine. We will drink -"

Mr. Fentolin broke off in the middle of his sentence. The august calm of the great house had been suddenly broken. From up-stairs came the tumult of raised voices, the slamming of a door, the falling of something heavy upon the floor. Mr. Fentolin listened with a grim change in his expression. His smile had departed, his lower lip was thrust out, his eyebrows met. He raised the little whistle which hung from his chain. At that moment, however, the door was opened. Doctor Sarson appeared.

"I am sorry to disturb you, Mr. Fentolin," he said, "but our patient is becoming a little difficult. The

E. Phillips Oppenheim

concussion has left him, as I feared it might, in a state of nervous excitability. He insists upon an interview with you."

Mr. Fentolin backed his little chair from the table. The doctor came over and laid his hand upon the handle.

"You will, I am sure, excuse me for a few moments, Mr. Hamel," his host begged. "My niece and nephew will do their best to entertain you. Now, Sarson, I am ready."

Mr. Fentolin glided across the dim, empty spaces of the splendid apartment, followed by the doctor; a ghostly little procession it seemed. The door was closed behind them. For a few moments a curious silence ensued. Gerald remained tense and apparently suffering from some sort of suppressed emotion. Esther for the first time moved in her place. She leaned towards Hamel. Her lips were slowly parted, her eyes sought the door as though in terror. Her voice, although save for themselves there was no one else in the whole of that great apartment, had sunk to the lowest of whispers.

"Are you a brave man, Mr. Hamel?" she asked.

He was staggered but he answered her promptly.

"I believe so."

"Don't give up the Tower - just yet. That is what - he has brought you here for. He wants you to give it up and go back. Don't!"

The earnestness of her words was unmistakable.

Hamel felt the thrill of coming events.

"Why not?"

"Don't ask me," she begged. "Only if you are brave, if you have feeling for others, keep the Tower, if it be for only a week. Hush!"

The door had been noiselessly opened. The doctor appeared and advanced to the table with a grave little bow.

"Mr. Fentolin," he said, "has been kind enough to suggest that I take a glass of wine with you. My presence is not needed up-stairs. Mr. Hamel," he added, "I am glad, sir, to make your acquaintance. I have for a long time been a great admirer of your father's work."

He took his place at the head of the table and, filling his glass, bowed towards Hamel. Once more Gerald and his sister relapsed almost automatically into an indifferent and cultivated silence. Hamel found civility towards the newcomer difficult. Unconsciously his attitude became that of the other two. He resented the intrusion. He found himself regarding the advent of Doctor Sarson as possessing some secondary significance. It was almost as though Mr. Fentolin preferred not to leave him alone with his niece and nephew.

Nevertheless, his voice, when he spoke, was clear and firm.

CHAPTER XIV

Mr. Fentolin, on leaving the dining-room, steered his chair with great precision through the open, wrought-iron doors of a small lift at the further end of the hall, which Doctor Sarson, who stepped in with him, promptly directed to the second floor. Here they made their way to the room in which Mr. Dunster was lying. Doctor Sarson opened the door and looked in. Almost immediately he stood at one side, out of sight of Mr. Dunster, and nodded to Mr. Fentolin.

"If there is any trouble," he whispered, "send for me. I am better away, for the present. My presence only excites him."

Mr. Fentolin nodded.

"You are right," he said. "Go down into the dining-room. I am not sure about that fellow Hamel, and Gerald is in a queer temper. Stay with them. See that they are not alone."

The doctor silently withdrew, and Mr. Fentolin promptly glided past him into the room. Mr. John P. Dunster, in his night clothes, was sitting on the side of the bed. Standing within a few feet of him, watching him all the time with the subtle intentness of a cat watching a mouse, stood Meekins. Mr. Dunster's head was still bound, although the bandage had slipped a little, apparently in some struggle. His face was chalklike, and he was breathing quickly.

"So you've come at last!" he exclaimed, a little truculently. "Are you Mr. Fentolin?"

Mr. Fentolin gravely admitted his identity. His eyes rested upon his guest with an air of tender interest. His face was almost beautiful.

"You are the owner of this house - I am underneath your roof - is that so?"

"This is certainly St. David's Hall," Mr. Fentolin replied. "It really appears as though your conclusions were correct."

"Then will you tell me why I am kept a prisoner here?"

Mr. Fentolin's expression was for a moment clouded. He seemed hurt.

"A prisoner," he repeated softly. "My dear Mr. Dunster, you have surely forgotten the circumstances which procured for me the pleasure of this visit; the condition in which you arrived here - only, after all, a very few hours ago?"

"The circumstances," Mr. Dunster declared drily, "are to me still inexplicable. At Liverpool Street Station I was accosted by a young man who informed me that his name was Gerald Fentolin, and that he was on his way to The Hague to play in a golf tournament. His story seemed entirely probable, and I permitted him a seat in the special train I had chartered for Harwich.

There was an accident and I received this blow to my head - only a trifling affair, after all. I come to my senses to find myself here. I do not know exactly what part of the world you call this, but from the fact that I can see the sea from my window, it must be some considerable distance from the scene of the accident. I find that my dressing-case has been opened, my pocket-book examined, and I am apparently a prisoner. I ask you, Mr. Fentolin, for an explanation."

Mr. Fentolin smiled reassuringly.

"My dear sir," he said, "my dear Mr. Dunster, I believe I may have the pleasure of calling you - your conclusions seem to me just a little melodramatic. My nephew - Gerald Fentolin - did what I consider the natural thing, under the circumstances. You had been courteous to him, and he repaid the obligation to the best of his ability. The accident to your train happened in a dreary part of the country, some thirty miles from here. My nephew adopted a course which I think, under the circumstances, was the natural and hospitable one. He brought you to his home. There was no hospital or town of any importance nearer."

"Very well," Mr. Dunster decided. "I will accept your version of the affair. I will, then, up to this point acknowledge myself your debtor. But will you tell me why my dressing-case has been opened, my clothes removed, and a pocket-book containing papers of great importance to me has been tampered with?"

"My dear Mr. Dunster," his host repelled calmly, "you surely cannot imagine that you are among thieves! Your dressing-case was opened and the contents of your pocket-book inspected with a view to ascertaining your address, or the names of some friends with whom we might communicate."

"Am I to understand that they are to be restored to me, then?" Mr. Dunster demanded.

"Without a doubt, yes!" Mr. Fentolin assured him. "You, however, are not fit for anything, at the present moment, but to return to your bed, from which I understand you rose rather suddenly a few minutes ago."

"On the contrary," Mr. Dunster insisted, "I am feeling absolutely well enough to travel. I have an appointment on the Continent of great importance, as you may judge by the fact that at Liverpool Street I chartered a special train. I trust that nothing in my manner may have given you offence, but I am anxious to get through with the business which brought me over to this side of the water. I have sent for you to ask that my pocket-book, dressing-case, and clothes be at once restored to me, and that I be provided with the means of continuing my journey without a moment's further delay."

Mr. Fentolin shook his head very gently, very regretfully, but also firmly.

"Mr. Dunster," he pleaded, "do be reasonable. Think of all you have been through. I can quite sympathise with you in your impatience, but I am forced to tell you that the doctor who has been attending you since the moment you were brought into this house has absolutely forbidden anything of the sort."

Mr. Dunster seemed, for a moment, to struggle

for composure.

"I am an American citizen," he declared. "I am willing to listen to the advice of any physician, but so long as I take the risk, I am not bound to follow it.

"In the present case I decline to follow it. I ask for facilities to leave this house at once."

Mr. Fentolin sighed.

"In your own interests," he said calmly, "they will not be granted to you."

Mr. Dunster had spoken all the time like a man struggling to preserve his self-control. There were signs now that his will was ceasing to serve him. His eyes flashed fire, his voice was raised.

"Will not be granted to me?" he repeated. "Do you mean to say, then, that I am to be kept here against my will?"

Mr. Fentolin made no immediate reply. With the delicate fingers of his right hand he pushed back the hair from his forehead. He looked at his questioner soothingly, as one might look at a spoiled child.

"Against my will?" Mr. Dunster repeated, raising his voice still higher. "Mr. Fentolin, if the truth must be told, I have heard of you before and been warned against you. I decline to accept any longer the hospitality of your roof. I insist upon leaving it. If you will not provide me with any means of doing so, I will walk."

He made a motion as though to rise from the bed. Meekins' hand very gently closed upon his arm. One could judge that the grip was like a grip of iron.

"Dear me," Mr. Fentolin said, "this is really very unreasonable of you! If you have heard of me, Mr. Dunster, you ought to understand that notwithstanding my unfortunate physical trouble, I am a person of consequence and position in this county. I am a magistrate, ex-high sheriff, and a great land-owner here. I think I may say without boasting that I represent one of the most ancient families in this country. Why, therefore, should you treat me as though it were to my interest to inveigle you under my roof and keep you there for some guilty purpose? Cannot you understand that it is for your own good I hesitate to part with you?"

"I understand nothing of the sort," Mr. Dunster exclaimed angrily. "Let us bring this nonsense to an end. I want my clothes, and if you won't lend me a car or a trap, I'll walk to the nearest railway station."

Mr. Fentolin shook his head.

"I am quite sure," he said, "that you are not in a position to travel. Even in the dining-room just now I heard a disturbance for which I was told that you were responsible."

"I simply insisted upon having my clothes," Mr. Dunster explained. "Your servant refused to fetch them. Perhaps I lost my temper. If so, I am sorry. I am not used to being thwarted."

"A few days' rest -" Mr. Fentolin began.

"A few days' rest be hanged!" Mr. Dunster interrupted fiercely. "Listen, Mr. Fentolin," he added, with the air of one making a last effort to preserve his temper, "the mission with which I am charged is one of greater importance than you can imagine. So much depends upon it that my own life, if that is in danger, would be a mere trifle in comparison with the issues involved. If I am not allowed to continue upon my journey at once, the consequences may be more serious than I can tell you, to you and yours, to your own country. There! - I am telling you a great deal, but I want you to understand that I am in earnest. I have a mission which I must perform, and which I must perform quickly."

"You are very mysterious," Mr. Fentolin murmured.

"I will leave nothing to chance," Mr. Dunster continued. "Send this man who seems to have constituted himself my jailer out of earshot, and I will tell you even more."

Mr. Fentolin turned to Meekins.

"You can leave the room for a moment," he ordered. "Wait upon the threshold."

Meekins very unwillingly turned to obey.

"You will excuse me, sir," he objected doubtfully, "but I am not at all sure that he is safe."

Mr. Fentolin smiled faintly.

"You need have no fear, Meekins," he declared. "I am quite sure that you are mistaken. I think that Mr. Dunster is incapable of any act of violence towards a person in my unfortunate position. I am willing to trust myself with him - perfectly willing, Meekins."

Meekins, with ponderous footsteps, left the room and closed the door behind him. Mr. Fentolin leaned a little forward in his chair. It seemed as though he were on springs. The fingers of his right hand had disappeared in the pocket of his black velvet dinner-coat. He was certainly prepared for all emergencies.

"Now, Mr. Dunster," he said softly, "you can speak to me without reserve."

Mr. Dunster dropped his voice. His tone became one of fierce eagerness.

"Look here," he exclaimed, "I don't think you ought to force me to give myself away like this, but, after all, you are an Englishman, with a stake in your country, and I presume you don't want her to take a back seat for the next few generations. Listen here. It's to save your country that I want to get to The Hague without a second's delay. I tell you that if I don't get there, if the message I convey doesn't reach its destination, you may find an agreement signed between certain Powers which will mean the greatest diplomatic humiliation which Great Britain has ever known. Aye, and more than that!" Mr. Dunster continued. "It may be that the bogey you've been setting before yourself for all these years may trot out into life, and you may find St. David's Hall a barrack for German soldiers before many months have passed."

Mr. Fentolin shook his head in gentle disbelief.

"You are speaking to one," he declared, "who knows

more of the political situation than you imagine. In my younger days I was in the Foreign Office. Since my unfortunate accident I have preserved the keenest interest in politics. I tell you frankly that I do not believe you. As the Powers are grouped at present, I do not believe in the possibility of a successful invasion of this country."

"Perhaps not," Mr. Dunster replied eagerly, "but the grouping of the Powers as it has existed during the last few years is on the eve of a great change. I cannot take you wholly into my confidence. I can only give you my word of honour as a friend to your country that the message I carry is her only salvation. Having told you as much as that, I do not think I am asking too much if I ask you for my clothes and dressing-case, and for the fastest motor-car you can furnish me with. I guess I can get from here to Yarmouth, and from there I can charter something which will take me to the other side."

Mr. Fentolin raised the little gold whistle to his lips and blew it very softly. Meekins at once entered, closing the door behind him. He moved silently to the side of the man who had risen now from the bed, and who was standing with his hand grasping the post and his eyes fixed upon Mr. Fentolin, as though awaiting his answer.

"Our conversation," the latter said calmly, "has reached a point, Mr. Dunster, at which I think we may leave it for the moment. You have told me some very surprising things. I perceive that you are a more interesting visitor even than I had thought."

He raised his left hand, and Meekins, who seemed to

have been waiting for some signal of the sort, suddenly, with a movement of his knee and right arm, flung Dunster hack upon the bed. The man opened his mouth to shout, but already, with lightning-like dexterity, his assailant had inserted a gag between his teeth. Treating his struggles as the struggles of a baby, Meekins next proceeded to secure his wrists with handcuffs. He then held his feet together while he quietly wound a coil of cord around them. Mr. Fentolin watched the proceedings from his chair with an air of pleased and critical interest.

"Very well done, Meekins - very neatly done, indeed!" he exclaimed. "As I was saying, Mr. Dunster," he continued, turning his chair, "our conversation has reached a point at which I think we may safely leave it for a time. We will discuss these matters again. Your pretext of a political mission is, of course, an absurd one, but fortunately you have fallen into good hands. Take good care of Mr. Dunster, Meekins. I can see that he is a very important personage. We must be careful not to lose sight of him."

Mr. Fentolin steered his chair to the door, opened it, and passed out. On the landing he blew his whistle; the lift almost immediately ascended. A moment or two later he glided into the dining-room. The three men were still seated around the table. A decanter of wine, almost empty, was before Doctor Sarson, whose pallid cheeks, however, were as yet unflushed.

"At last, my dear guest," Mr. Fentolin exclaimed, turning to Hamel, "I am able to return to you. If you will drink no more wine, let us have our coffee in the library, you and I. I want to talk to you about the Tower."

E. Phillips Oppenheim

CHAPTER XV

Mr. Fentolin led the way to a delightful little corner of his library, where before the open grate, recently piled with hissing logs, an easy chair had been drawn. He wheeled himself up to the other side of the hearthrug and leaned back with a little air of exhaustion. The butler, who seemed to have appeared unsummoned from somewhere among the shadows, served coffee and poured some old brandy into large and wonderfully thin glasses.

"Why my house should be turned into an asylum to gratify the hospitable instincts of my young nephew, I cannot imagine," Mr. Fentolin grumbled. "A most extraordinary person, our visitor, I can assure you. Quite violent, too, he was at first."

"Have you had any outside advice about his condition?" Hamel inquired.

Mr. Fentolin glanced across those few feet of space and looked at Hamel with swift suspicion.

"Why should I?" he asked. "Doctor Sarson is fully qualified, and the case seems to present no unusual characteristics."

Hamel sipped his brandy thoughtfully.

"I don't know why I suggested it," he admitted. "I only thought that an outside doctor might help you to get rid of the fellow."

Mr. Fentolin shrugged his shoulders.

"After all," he said, "the matter is of no real consequence. Doctor Sarson assures me that we shall be able to send him on his way very shortly. In the meantime, Mr. Hamel, what about the Tower?"

"What about it?" Hamel asked, selecting a cigar from the box which had been pushed to his side. "I am sure I haven't any wish to inconvenience you."

"I will be quite frank," Mr. Fentolin declared. "I do not dispute your right for a moment. On the other hand, my few hours daily down there have become a habit with me. I do not wish to give them up. Stay here with us, Mr. Hamel. You will be doing us a great kindness. My nephew and niece have too little congenial society. Make up your mind to give us a fortnight of your time, and I can assure you that we will do our best to make yours a pleasant stay."

Hamel was a little taken aback.

"Mr. Fentolin," he said, "I couldn't think of accepting your hospitality to such an extent. My idea in coming here was simply to fulfil an old promise to my father and to rough it at the Tower for a week or so, and when that was over, I don't suppose I should ever be likely to come back again. You had better let me carry out that plan, and afterwards the place shall be entirely at your disposal."

"You don't quite understand," Mr. Fentolin persisted, a little irritably. "I sit there every morning. I want, for instance, to be there to-morrow morning, and the next morning, and the morning afterwards, to finish a little seascape I have commenced. Nowhere else will do. Call it a whim or what you will I have begun the picture, and I want to finish it."

"Well, you can sit there all right," Hamel assured him. "I shall be out playing golf or fishing. I shall do nothing but sleep there."

"And very uncomfortable you will be," Mr. Fentolin pointed out. "You have no servant, I understand, and there is no one in the village fit to look after you. Think of my thirty-nine empty rooms, my books here, my gardens, my motor-cars, my young people, entirely at your service. You can have a suite to yourself. You can disappear when you like. To all effects and purposes you will be the master of St. David's Hall. Be reasonable. Don't you think, now, that you can spend a fortnight more pleasantly under such circumstances than by playing the misanthrope down at the Tower?"

"Please don't think," Hamel begged, "that I don't appreciate your hospitality. I should feel uncomfortable, however, if I paid you a visit of the length you have suggested. Come, I don't see," he added, "why my occupation of the Tower should interfere with you. I should be away from it by about nine or ten o'clock every morning. I should probably only sleep there. Can't you accept the use of it all the rest of the time? I can assure you that you will be welcome to come and go as though it were entirely your own."

Mr. Fentolin had lit a cigarette and was watching the

blue smoke curl upwards to the ceiling.

"You're an obstinate man, Mr. Hamel," he sighed, "but I suppose you must have your own way. By-the-by, you would only need to use the up-stairs room and the sitting-room. You will not need the outhouse - rather more than an outhouse, though isn't it? I mean the shed which leads out from the kitchen, where the lifeboat used to be kept?"

"I don't think I shall need that," Hamel admitted, a little hesitatingly.

"To tell you the truth," Mr. Fentolin continued, "among my other hobbies I have done a little inventing. I work sometimes at a model there. It is foolish, perhaps, but I wish no one to see it. Do you mind if I keep the keys of the place?"

"Not in the least," Hamel replied. "Tell me, what direction do your inventions take, Mr. Fentolin?"

"Before you go," Mr. Fentolin promised, "I will show you my little model at work. Until then we will not talk of it. Now come, be frank with me. Shall we exchange ideas for a little time? Will you talk of books? They are my daily friends. I have thousands of them, beloved companions on every side. Or will you talk of politics or travel? Or would you rather be frivolous with my niece and nephew? That, I think, is Esther playing."

"To be quite frank," Hamel declared bluntly, "I should like to talk to your niece."

Mr. Fentolin smiled as though amused. His amusement, however, was perfectly good-natured.

"If you will open this door," he said, "you will see another one exactly opposite to you. That is the drawing-room. You will find Esther there. Before you go, will you pass me the Quarterly Review? Thank you."

Hamel crossed the hail, opened the door of the room to which he had been directed, and made his way towards the piano. Esther was there, playing softly to herself with eyes half closed. He came and stood by her side, and she stopped abruptly. Her eyes questioned him. Then her fingers stole once more over the keys, more softly still.

"I have just left your uncle," Hamel said. "He told me that I might come in here."

"Yes?" she murmured.

"He was very hospitable," Hamel continued. "He wanted me to remain here as a guest and not go to the Tower at all."

"And you?"

"I am going to the Tower," he said. "I am going there to-morrow or the day after."

The music swelled beneath her fingers.

"For how long?"

"For a week or so. I am just giving your uncle time to clear out his belongings. I am leaving him the outhouse."

"He asked you to leave him that?" she whispered.

"Yes!"

"You are not going in there at all?"

"Not at all."

Again she played a little more loudly for a few moments. Then the music died away once more.

"What reason did he give for keeping possession of that?"

"Another hobby," Hamel replied. "He is an inventor, it seems. He has the model of something there; he would not tell me what."

She shivered a little, and her music drifted away. She bent over the keys, her face hidden from him.

"You will not go away just yet?" she asked softly. "You are going to stay for a few days, at any rate?"

"Without a doubt," he assured her. "I am altogether my own master."

"Thank God," she murmured.

He leaned with his elbow against the top of the piano, looking down at her. Since dinnertime she had fastened a large red rose in the front of her gown.

"Do you know that this is all rather mysterious?" he said calmly.

"What is mysterious?" she demanded.

"The atmosphere of the place: your uncle's queer aversion to my having the Tower; your visitor up-stairs, who fights with the servants while we are at dinner; your uncle himself, whose will seems to be law not only to you but to your brother, who must be of age, I should think, and who seems to have plenty of spirit."

"We live here, both of us," she told him. "He is our guardian."

"Naturally," Hamel replied, "and yet, it may have been my fancy, of course, but at dinnertime I seemed to get a queer impression."

"Tell it me?" she insisted, her fingers breaking suddenly into a livelier melody. "Tell it me at once? You were there all the time. I could see you watching. Tell me what you thought?"

She had turned her head now, and her eyes were fixed upon his. They were large and soft, capable, he knew, of infinite expression. Yet at that moment the light that shone from them was simply one of fear, half curious, half shrinking.

"My impression," he said, "was that both of you disliked and feared Mr. Fentolin, yet for some reason or other that you were his abject slaves."

Her fingers seemed suddenly inspired with diabolical strength and energy. Strange chords crashed and broke beneath them. She played some unfamiliar music with tense and fierce energy. Suddenly she paused and rose to her feet.

"Come out on to the terrace," she invited. "You are not afraid of cold?"

He followed her without a word. She opened the French windows, and they stepped out on to the long, broad stone promenade. The night was dark, and there was little to be seen. The light was burning at the entrance to the waterway; a few lights were twinkling from the village. The soft moaning of the sea was distinctly audible. She moved to the edge of the palisading. He followed her closely.

"You are right, Mr. Hamel," she said. "I think that I am more afraid of him than any woman ever was of any man in this world."

"Then why do you live here?" he protested. "You must have other relations to whom you could go. And your brother - why doesn't he do something - go into one of the professions? He could surely leave easily enough?"

"I will tell you a secret," she answered calmly. "Perhaps it will help you to understand. You know my uncle's condition. You know that it was the result of an accident?"

"I have heard so," he replied gravely.

She clutched at his arm.

"Come," she said.

Side by side they walked the entire length of the terrace. When they reached the corner, they were met with a fierce gust of wind. She battled along, and he followed her. They were looking inland now. There were no lights visible - nothing but dark, chaotic emptiness. From somewhere below him he could hear the wind in the tree-tops.

"This way," she directed. "Be careful."

They walked to the very edge of the palisading. It was scarcely more than a couple of feet high. She pointed downwards.

"Can you see?" she whispered.

By degrees his eyes faintly penetrated the darkness. It was as though they were looking down a precipice. The descent was perfectly sheer for nearly a hundred feet. At the bottom were the pine trees.

"Come here again in the morning," she whispered. "You will see then. I brought you here to show you the place. It was here that the accident happened."

"What accident?"

"Mr. Fentolin's," she continued. "It was here that he went over. He was picked up with both his legs broken. They never thought that he would live."

Hamel shivered a little. As his eyes grew accustomed to the darkness, he saw more distinctly than ever the sheer fall, the tops of the bending trees below.

"What a horrible thing!" he exclaimed.

"It was more horrible than you know," she continued,

dropping her voice a little, almost whispering in his ear. "I do not know why I tell you this - you, a stranger - but if I do not tell some one, I think that the memory of it will drive me mad. It was no accident at all. Mr. Fentolin was thrown over!"

"By whom?" he asked.

She clung to his arm for a moment.

"Ah, don't ask me!" she begged. "No one knows. My uncle gave out, as soon as he was conscious, that it was an accident."

"That, at any rate, was fine of him," Hamel declared.

She shivered.

"He was proud, at least, of our family name. Whatever credit he deserves for it, he must have. It was owing to that accident that we became his slaves: nothing but that - his absolute slaves, to wait upon him, if he would, hand and foot. You see, he has never been able to marry. His life was, of course, ruined. So the burden came to us. We took it up, little thinking what was in store for us. Five years ago we came here to live. Gerald wanted to go into the army; I wanted to travel with my mother. Gerald has done all the work secretly, but he has never been allowed to pass his examinations. I have never left England except to spend two years at the strictest boarding-school in Paris, to which I was taken and fetched away by one of his creatures. We live here, with the shadow of this thing always with us. We are his puppets. If we hesitate to do his bidding, he reminds us. So far, we have been his creatures, body and soul. Whether it will go on, I cannot say - oh, I cannot say! It is bad for us, but - there is mother, too. He makes her life a perfect hell!"

A roar of wind came booming once more across the marshes, bending the trees which grew so thickly beneath them and which ascended precipitately to the back of the house. The French windows behind rattled. She looked around nervously.

"I am afraid of him all the time," she murmured. "He seems to overhear everything - he or his creatures. Listen!"

They were silent for several moments. He whispered in her ear so closely that through the darkness he could, see the fire in her eyes.

"You are telling me half," he said. "Tell me everything. Who threw your uncle over the parapet?"

She stood by his side, motionless and trembling.

"It was the passion of a moment," she said at last, speaking hoarsely. "I cannot tell you. Listen! Listen!"

"There is no one near," Hamel assured her. "It is the wind which shakes the windows. I wish that you would tell me everything. I would like to be your friend. Believe me, I have that desire, really. There are so many things which I do not understand. That it is dull here for you, of course, is natural, but there is something more than that. You seem always to fear something. Your uncle is a selfish man, naturally, although to look at him he seems to have the disposition of an angel. But beyond that, is there anything of which you are afraid? You seem all the time to live in fear."

She suddenly clutched his hand. There was nothing of affection in her touch, and yet he felt a thrill of delight.

"There are strange things which happen here," she whispered, "things which neither Gerald nor I understand. Yet they terrify us. I think that very soon the end will come. Neither of us can stand it very much longer. We have no friends. Somehow or other, he seems to manage to keep us always isolated."

"I shall not go away from here," Hamel said firmly, "at present. Mind, I am not at all sure that, living this solitary life as you do, you have not become a little over-nervous; that you have not exaggerated the fear of some things. To me your uncle seems merely quixotic and egregiously selfish. However that may be, I am going to remain." She clutched once, more at his arm, her finger was upraised. They listened together. From somewhere behind them came the clear, low wailing of a violin.

"It is Mr. Fentolin," she whispered. "Please come in; let us go in at once. He only plays when he is excited. I am afraid! Oh, I am afraid that something is going to happen!"

She was already round the corner and on her way to the main terrace. He followed her closely.

CHAPTER XVI

"Let us follow the example of all great golfers," Hamel said. "Let us for this morning, at any rate, imagine that your whole world is encompassed within these eighteen holes. We have been sent here in a moment of good humour by your tyrant uncle. The sun shines, and the wind is from the west. Why not?"

"That is all very well for you," she retorted, smiling, "but I have topped my drive."

"Purely an incident," he assured her. "The vicissitudes of the game do not enter into the question. I have driven a ball far above my usual form, but I am not gloating over it. I prefer to remember only that I am going to spend the next two hours with you."

She played her shot, and they walked for a little way together. She was suddenly silent.

"Do you know," she said finally, just a little gravely, "I am not at all used to speeches of this sort."

"Then you ought to be," he declared. "Nothing but the lonely life you have been living has kept you from hearing them continually."

She laughed a little at the impotence of her rebuff and

paused for a moment to make her next shot. Hamel, standing a little on one side, watched her appraisingly. Her short, grey tweed skirt was obviously the handi-work of an accomplished tailor. Her grey stockings and suede shoes were immaculate and showed a care for her appearance which pleased him. Her swing, too, revealed a grace, the grace of long arms and a supple body, at which previously he had only guessed. The sunshine seemed to have brought out a copper tinge from her abundant brown hair.

"Do you know," he remarked, "I think I am beginning to like your uncle. Great idea of his, sending us off here directly after breakfast."

Her face darkened for a moment, and he realised his error. The same thought, indeed, had been in both their minds. Mr. Fentolin's courteous suggestion had been offered to them almost in the shape of a command. It was scarcely possible to escape from the reflection that he had desired to rid himself of their presence for the morning.

"Of course," he went on, "I knew that these links were good - quite famous, aren't they?"

"I have played on so few others," she told him. "I learned my golf here with King, the professional."

He took off his cap and handed it to his caddy. He himself was beginning already to look younger. The long blue waves came rippling up the creeks. The salt wind, soft with sunshine, blew in their faces. The marshes on the landward side were mauve with lavender blossom. In the distance, the red-tiled cottages nestled deep among a background of green trees and rising fields.

"This indeed is a land of peace," he declared. "If I hadn't to give you quite so many strokes, I should be really enjoying myself."

"You don't play like a man who has been living abroad for a great many years," she remarked. "Tell me about some of the places you have visited?"

"Don't let us talk seriously," he begged. "I'll tell you of them but let it be later on. This morning I feel that the spring air is getting into my head. I have an absurd desire to talk nonsense."

"So far," she admitted, "you haven't been altogether unsuccessful."

"If you are alluding," he replied, "to the personal remarks I was emboldened to make on my way here, I can only say that they were excused by their truthfulness."

"I am not at all sure that you have known me long enough to tell me what colours suit me," she demurred.

"Then what will you say," he enquired, "if I admire the angle of that quill in your hat?"

"Don't do it," she laughed. "If you continue like this, I may have to go home."

"You have sent the car away," he reminded her cheerfully. "You would simply have to sit upon the balcony and reflect upon your wasted morning."

"I decline to talk upon the putting green," she said. "It puts me off. If you will stand perfectly quiet and say nothing, I will play the like."

They moved off presently to the next teeing ground.

"I don't believe this nonsense is good for our golf," she said.

"It is immensely good for us as human beings," he protested.

They had played the ninth hole and turned for home. On their right now was a shimmering stretch of wet sand and a thin line of sea, in the distance. The tide, receding, had left little islands of virgin sand, grass tufted, the home of countless sea-gulls. A brown-sailed fishing boat was racing for the narrow entrance to the tidal way.

"I am beginning to understand what there is about this coast which fascinated my father so," he remarked.

"Are you?" she answered gravely. "Years ago I used to love it, but not now."

He tried to change the subject, but the gloom had settled upon her face once more.

"You don't know what it is like," she went on, as they walked side by side after their balls, "to live day and night in fear, with no one to talk to - no one, that is to say, who is not under the same shadow. Even the voices of the wind and the sea, and the screaming of the birds, seem to bring always an evil message. There is nothing kindly or hopeful even in the sunshine. At night, when the tide comes thundering in as it does so often at this time of the year, one is afraid. There is so much to make one afraid!"

She had turned pale again, notwithstanding the sunshine and the freshening wind. He laid his hand lightly upon her arm. She suffered his touch without appearing to notice it.

"Ah, you mustn't talk like that!" he pleaded. "Do you know what you make me feel like?"

She came back from the world of her own unhappy imaginings.

"Really, I forgot myself," she declared, with a little smile. "Never mind, it does one good sometimes. One up, are you? Henceforth, then, golf - all the rigour of the game, mind."

He fell in with her mood, and their conversation touched only upon the game. On the last green he suffered defeat and acknowledged it with a little grimace.

"If I might say so, Miss Fentolin," he protested, "you are a little too good for your handicap. I used to play a very reasonable scratch myself, but I can't give you the strokes."

She smiled.

"Doubtless your long absence abroad," she began slowly, "has affected your game."

"I was round in eighty-one," he grumbled.

"You must have travelled in many countries," she continued, "where golf was an impossibility."

"Naturally," he admitted. "Let us stay and have lunch and try again."

She shook her head with a little sigh of regret.

"You see, the car is waiting," she pointed out. "We are expected home. I shan't be a minute putting my clubs away."

They sped swiftly along the level road towards St. David's Hall. Far in the distance they saw it, built upon that strange hill, with the sunlight flashing in its windows. He looked at it long and curiously.

"I think," he said, "that yours is the most extraordinarily situated house I have ever seen. Fancy a gigantic mound like that in the midst of an absolutely flat marsh."

She nodded.

"There is no other house quite like it in England," she said. "I suppose it is really a wonderful place. Have you looked at the pictures?"

"Not carefully," he told her.

"You must before you leave," she insisted. "Mr. Fentolin is a great judge, and so was his father."

Their road curved a little to the sea, and at its last bend they were close to the pebbly ridge on which the Tower was built. He touched the electric bell and stopped the car.

"Do let us walk along and have a look at my queer possession once more," he begged. "Luncheon, you told me, is not till half-past one, and it is a quarter to now."

She hesitated for a moment and then assented. They left the car and walked along the little track, bordered with white posts, which led on to the ridge. To their right was the village, separated from them only by one level stretch of meadowland; in the background, the hall. They turned along the raised dike just inside the pebbly beach, and she showed her companion the narrow waterway up to the village. At its entrance was a tall iron upright, with a ladder attached and a great lamp at the top.

"That is to show them the way in at night, isn't it?" he asked.

She nodded.

"Yes," she told him. "Mr. Fentolin had it placed there. And yet," she went on, "curiously enough, since it was erected, there have been more wrecks than ever."

"It doesn't seem a dangerous beach," he remarked.

She pointed to a spot about fifty yards from the Tower. It was the spot to which the woman whom he had met on the day of his arrival had pointed.

"You can't see them," she said; "they are always out of sight, even when the tide is at the lowest - but there are some hideous sunken rocks there. 'The Daggers,' they call them. One or two fishing boats have been lost on them, trying to make the village. When Mr. Fentolin put up the lamp, every one thought that it would be quite safe to try and get in at night. This winter, though, there have been three wrecks which no one could understand. It must be something in the currents, or a sort of optical illusion, because in the last shipwreck one man was saved, and he swore that at the time they struck the rock, they were headed straight for the light."

They had reached the Tower now. Hamel became a little absorbed. They walked around it, and he tried the front door. He found, as he had expected, that it opened readily. He looked around him for several moments.

"Your uncle has been here this morning," he remarked quietly.

"Very likely."

"That outhouse," he continued, "must be quite a large place. Have you any idea what it is he works upon there?"

"None," she answered.

He looked around him once more.

"Mr. Fentolin has been preparing for my coming," he observed. "I see that he has moved a few of his personal things."

She made no reply, only she shivered a little as she stepped back into the sunshine.

E. Phillips Oppenheim

"I don't believe you like my little domicile," he remarked, as they started off homeward.

"I don't," she admitted curtly.

"In the train," he reminded her, "you seemed rather to discourage my coming here. Yet last night, after dinner -"

"I was wrong," she interrupted. "I should have said nothing, and yet I couldn't help it. I don't suppose it will make any difference."

"Make any difference to what?"

"I cannot tell you," she confessed. "Only I have a strange antipathy to the place. I don't like it. My uncle sometimes shuts himself up here for quite a long time. We have an idea, Gerald and I, that things happen here sometimes which no one knows of. When he comes back, he is moody and ill-tempered, or else half mad with excitement. He isn't always the amiable creature whom you have met. He has the face of an angel, but there are times -"

"Well, don't let's talk about him," Hamel begged, as her voice faltered. "Now that I am going to stay in the neighbourhood for a few days, you must please remember that it is partly your responsibility. You are not going to shut yourself up, are you? You'll come and play golf again?"

"If he will let me," she promised.

"I think he will let you, right enough," Hamel observed. "Between you and me, I rather think he hates having me down at the Tower at all. He will encourage anything that takes me away, even as far as the Golf Club."

They were approaching the Hall now. She was looking once more as she had looked last night. She had lost her colour, her walk was no longer buoyant. She had the air of a prisoner who, after a brief spell of liberty, enters once more the place of his confinement. Gerald came out to meet them as they climbed the stone steps which led on to the terrace. He glanced behind as he greeted them, and then almost stealthily took a telegram from his pocket.

"This came for you," he remarked, handing it to Hamel. "I met the boy bringing it out of the office."

Hamel tore it open, with a word of thanks. Gerald stood in front of him as he read.

"If you wouldn't mind putting it away at once," he asked, a little uncomfortably. "You see, the telegraph office is in the place, and my uncle has a queer rule that every telegram is brought to him before it is delivered."

Hamel did not speak for a moment. He was looking at the few words scrawled across the pink sheet with a heavy black pencil:

"Make every enquiry in your neighbourhood for an American, John P. Dunster, entrusted with message of great importance, addressed to Von Dusenberg, The Hague. Is believed to have been in railway accident near Wymondham and to have been taken from inn by young man in motor-car.

Suggest that he is being improperly detained."

Hamel crumpled up the telegram and thrust it into his pocket.

"By-the-by," he asked, as they ascended the steps, "what did you say the name of this poor fellow was who is lying ill up-stairs?"

Gerald hesitated for a moment. Then he answered as though a species of recklessness had seized him.

"He called himself Mr. John P. Dunster."

CHAPTER XVII

Mr. Fentolin, having succeeded in getting rid of his niece and his somewhat embarrassing guest for at least two hours, was seated in his study, planning out a somewhat strenuous morning, when his privacy was invaded by Doctor Sarson.

"Our guest," the latter announced, in his usual cold and measured tones, "has sent me to request that you will favour him with an interview."

Mr. Fentolin laid his pen deliberately down.

"So soon," he murmured. "Very well, Sarson, I am at his service. Say that I will come at once."

Mr. Fentolin lost no time in paying this suggested visit. Mr. John P. Dunster, shaved and clothed, was seated in an easy-chair drawn up to the window of his room, smoking what he was forced to confess was a very excellent cigar. He turned his head as the door opened, and Mr. Fentolin waved his hand pleasantly.

"Really," he declared, "this is most agreeable. I had an idea, Mr. Dunster, that I should find you a reasonable person. Men of your eminence in their profession usually are."

Mr. Dunster looked at the speaker curiously.

"And what might my profession be, Mr. Fentolin?" he asked. "You seem to know a great deal about me."

"It is true," Mr. Fentolin admitted. "I do know a great deal."

Mr. Dunster knocked the ash from his cigar.

"Well," he said, "I have been the hearer of several important communications from my side of the Atlantic to England and to the Continent, and I have always known that there was a certain amount of risk in the business. Once I had an exceedingly narrow shave," he continued reminiscently, "but this is the first time I have ever been dead up against it, and I don't mind confessing that you've fairly got me puzzled. Who the mischief are you, Mr. Fentolin, and what are you interfering about?"

Mr. Fentolin smiled queerly.

"I am what you see," he replied. "I am one of those unfortunate human beings who, by reason of their physical misfortunes, are cut off from the world of actual life. I have been compelled to seek distraction in strange quarters. I have wealth - great wealth I suppose I should say; an inordinate curiosity, a talent for intrigue. As to the direction in which I carry on my intrigues, or even as to the direct interests which I study, that is a matter, Mr. Dunster, upon which I shall not gratify your curiosity nor anybody else's. But, you see, I am admitting freely that it does interest me to interfere in great affairs."

"But how on earth did you get to know about me," Mr. Dunster asked, "and my errand? You couldn't possibly have got me here in an ordinary way. It was an entire fluke."

"There, you speak with some show of reason. I have a nephew whom you have met, who is devoted to me."

"Mr. Gerald Fentolin," Mr. Dunster remarked drily.

"Precisely," Mr. Fentolin declared. "Well, I admit frankly the truth of what you say. Your - shall we say capture, was by way of being a gigantic fluke. My nephew's instructions simply were to travel down by the train to Harwich with you, to endeavour to make your acquaintance, to follow you on to your destination, and, if any chance to do so occurred, to relieve you of your pocket-book. That, however, I never ventured to expect. What really happened was, as you have yourself suggested, almost in the nature of a miracle. My nephew showed himself to be possessed of gifts which were a revelation to me. He not only succeeded in travelling with you by the special train, but after its wreck he was clever enough to bring you here, instead of delivering you over to the mercies of a village doctor. I really cannot find words to express my appreciation of my nephew's conduct."

"I could," Mr. Dunster muttered, "very easily!"

Mr. Fentolin sighed gently.

"Perhaps our points of view might differ."

"We have spent a very agreeable few minutes in explanations," Mr. Dunster continued. "Would it be asking too much if I now suggest that we remove the buttons from our foils?"

"Why not?" Mr. Fentolin assented smoothly. "Your first question to yourself, under these circumstances, would naturally be: 'What does Mr. Fentolin want with me?' I will answer that question for you. All that I ask - it is really very little - is the word agreed upon."

Mr. Dunster held his cigar a little way off and looked steadfastly at his host for a moment. "So you have interpreted my cipher?"

Mr. Fentolin spread out the palms of his hands in a delicate gesture.

"My dear Mr. Dunster," he said, "one of the simplest, I think, that was ever strung together. I am somewhat of an authority upon ciphers."

"I gather," Mr. Dunster went on, although his cigar was burning itself out, "that you have broken the seal of my dispatches?"

Mr. Fentolin closed his eyes as though he had heard a discord.

"Nothing so clumsy as that, I hope," he murmured gently. "I will not insult a person of your experience and intelligence by enumerating the various ways in which the seal of a dispatch may be liquefied. It is quite true that I have read with much pleasure the letter which you are carrying from a certain group of very distinguished men to a certain person now in The Hague. The letter, however, is replaced in its envelope; the seal is still there. You need have no fears whatever concerning it. All that I require is that one word from you."

"And if I give you that one word?" Mr. Dunster asked.

"If you give it me, as I think you will," Mr. Fentolin replied suavely, "I shall then telegraph to my agent, or rather I should say to a dear friend of mine who lives at The Hague, and that single word will be cabled by him from The Hague to New York."

"And in that case," Mr. Dunster enquired, "what would become of me?"

"You would give us the great pleasure of your company here for a very brief visit," Mr. Fentolin answered. "We should, I can assure you, do our very best to entertain you."

"And the dispatch which I am carrying to The Hague?"

"Would remain here with you."

Mr. Dunster knocked the ash from his cigar. Without being a man of great parts, he was a shrewd person, possessed of an abundant stock of common sense. He applied himself, for a few moments, to a consideration of this affair, without arriving at any satisfactory conclusion.

"Come, Mr. Fentolin," he said at last, "you must really forgive me, but I can't see what you're driving at. You are an Englishman, are you not?"

"I am an Englishman," Mr. Fentolin confessed "or rather , " he added, with ghastly humour, "I am half an Englishman."

"You are, I am sure," Mr. Dunster continued, "a person of intelligence, a well-read person, a person of perceptions. Surely you can see and appreciate the danger with which your country is threatened?"

"With regard to political affairs," Mr. Fentolin admitted, "I consider myself unusually well posted - in fact, the study of the diplomatic methods of the various great Powers is rather a hobby of mine."

"Yet," Mr. Dunster persisted, "you do not wish this letter delivered to that little conference in The Hague, which you must be aware is now sitting practically to determine the fate of your nation?"

"I do not wish," Mr. Fentolin replied, "I do not intend, that that letter shall be delivered. Why do you worry about my point of view? I may have a dozen reasons. I may believe that it will be good for my country to suffer a little chastisement."

"Or you may," Mr. Dunster suggested, glancing keenly at his host, "be the paid agent of some foreign Power."

Mr. Fentolin shook his head.

"My means," he pointed out, "should place me above such suspicion. My income, I really believe, is rather more than fifty thousand pounds a year. I should not enter into these adventures, which naturally are not entirely dissociated from a certain amount of risk, for the purposes of financial gain."

Mr. Dunster was still mystified.

"Granted that you do so from pure love of adventure," he declared, "I still cannot see why you should range yourself on the side of your country's enemies.

"In time," Mr. Fentolin observed, "even that may become clear to you. At present, well - just that word, if you please?"

Mr. Dunster shook his head.

"No," he decided, "I do not think so. I cannot make up my mind to tell you that word."

Mr. Fentolin gave no sign of annoyance or even disappointment. He simply sighed. His eyes were full of a gentle sympathy, his face indicated a certain amount of concern.

"You distress me," he declared. "Perhaps it is my fault. I have not made myself sufficiently clear. The knowledge of that word is a necessity to me. Without it I cannot complete my plans. Without it I very much fear, dear Mr. Dunster, that your sojourn among us may be longer than you have any idea of."

Mr. Dunster laughed a little derisively.

"We've passed those days," he remarked. "I've done my best to enter into the humour of this situation, but there are limits. You can't keep prisoners in English country houses, nowadays. There are a dozen ways of communicating with the outside world, and when that's once done, it seems to me that the position of Squire Fentolin of St. David's Hall might be a little peculiar."

Mr. Fentolin smiled, very slightly, still very blandly.

"Alas, my stalwart friend, I fear that you are by nature an optimist! I am not a betting man, but I am prepared to bet you a hundred pounds to one that you have made your last communication with the outside world until I say the word."

Mr. Dunster was obviously plentifully supplied with either courage or bravado, for he only laughed.

"Then you had better make up your mind at once, Mr. Fentolin, how soon that word is to be spoken, or you may lose your money," he remarked.

Mr. Fentolin sat very quietly in his chair.

"You mean, then," he asked, "that you do not intend to humour me in this little matter?"

"I do not intend," Mr. Dunster assured him, "to part with that word to you or to any one else in the the world. When my message has been presented to the person to whom it has been addressed, when my trust is discharged, then and then only shall I send that cablegram. That moment can only arrive at the end of my journey."

Mr. Fentolin leaned now a little forward in his chair. His face was still smooth and expressionless, but there was a queer sort of meaning in his words.

"The end of your journey," he said grimly, "may be nearer than you think."

"If I am not heard of in The Hague to-morrow at the latest," Mr. Dunster pointed out, "remember that before many more hours have passed, I shall be searched for, even to the far corners of the earth."

"Let me assure you," Mr. Fentolin promised serenely, "that though your friends search for you up in the skies or down in the bowels of the earth, they will not find you. My hiding-places are not as other people's."

Mr. Dunster beat lightly with his square, blunt forefinger upon the table which stood by his side.

"That's not the sort of talk I understand," he declared curtly. "Let us understand one another, if we can. What is to happen to me, if I refuse to give you that word?"

Mr. Fentolin held his hand in front of his eyes, as though to shut out some unwelcome vision.

"Dear me," he exclaimed, "how unpleasant! Why should you force me to disclose my plans? Be content, dear Mr. Dunster, with the knowledge of this one fact: we cannot part with you. I have thought it over from every point of view, and I have come to that conclusion; always presuming," he went on, "that the knowledge of that little word of which we have spoken remains in its secret chamber of your memory."

Mr. Dunster smoked in silence for a few minutes.

"I am very comfortable here," he remarked.

"You delight me," Mr. Fentolin murmured.

"Your cook," Mr. Dunster continued, "has won my heartfelt appreciation. Your cigars and wines are fit for any nobleman. Perhaps, after all, this little rest is good for me."

Mr. Fentolin listened attentively.

"Do not forget," he said, "that there is always a limit fixed, whether it be one day, two days, or three days."

"A limit to your complacence, I presume?"

Mr. Fentolin assented.

"Obviously, then," Mr. Dunster concluded, "you wish those who sent me to believe that my message has been delivered. Yet there I must confess that you puzzle me. What I cannot see is, to put it bluntly, where you come in. Any one of the countries represented at this little conference would only be the gainers by the miscarriage of my message, which is, without doubt, so far as they are concerned, of a distasteful nature. Your own country alone could be the sufferer. Now what interest in the world, then, is there left - what interest in the world can you possibly represent - which can be the gainer by your present action?"

Mr. Fentolin's eyes grew suddenly a little brighter. There was a light upon his face strange to witness.

"The power which is to be the gainer," he said quietly, "is the power encompassed by these walls,"

He touched his chest; his long, slim fingers were folded upon it.

"When I meet a man whom I like," he continued softly, "I take him into my confidence. Picture me, if you will, as a kind of Puck. Haven't you heard that with the decay of the body comes sometimes a malignant growth in the brain; a Caliban-like desire for evil to fall upon the world; a desire to escape from the loneliness of suffering, the isolation of black misery?"

Mr. John P. Dunster let his cigar burn out. He looked steadfastly at this strange little figure whose chair had imperceptibly moved a little nearer to his.

"You know what the withholding of this message you carry may mean," Mr. Fentolin proceeded. "You come here, bearing to Europe the word of a great people, a people whose voice is powerful enough even to still the gathering furies. I have read your ciphered message. It is what I feared. It is my will, mine - Miles Fentolin's - that that message be not delivered."

"I wonder," Mr. Dunster muttered under his breath, "whether you are in earnest."

"In your heart," Mr. Fentolin told him, "you know that I am. I can see the truth in your face. Now, for the first time, you begin to understand."

"To a certain extent," Mr. Dunster admitted. "Where I am still in the dark, however, is why you should expect that I should become your confederate. It is true that by holding me up and obstructing my message, you may bring about the evil you seek, but unless that word is cabled back to New York, and my senders believe that my message has been delivered, there can be no certainty. What has been trusted to me as the safest means of transmission, might, in an emergency, be committed to a cable."

"Excellent reasoning," Fentolin agreed. "For the very reasons you name that word will be given."

Mr. Dunster's face was momentarily troubled. There was something in the still, cold emphasis of this man's voice which made him shiver.

"Do you think," Mr. Fentolin went on, "that I spend a great fortune buying the secrets of the world, that I live from day to day with the risk of ignominious detection always hovering about me - do you think that I do this and am yet unprepared to run the final risks of life and death? Have you ever talked with a murderer, Mr. Dunster? Has curiosity ever taken you within the walls of Sing Sing? Have you sat within the cell of a doomed man and felt the thrill of his touch, of his close presence? Well, I will not ask you those questions. I will simply tell you that you are talking to one now."

Mr. Dunster had forgotten his extinct cigar. He found it difficult to remove his eyes from Mr. Fentolin's face. He was half fascinated, half stirred with a vague, mysterious fear. Underneath these wild words ran always that hard note of truth.

"You seem to be in earnest," he muttered.

"I am," Mr. Fentolin assured him quietly. "I have more than once been instrumental in bringing about the death of those who have crossed my purposes. I plead guilty to the weakness of Nero. Suffering and death are things of joy to me. There!"

"I am not sure," Mr. Dunster said slowly, "that I ought not to wring your neck."

Mr. Fentolin smiled. His chair receded an inch or two. There was never a time when his expression had seemed more seraphic.

"There is no emergency of that sort," he remarked, "for which I am not prepared."

His little revolver gleamed for a minute beneath his cuff. He backed his chair slowly and with wonderful skill towards the door.

"We will fix the period of your probation, Mr. Dunster, at - say, twenty-four hours," he decided. "Please make yourself until then entirely at home. My cook, my cellar, my cigar cabinets, are at your disposal. If some happy impulse," he concluded, "should show you the only reasonable course by dinnertime, it would give me the utmost pleasure to have you join us at that meal. I can promise you a cheque beneath your plate which even you might think worth considering, wine in your glass which kings might sigh for, cigars by your side which even your Mr. Pierpont Morgan could not buy. Au revoir!"

The door opened and closed. Mr. Dunster sat staring into the open space like a man still a little dazed.

CHAPTER XVIII

The beautiful but somewhat austere front of St. David's Hall seemed, in a sense, transformed, as Hamel and his companion climbed the worn grey steps which led on to the broad sweep of terrace. Evidently visitors had recently arrived. A dark, rather good-looking woman, with pleasant round face and a ceaseless flow of conversation, was chattering away to Mr. Fentolin. By her side stood another woman who was a stranger to Hamel - thin, still elegant, with tired, worn face, and the shadow of something in her eyes which reminded him at once of Esther. She wore a large picture hat and carried a little Pomeranian dog under her arm. In the background, an insignificant-looking man with grey side-whiskers and spectacles was beaming upon everybody. Mr. Fentolin waved his hand and beckoned to Hamel and Esther as they somewhat hesitatingly approached.

"This is one of my fortunate mornings, you see, Esther!" he exclaimed, smiling. "Lady Saxthorpe has brought her husband over to lunch. Lady Saxthorpe," he added, turning to the woman at his side, "let me present to you the son of one of the first men to realise the elusive beauty of our coast. This is Mr. Hamel, son of Peter Hamel, R.A. - the Countess of Saxthorpe."

Lady Saxthorpe, who had been engaged in greeting

Esther, held out her hand and smiled good-humouredly at Hamel.

"I know your father's work quite well," she declared, "and I don't wonder that you have made a pilgrimage here. They tell me that he painted nineteen pictures - pictures of importance, that is to say - within this little area of ten miles. Do you paint, Mr. Hamel?"

"Not at all," Hamel answered.

"Our friend Hamel," Mr. Fentolin intervened, "woos other and sterner muses. He fights nature in distant countries, spans her gorges with iron bridges, stems the fury of her rivers, and carries to the boundary of the world that little twin line of metal which brings men like ants to the work-heaps of the universe. My dear Florence," he added, suddenly turning to the woman at his other side, "for the moment I had forgotten. You have not met our guest yet. Hamel, this is my sister-in-law, Mrs. Seymour Fentolin."

She held out her hand to him, unnaturally thin and white, covered with jewels. Again he saw something in her eyes which stirred him vaguely.

"It is so nice that you are able to spend a few days with us, Mr. Hamel," she said quietly. "I am sorry that I have been too indisposed to make your acquaintance earlier."

"And," Mr. Fentolin continued, "you must know my young friend here, too. Mr. Hamel - Lord Saxthorpe."

The latter shook hands heartily with the young man.

"I knew your father quite well," he announced. "Queer thing, he used to hang out for months at a time at that little shanty on the beach there. Hardest work in the world to get him away. He came over to dine with us once or twice, but we saw scarcely anything of him. I hope his son will not prove so obdurate."

"You are very kind," Hamel murmured.

"Mr. Hamel came into these parts to claim his father's property," Mr. Fentolin said. "However, I have persuaded him to spend a day or two up here before he transforms himself into a misanthrope. What of his golf, Esther, eh?"

"Mr. Hamel plays very well, indeed," the girl replied.

"Your niece was too good for me," Hamel confessed.

Mr. Fentolin smiled.

"The politeness of this younger generation," he remarked, "keeps the truth sometimes hidden from us. I perceive that I shall not be told who won. Lady Saxthorpe, you are fortunate indeed in the morning you have chosen for your visit. There is no sun in the world like an April sun, and no corner of the earth where it shines with such effect as here. Look steadily to the eastward of that second dike and you will see the pink light upon the sands, which baffled every one until our friend Hamel came and caught it on his canvas."

"I do see it," Lady Saxthorpe murmured. "What eyes you have, Mr. Fentolin! What perception for colour!"

"Dear lady," Mr. Fentolin said, "I am one of those who

benefit by the law of compensations. On a morning like this I can spend hours merely feasting my eyes upon this prospect, and I can find, if not happiness, the next best thing. The world is full of beautiful places, but the strange part of it is that beauty has countless phases, and each phase differs in some subtle and unexplainable manner from all others. Look with me fixedly, dear Lady Saxthorpe. Look, indeed, with more than your eyes. Look at that flush of wild lavender, where it fades into the sands on one side, and strikes the emerald green of that wet seamoss on the other. Look at the liquid blue of that tongue of sea which creeps along its bed through the yellow sands, through the dark meadowland, which creeps and oozes and widens till in an hour's time it will have become a river. Look at my sand islands, virgin from the foot of man, the home of sea-gulls, the islands of a day. There may be other and more beautiful places. There is none quite like this."

"I pity you no longer," Lady Saxthorpe asserted fervently. "The eyes of the artist are a finer possession than the limbs of the athlete."

The butler announced luncheon, and they all trooped in. Hamel found himself next to Lady Saxthorpe.

"Dear Mr. Fentolin has been so kind," she confided to him as they took their places. "I came in fear and trembling to ask for a very small cheque for my dear brother's diocese. My brother is a colonial bishop, you know. Can you imagine what Mr. Fentolin has given me?"

Hamel wondered politely. Lady Saxthorpe continued with an air of triumph.

"A thousand pounds! Just fancy that - a thousand pounds! And some people say he is so difficult," she went on, dropping her voice. "Mrs. Hungerford came all the way over from Norwich to beg for the infirmary there, and he gave her nothing."

"What was his excuse?" Hamel asked.

"I think he told her that it was against his principles to give to hospitals," Lady Saxthorpe replied. "He thinks that they should be supported out of the rates."

"Some people have queer ideas of charity," Hamel remarked. "Now I am afraid that if I had been Mr. Fentolin, I would have given the thousand pounds willingly to a hospital, but not a penny to a mission."

Mr. Fentolin looked suddenly down the table. He was some distance away, but his hearing was wonderful.

"Ah, my dear Hamel," he said, "believe me, missions are very wonderful things. It is only from a very careful study of their results that I have brought myself to be a considerable supporter of those where I have some personal knowledge of the organisation. Hospitals, on the other hand, provide for the poor what they ought to be able to provide for themselves. The one thing to avoid in the giving away of money is pauperisation. What do you think, Florence?"

His sister-in-law, who was seated at the other end of the table, looked across at him with a bright but stereotyped smile.

"I agree with you, of course, Miles. I always agree with you. Mr. Fentolin has the knack of being right about most things," she continued, turning to Lord Saxthorpe. "His judgment is really wonderful."

"Wish we could get him to come and sit on the bench sometimes, then," Lord Saxthorpe remarked heartily. "Our neighbours in this part of the world are not overburdened with brains. By-the-by," he went on, "that reminds me. You haven't got such a thing as a mysterious invalid in the house, have you?"

There was a moment's rather curious silence. Mr. Fentolin was sitting like a carved figure, with a glass of wine half raised to his lips. Gerald had broken off in the middle of a sentence and was staring at Lord Saxthorpe. Esther was sitting perfectly still, her face grave and calm, her eyes alone full of fear. Lord Saxthorpe was not an observant man and he continued, quite unconscious of the sensation which his question had aroused.

"Sounds a silly thing to ask you, doesn't it? They're all full of it at Wells, though. I sat on the bench this morning and went into the police-station for a moment first. Seems they've got a long dispatch from Scotland Yard about a missing man who is supposed to be in this part of the world. He came down in a special train on Tuesday night - the night of the great flood - and his train was wrecked at Wymondham. After that he was taken on by some one in a motor-car. Colonel Renshaw wanted me to allude to the matter from the bench, but it seemed to me that it was an affair entirely for the police."

As though suddenly realising the unexpected interest which his words had caused, Lord Saxthorpe brought his sentence to a conclusion and glanced enquiringly around the table.

"A man could scarcely disappear in a civilised neighbourhood like this," Mr. Fentolin remarked quietly, "but there is a certain amount of coincidence about your question. May I ask whether it was altogether a haphazard one?"

"Absolutely," Lord Saxthorpe declared. "The idea seems to be that the fellow was brought to one of the houses in the neighbourhood, and we were all rather chaffing one another this morning about it. Inspector Yardley - the stout fellow with the beard, you know - was just starting off in his dog-cart to make enquiries round the neighbourhood. If any one in fiction wants a type of the ridiculous detective, there he is, ready-made."

"The coincidence of your question," Mr. Fentolin said smoothly, "is certainly a strange one. The mysterious stranger is within our gates."

Lady Saxthorpe, who had been out of the conversation for far too long, laid down her knife and fork.

"My dear Mr. Fentolin!" she exclaimed. "My dear Mrs. Fentolin! This is really most exciting! Do tell us all about it at once. I thought that the man was supposed to have been decoyed away in a motor-car. Do you know his name and all about him?"

"There are a few minor points," Mr. Fentolin murmured, "such as his religious convictions and his size in boots, which I could not swear about, but so far as regards his name and his occupation, I think I can gratify your curiosity. He is a Mr. John P. Dunster, and he appears to be the representative of an American firm of bankers, on his way to Germany to conclude a loan."

"God bless my soul!" Lord Saxthorpe exclaimed wonderingly. "The fellow is actually here under this roof! But who brought him? How did he find his way?"

"Better ask Gerald," Mr. Fentolin replied. "He is the abductor. It seems that they both missed the train from Liverpool Street, and Mr. Dunster invited Gerald to travel down in his special train. Very kind of him, but might have been very unlucky for Gerald. As you know, they got smashed up at Wymondham, and Gerald, feeling in a way responsible for him, brought him on here; quite properly, I think. Sarson has been looking after him, but I am afraid he has slight concussion of the brain."

"I shall remember this all my life," Lord Saxthorpe declared solemnly, "as one of the most singular coincidences which has ever come within my personal knowledge. Perhaps after lunch, Mr. Fentolin, you will let some of your people telephone to the police-station at Wells? There really is an important enquiry respecting this man. I should not be surprised," he added, dropping his voice a little for the benefit of the servants, "to find that Scotland Yard needed him on their own account."

"In that case," Mr. Fentolin remarked, "he is quite safe, for Sarson tells me there is no chance of his being able to travel, at any rate for twenty-four hours."

Lady Saxthorpe shivered.

"Aren't you afraid to have him in the house?" she asked, "a man who is really and actually wanted by Scotland Yard? When one considers that nothing ever happens here except an occasional shipwreck in the winter and a flower-show in the summer, it does sound positively thrilling. I wonder what he has done."

They discussed the subject of Mr. Dunster's possible iniquities. Meanwhile, a young man carrying his hat in his hand had slipped in past the servants and was leaning over Mr. Fentolin's chair. He laid two or three sheets of paper upon the table and waited while his employer glanced them through and dismissed him with a little nod.

"My wireless has been busy this morning," Mr. Fentolin remarked. "We seem to have collected about forty messages from different battleships and cruisers. There must be a whole squadron barely thirty miles out."

"You don't really think," Lady Saxthorpe asked, "that there is any fear of war, do you, Mr. Fentolin?"

He answered her with a certain amount of gravity. "Who can tell? The papers this morning were bad. This conference at The Hague is still unexplained. France's attitude in the matter is especially mysterious."

"I am a strong supporter of Lord Roberts," Lord Saxthorpe said, "and I believe in the vital necessity of some scheme for national service. At the same time, I find it hard to believe that a successful invasion of this country is within the bounds of possibility."

"I quite agree with you, Lord Saxthorpe," Mr. Fentolin

declared smoothly. "All the same, this Hague Conference is a most mysterious affair. The papers this morning are ominously silent about the fleet. From the tangle of messages we have picked up, I should say, without a doubt, that some form of mobilisation is going on in the North Sea. If Lady Saxthorpe thinks it warm enough, shall we take our coffee upon the terrace?"

"The terrace, by all means," her ladyship assented, rising from her place. "What a wonderful man you are, Mr. Fentolin, with your wireless telegraphy, and your telegraph office in the house, and telephones. Does it really amuse you to be so modern?"

"To a certain extent, yes," Mr. Fentolin sighed, as he guided his chair along the hall. "When my misfortune first came, I used to speculate a good deal upon the Stock Exchange. That was really the reason I went in for all these modern appliances."

"And now?" she asked. "What use do you make of them now?"

Mr. Fentolin smiled quietly. He looked out sea-ward, beyond the sky-line, from whence had come to him, through the clouds, that tangle of messages.

"I like to feel," he said, "that the turning wheel of life is not altogether out of earshot. I like to dabble just a little in the knowledge of these things."

Lord Saxthorpe came strolling up to them.

"You won't forget to telephone about this guest of yours?" he asked fussily.

"It is already done," Mr. Fentolin assured him. "My dear sister, why so silent?"

Mrs. Fentolin turned slowly towards him. She, too, had been standing with her eyes fixed upon the distant sea-line. Her face seemed suddenly to have aged, her forced vivacity to have departed. Her little Pomeranian rubbed against her feet in vain. Yet at the sound of Mr. Fentolin's voice, she seemed to come back to herself as though by magic.

"I was looking where you were looking," she declared lightly, "just trying to see a little way beyond. So silly, isn't it? Chow-Chow, you bad little dog, come and you shall have your dinner."

She strolled off, humming a tune to herself. Lord Saxthorpe watched her with a shadow upon his plain, good-humoured face.

"Somehow or other," he remarked quietly, "Mrs. Fentolin never seems to have got over the loss of her husband, does she? How long is it since he died?"

"Eight years," Mr. Fentolin replied. "It was just six months after my own accident."

"I am losing a great deal of sympathy for you, Mr. Fentolin," Lady Saxthorpe confessed, coming over to his side. "You have so many resources, there is so much in life which you can do. You paint, as we all know, exquisitely. They tell me that you play the violin like a master. You have unlimited time for reading, and they say that you are one of the greatest living authorities upon the politics of Europe. Your morning paper must bring you so much that is interesting."

"It is true," Mr. Fentolin admitted, "that I have compensations which no one can guess at, compensations which appeal to me more as time steals on. And yet -"

He stopped short.

"And yet?" Lady Saxthorpe repeated interrogatively.

Mr. Fentolin was watching Gerald drive golf balls from the lawn beneath. He pointed downwards.

"I was like that when I was his age," he said quietly.

E. Phillips Oppenheim

CHAPTER XIX

Mr. Fentolin remained upon the terrace long after the departure of his guests. He had found a sunny corner out of the wind, and he sat there with a telescope by his side and a budget of newspapers upon his knee. On some pretext or another he had detained all the others of the household so that they formed a little court around him. Even Hamel, who had said something about a walk, had been induced to stop by an appealing glance from Esther. Mr. Fentolin was in one of his most loquacious moods. For some reason or other, the visit of the Saxthorpes seemed to have excited him. He talked continually, with the briefest pauses. Every now and then he gazed steadily across the marshes through his telescope.

"Lord Saxthorpe," he remarked, "has, I must confess, greatly excited my curiosity as to the identity of our visitor. Such a harmless-looking person, he seems, to be causing such a commotion. Gerald, don't you feel your responsibility in the matter?"

"Yes, sir, I do!" Gerald replied, with unexpected grimness. "I feel my responsibility deeply."

Mr. Fentolin, who was holding the telescope to his eye, touched Hamel on the shoulder.

"My young friend," he said, "your eyes are better than mine. You see the road there? Look along it, between the white posts, as far as you can. What do you make of that black speck?"

Hamel held the telescope to his eye and steadied it upon the little tripod stand.

"It looks like a horse and trap," he announced. "Good!" Mr. Fentolin declared. "It seemed so to me, but I was not sure. My eyes are weak this afternoon. How many people are in the trap?"

"Two," Hamel answered. "I can see them distinctly now. One man is driving, another is sitting by his side. They are coming this way."

Mr. Fentolin blew his whistle. Meekins appeared almost directly. His master whispered a word in his ear. The man at once departed.

"Let me make use of your eyes once more," Mr. Fentolin begged. "About these two men in the trap, Mr. Hamel. Is one of them, by any chance, wearing a uniform?"

"They both are," Hamel replied. "The man who is driving is wearing a peaked hat. He looks like a police inspector. The man by his side is an ordinary policeman."

Mr. Fentolin sighed gently.

"It is very interesting," he said. "Let us hope that we shall not see an arrest under my roof. I should feel it a reflection upon my hospitality. I trust, I sincerely trust, that this visit does not bode any harm to Mr. John P. Dunster."

Gerald rose impatiently to his feet and swung across the terrace. Mr. Fentolin, however, called him back.

"Gerald," he advised, "better not go away. The inspector may desire to ask you questions. You will have nothing to conceal. It was a natural and delightful impulse of yours to bring the man who had befriended you, and who was your companion in that disaster, straight to your own home for treatment and care. It was an admirable impulse, my boy. You have nothing to be ashamed of."

"Shall I tell him, too -" Gerald began.

"Be careful, Gerald."

Mr. Fentolin's words seemed to be charged with a swift, rapier-like note. The boy broke off in his speech. He looked at Hamel and was silent.

"Dear me," Mrs. Fentolin murmured, "I am sure there is no need for us to talk about this poor man as though anybody had done anything wrong in having him here. This, I suppose, must be the Inspector Yardley whom Lord Saxthorpe spoke of."

"A very intelligent-looking officer, I am sure," Mr. Fentolin remarked. "Gerald, go and meet him, if you please. I should like to speak to him out here."

The dog-cart had drawn up at the front door, and the inspector had already alighted. Gerald intervened as he was in the act of questioning the butler.

"Mr. Fentolin would like to speak to you, inspector," he said, "if you will come this way."

The inspector followed Gerald and saluted the little group solemnly. Mr. Fentolin held out his hand.

"You got my telephone message, inspector?" he asked.

"We have not received any message that I know of, sir," the inspector replied. "I have come over here in accordance with instructions received from head-quarters - in fact from Scotland Yard."

"Quite so," Mr. Fentolin assented. "You've come over, I presume, to make enquiries concerning Mr. John P. Dunster?"

"That is the name of the gentleman, sir."

"I only understood to-day from my friend Lord Saxthorpe," Mr. Fentolin continued, "that Mr. Dunster was being enquired about as though he had disappeared. My nephew brought him here after the railway accident at Wymondham, since when he has been under the care of my own physician. I trust that you have nothing serious against him?"

"My first duty, sir," the inspector pronounced, "is to see the gentleman in question."

"By all means," Mr. Fentolin agreed. "Gerald, will you take the inspector up to Mr. Dunster's rooms? Or stop, I will go myself."

Mr. Fentolin started his chair and beckoned the inspector to follow him. Meekins, who was waiting inside the hall, escorted them by means of the lift to the second floor. They made their way to Mr. Dunster's room. Mr. Fentolin knocked softly at the door. It was opened by the nurse.

"How is the patient?" Mr. Fentolin enquired.

Doctor Sarson appeared from the interior of the room.

"Still unconscious," he reported. "Otherwise, the symptoms are favourable. He is quite unfit," the doctor added, looking steadily at the inspector, "to be removed or questioned."

"There is no idea of anything of the sort," Mr. Fentolin explained. "It is Inspector Yardley's duty to satisfy himself that Mr. Dunster is here. It is necessary for the inspector to see your patient, so that he can make his report at headquarters."

Doctor Sarson bowed.

"That is quite simple, sir," he said. "Please step in."

They all entered the room, which was large and handsomely furnished. Through the open windows came a gentle current of fresh air. Mr. Dunster lay in the midst of all the luxury of fine linen sheets and embroidered pillow-cases. The inspector looked at him stolidly.

"Is he asleep?" he asked.

The doctor shook his head.

"It is the third day of his concussion," he whispered.

"He is still unconscious. He will remain in the same condition for another two days. After that he will begin to recover."

Mr. Fentolin touched the inspector on the arm.

"You see his clothing at the foot of the bed," he pointed out. "His linen is marked with his name. That is his dressing-case with his name painted on it."

"I am quite satisfied, sir," the inspector announced. "I will not intrude any further."

They left the room. Mr. Fentolin himself escorted the inspector into the library and ordered whisky and cigars.

"I don't know whether I am unreasonably curious," Mr. Fentolin remarked, "but is it really true that you have had enquiries from Scotland Yard about the poor fellow up-stairs?"

"We had a very important enquiry indeed, sir," the inspector replied. "I have instructions to telegraph all I have been able to discover, immediately."

"Pardon my putting it plainly," Mr. Fentolin asked, "but is our friend a criminal?"

"I wouldn't go so far as that, sir," the inspector answered. "I know of no charge against him. I don't know that I have the right to say so much," he added, sipping his whisky and soda, "but putting two and two together, I should rather come to the conclusion that he was a person of some political importance."

"Not a criminal at all?"

"Not as I know of," the inspector assented.
"That isn't the way I read the enquiries at all."

"You relieve me," Mr. Fentolin declared. "Now what about his possessions?"

"There's a man coming down shortly from Scotland Yard," the inspector announced, a little gloomily. "My orders were to touch nothing, but to locate him."

"Well, you've succeeded so far," Mr. Fentolin remarked. "Here he is, and here I think he will stay until some days after your friend from Scotland Yard can get here."

"It does seem so, indeed," the inspector agreed. "To me he looks terrible ill. But there's one thing sure, he's having all the care and attention that's possible. And now, sir, I'll not intrude further upon your time. I'll just make my report, and you'll probably have a visit from the Scotland Yard man sometime within the next few days."

Mr. Fentolin escorted the inspector to his dog-cart, shook hands with him, and watched him drive off. Only Mrs. Seymour Fentolin remained upon the terrace. He glided over to her side.

"My dear Florence," he asked, "where are the others?"

"Mr. Hamel and Esther have gone for a walk," she answered. "Gerald has disappeared somewhere. Has anything - is everything all right?"

"Naturally," Mr. Fentolin replied easily. "All that the inspector desired was to see Mr. Dunster. He has seen him. The poor fellow was unfortunately unconscious, but our friend will at least be able to report that he was in good hands and well cared for."

"Unconscious," Mrs. Fentolin repeated. "I thought that he was better."

"One is always subject to those slight relapses in an affair of concussion," Mr. Fentolin explained.

Mrs. Fentolin laid down her work and leaned a little towards her brother-in-law. Her hand rested upon his. Her voice had fallen to a whisper.

"Miles," she said, "forgive me, but are you sure that you are not getting a little out of your depth? Remember that there are some risks which are not worth while."

"Quite true," he answered. "And there are some risks, my dear Florence, which are worth every drop of blood in a man's body, and every breath of life. The peace of Europe turns upon that man up-stairs. It is worth taking a little risk for, worth a little danger. I have made my plans, and I mean to carry them through. Tell me, when I was up-stairs, this fellow Hamel - was he talking confidentially to Gerald?"

"Not particularly."

"I am not sure that I trust him," Mr. Fentolin continued. "He had a telegram yesterday from a man in the Foreign Office, a telegram which I did not see. He took the trouble to walk three miles to send the reply to it from another office."

"But after all," Mrs. Fentolin protested, "you know who he is. You know that he is Peter Hamel's son. He had a definite purpose in coming here."

Mr. Fentolin nodded.

"Quite true," he admitted. "But for that, Mr. Hamel would have found a little trouble before now. As it is, he must be watched. If any one comes between me and the things for which I am scheming to-day, they will risk death."

Mrs. Fentolin sighed. She was watching the figures of Esther and Hamel far away in the distance, picking their way across the last strip of marshland which lay between them and the sea.

"Miles," she said earnestly, "you take advice from no one. You will go your own way, I know. And yet, it seems to me that life holds so many compensations for you without your taking these terrible risks. I am not thinking of any one else. I am not pleading to you for the sake of any one else. I am thinking only of yourself. I have had a sort of feeling ever since this man was brought into the house, that trouble would come of it. To me the trouble seems to be gathering even now."

Mr. Fentolin laughed softly, a little contemptuously.

"Presentiments," he scoffed, "are the excuses of cowards. Don't be afraid, Florence. Remember always that I look ahead. Do you think that I could stay here contented with what you call my compensations - my

art, the study of beautiful things, the calm epicurea-
nism of the sedate and simple life? You know very
well that I could not do that. The craving for other
things is in my heart and blood. The excitement which
I cannot have in one way, I must find in another, and I
think that before many nights have passed, I shall lie
on my pillow and hear the guns roar, hear the footsteps
of the great armies of the world moving into battle. It
is for that I live, Florence."

She took up her knitting again. Her eyes were fixed
upon the sky-line. Twice she opened her lips, but twice
no words came.

"You understand?" he whispered. "You begin to
understand, don't you?"

She looked at him only for a moment and back at her
work.

"I suppose so," she sighed.

CHAPTER XX

In the middle of that night Hamel sat up in bed, awakened with a sudden start by some sound, only the faintest echo of which remained in his consciousness. His nerves were tingling with a sense of excitement. He sat up in bed and listened. Suddenly it came again - a long, low moan of pain, stifled at the end as though repressed by some outside agency. He leaped from his bed, hurried on a few clothes, and stepped out on to the landing. The cry had seemed to him to come from the further end of the long corridor - in the direction, indeed, of the room where Mr. Dunster lay. He made his way there, walking on tiptoe, although his feet fell noiselessly upon the thick carpet. A single light was burning from a bracket in the wall, insufficient to illuminate the empty spaces, but enough to keep him from stumbling. The corridor towards the south end gradually widened, terminating in a splendid high window with stained glass, a broad seat, and a table. On the right, the end room was Mr. Dunster's apartment, and on the left a flight of stairs led to the floor above. Hamel stood quite still, listening. There was a light in the room, as he could see from under the door, but there was no sound of any one moving. Hamel listened intently, every sense strained. Then the sound of a stair creaking behind diverted his attention. He looked quickly around. Gerald was descending. The boy's face was white, and his eyes were filled with fear. Hamel stepped softly back from the door and met him at the foot of the stairs.

"Did you hear that cry?" he whispered.

Gerald nodded.

"It woke me up. What do you suppose it was?" Hamel shook his head.

"Some one in pain," he replied. "I don't understand it. It came from this room."

"You know who sleeps there?" Gerald asked hoarsely.

Hamel nodded.

"A man with concussion of the brain doesn't cry out like that. Besides, did you hear the end of it? It sounded as though some one were choking him. Hush!"

They had spoken only in bated breath, but the door of the room before which they were standing was suddenly opened. Meekins stood there, fully dressed, his dark, heavy face full of somber warning. He started a little as he saw the two whispering together. Gerald addressed him almost apologetically.

"We both heard the same sound, Meekins. Is any one ill? It sounded like some one in pain."

The man hesitated. Then from behind his shoulder came Mr. Fentolin's still, soft voice. There was a little click, and Meekins, as though obeying an unseen gesture, stepped back. Mr. Fentolin glided on to the threshold. He was still dressed. He propelled his chair a few yards down the corridor and beckoned them to approach.

"I am so sorry," he said softly, "that you should have been disturbed, Mr. Hamel. We have been a little anxious about our mysterious guest. Doctor Sarson fetched me an hour ago. He discovered that it was necessary to perform a very slight operation, merely the extraction of a splinter of wood. It is all over now, and I think that he will do very well."

Notwithstanding this very plausible explanation, Hamel was conscious of the remains of an uneasiness which he scarcely knew how to put into words.

"It was a most distressing cry," he observed doubtfully, "a cry of fear as well as of pain."

"Poor fellow!" Mr. Fentolin remarked compassionately. "I am afraid that for a moment or two he must have suffered acutely. Doctor Sarson is very clever, however, and there is no doubt that what he did was for the best. His opinion is that by to-morrow morning there will be a marvellous change. Good night, Mr. Hamel. I am quite sure that you will not be disturbed again."

Hamel neither felt nor showed any disposition to depart.

"Mr. Fentolin," he said, "I hope that you will not think that I am officious or in any way abusing your hospitality, but I cannot help suggesting that as Dr. Sarson is purely your household physician, the relatives of this man Dunster might be better satisfied if some second opinion were called in. Might I suggest that you telephone to Norwich for a surgeon?"

Mr. Fentolin showed no signs of displeasure. He was silent for a moment, as though considering the matter.

"I am not at all sure, Mr. Hamel, that you are not right," he admitted frankly. "I believe that the case is quite a simple one, but on the other hand it would perhaps be more satisfactory to have an outside opinion. If Mr. Dunster is not conscious in the morning, we will telephone to the Norwich Infirmary."

"I think it would be advisable," Hamel agreed.

"Good night!" Mr. Fentolin said once more. "I am sorry that your rest has been disturbed."

Hamel, however, still refused to take the hint. His eyes were fixed upon that closed door.

"Mr. Fentolin," he asked, "have you any objection to my seeing Mr. Dunster?"

There was a moment's intense silence. A sudden light had burned in Mr. Fentolin's eyes. His fingers gripped the side of his chair. Yet when he spoke there were no signs of anger in his tone. It was a marvellous effort of self-control.

"There is no reason, Mr. Hamel," he said, "why your curiosity should not be gratified. Knock softly at the door, Gerald."

The boy obeyed. In a moment or two Doctor Sarson appeared on the threshold.

"Our guest, Mr. Hamel," Mr. Fentolin explained in a whisper, "has been awakened by this poor fellow's cry. He would like to see him for a moment."

Doctor Sarson opened the door. They all passed in on tiptoe. The doctor led the way towards the bed upon which Mr. Dunster was lying, quite still. His head was bandaged, and his eyes closed. His face was ghastly. Gerald gave vent to a little muttered exclamation. Mr. Fentolin turned to him quickly.

"Gerald!"

The boy stood still, trembling, speechless. Mr. Fentolin's eyes were riveted upon him. The doctor was standing, still and dark, a motionless image.

"Is he asleep?" Hamel asked.

"He is under the influence of a mild anaesthetic," Doctor Sarson explained. "He is doing very well. His case is quite simple. By to-morrow morning he will be able to sit up and walk about if he wishes to."

Hamel looked steadily at the figure upon the bed. Mr. Dunster's breathing was regular, and his eyes were closed, but his colour was ghastly.

"He doesn't look like getting up for a good many days to come," Hamel observed.

The doctor led the way towards the door.

"The man has a fine constitution," he said. "I feel sure that if you wish you will be able to talk to him to-morrow."

They separated outside in the passage. Mr. Fentolin bade his guest a somewhat restrained good night, and Gerald mounted the staircase to his room. Hamel, however, had scarcely reached his door before Gerald reappeared. He had descended the stair-case at the other end of the corridor. He stood for a moment looking down the passage. The doors were all closed. Even the light had been extinguished.

"May I come in for a moment, please?" he whispered.

Hamel nodded.

"With pleasure! Come in and have a cigarette if you will. I shan't feel like sleep for some time."

They entered the room, and Gerald threw himself into an easy-chair near the window. Hamel wheeled up another chair and produced a box of cigarettes.

"Queer thing your dropping across that fellow in the way you did," he remarked. "Just shows how one may disappear from the world altogether, and no one be a bit the wiser."

The boy was sitting with folded arms. His expression was one of deep gloom.

"I only wish I'd never brought him here," he muttered. "I ought to have known better."

Hamel raised his eyebrows. "Isn't he as well off here as anywhere else?"

"Do you think that he is?" Gerald demanded, looking across at Hamel.

There was a brief silence.

"We can scarcely do your uncle the injustice," Hamel remarked, "of imagining that he can possibly have any reason or any desire to deal with that man except as a guest."

"Do you really believe that?" Gerald asked.

Hamel rose to his feet.

"Look here, young man," he said, "this is getting serious. You and I are at cross-purposes. If you like, you shall have the truth from me."

"Go on."

"I was warned about your uncle before I came down into this part of the world," Hamel continued quietly. "I was told that he is a dangerous conspirator, a man who sticks at nothing to gain his ends, a person altogether out of place in these days. It sounds melodramatic, but I had it straight from a friend. Since I have been here, I have had a telegram - you brought it to me yourself - asking for information about this man Dunster. It was I who wired to London that he was here. It was through me that Scotland Yard communicated with the police station at Wells, through me that a man is to be sent down from London. I didn't come here as a spy - don't think that; I was coming here, anyhow. On the other hand, I believe that your uncle is playing a dangerous game. I am going to have Mr. John P. Dunster put in charge of a Norwich physician to-morrow."

"Thank God!" the boy murmured.

"Look here," Hamel continued, "what are you doing in this business, anyway? You are old enough to know your own mind and to go your own way."

"You say that because you don't know," Gerald declared bitterly.

"In a sense I don't," Hamel admitted, "and yet your sister hinted to me only this afternoon that you and she -"

"Oh, I know what she told you!" the boy interrupted. "We've worn the chains for the last eight years. They are breaking her. They've broken my mother. Sometimes I think they are breaking me. But, you know, there comes a time - there comes a time when one can't go on. I've seen some strange things here, some that I've half understood, some that I haven't understood at all. I've closed my eyes. I've kept my promise. I've done his bidding, where ever it has led me. But you know there is a time - there is a limit to all things. I can't go on. I spied on this man Dunster. I brought him here. It is I who am responsible for anything that may happen to him. It's the last time!"

Gerald's face was white with pain. Hamel laid his hand upon his shoulder.

"My boy," he said, "there are worse things in the world than breaking a promise. When you gave it, the conditions which were existing at the time made it, perhaps, a right and reasonable undertaking, but sometimes the whole of the conditions under which a promise was given, change. Then one must have courage enough to be false even to one's word."

E. Phillips Oppenheim

"Have you talked to my sister like that?" Gerald asked eagerly.

"I have and I will again," Hamel declared. "To-morrow morning I leave this house, but before I go I mean to have the affair of this man Dunster cleared up. Your uncle will be very angry with me, without a doubt. I don't care. But I do want you to trust me, if you will, and your sister. I should like to be your friend."

"God knows we need one!" the boy said simply. "Good night!"

Once more the house was quiet. Hamel pushed his window wide open and looked out into the night. The air was absolutely still, there was no wind. The only sound was the falling of the low waves upon the stony beach and the faint scrunching of the pebbles drawn back by the ebb. He looked along the row of windows, all dark and silent now. A rush of pleasant fancies suddenly chased away the grim depression of the last few minutes. Out of all this sordidness and mystery there remained at least something in life for him to do. A certain aimlessness of purpose which had troubled him during the last few months had disappeared. He had found an object in life.

CHAPTER XXI

"To-day," Hamel declared, as he stood at the sideboard the following morning at breakfast-time and helped himself to bacon and eggs, "I am positively going to begin reading. I have a case full of books down at the Tower which I haven't unpacked yet."

Esther made a little grimace.

"Look at the sunshine," she said. "There isn't a breath of wind, either. I think to-day that I could play from the men's tees."

Hamel sighed as he returned to his place.

"My good intentions are already half dissipated," he admitted.

She laughed.

"How can we attack the other half?" she asked.

Gerald, who was also on his way to the sideboard, suddenly stopped.

"Hullo!" he exclaimed, looking out of the window. "Who's going away this morning, I wonder? There's the Rolls-Royce at the door."

E. Phillips Oppenheim

Hamel, too, rose once more to his feet. The two exchanged swift glances. Moved by a common thought, they both started for the door, only to find it suddenly opened before them. Mr. Fentolin glided into the room.

"Uncle!" Gerald exclaimed.

Mr. Fentolin glanced keenly around the room.

"Good morning, everybody," he said. "My appearance at this hour of the morning naturally surprises you. As a matter of fact, I have been up for quite a long time. Esther dear, give me some coffee, will you, and be sure that it is hot. If any of you want to say good-by to Mr. John P. Dunster, you'd better hurry out."

"You mean that he is going?" Hamel asked incredulously.

"He is going," Mr. Fentolin admitted. "I wash my hands of the man. He has given us an infinite amount of trouble, has monopolised Doctor Sarson when he ought to have been attending upon me - a little more hot milk, if you please, Esther - and now, although he really is not fit to leave his room, he insists upon hurrying off to keep an appointment somewhere on the Continent. The little operation we spoke of last night was successful, as Doctor Sarson prophesied, and Mr. Dunster was quite conscious and able to sit up early this morning. We telephoned at six o'clock to Norwich for a surgeon, who is now on his way over here, but he will not wait even to see him. What can you do with a man so obstinate!"

Neither Hamel nor Gerald had resumed their places.

The former, after a moment's hesitation, turned towards the door.

"I think," he said, "that I should like to see the last of Mr. Dunster."

"Pray do," Mr. Fentolin begged. "I have said good-by to him myself, and all that I hope is that next time you offer a wayfarer the hospitality of St. David's Hall, Gerald, he may be a more tractable person. This morning I shall give myself a treat. I shall eat an old-fashioned English breakfast. Close the door after you, if you please, Gerald."

Hamel, with Gerald by his side, hurried out into the hall. Just as they crossed the threshold they saw Mr. Dunster, wrapped from head to foot in his long ulster, a soft hat upon his head and one of Mr. Fentolin's cigars in his mouth, step from the bottom stair into the hall and make his way with somewhat uncertain footsteps towards the front door. Doctor Sarson walked on one side, and Meekins held him by the arm. He glanced towards Gerald and his companion and waved the hand which held his cigar.

"So long, my young friend!" he exclaimed. "You see, I've got them to let me make a start. Next time we go about the country in a saloon car together, I hope we'll have better luck. Say, but I'm groggy about the knees!"

"You'd better save your breath," Doctor Sarson advised him grimly. "You haven't any to spare now, and you'll want more than you have before you get to the end of your journey. Carefully down the steps, mind."

They helped him into the car. Hamel and Gerald stood

E. Phillips Oppenheim

under the great stone portico, watching.

"Well, I'm jiggered!" the boy exclaimed, under his breath.

Hamel was watching the proceedings with a puzzled frown. To his surprise, neither Doctor Sarson nor Meekins were accompanying the departing man.

"He's off, right enough," Hamel declared, as the car glided away. "Do you understand it? I don't."

Gerald did not speak for several moments. His eyes were still fixed upon the back of the disappearing car. Then he turned towards Hamel.

"There isn't much," he said softly, "that Mr. Fentolin doesn't know. If that detective was really on his way here, there wasn't any chance of keeping Mr. Dunster to himself. You see, the whole story is common property. And yet, there's something about the affair that bothers me."

"And me," Hamel admitted, watching the car until it became a speck in the distance.

"He was fairly well cornered," Gerald concluded, as they made their way back to the dining-room, "but it isn't like him to let go of anything so easily."

"So you've seen the last of our guest," Mr. Fentolin remarked, as Hamel and Gerald re-entered the dining-room. "A queer fellow - almost a new type to me. Dogged and industrious, I should think. He hadn't the least right to travel, you know, and I think so long as we had taken the trouble to telephone to Norwich, he might have waited to see the physician. Sarson was very angry about it, but what can you do with these fellows who are never ill? They scarcely know what physical disability means. Well, Mr. Hamel, and how are you going to amuse yourself to-day?"

"I had thought of commencing some reading I brought with me," Hamel replied, "but Miss Esther has challenged me to another game of golf."

"Excellent!" Mr. Fentolin declared. "It is very kind of you indeed, Mr. Hamel. It is always a matter of regret for me that society in these parts is so restricted. My nephew and niece have little opportunity for enjoying themselves. Play golf with Mr. Hamel, by all means, my dear child," he continued, turning to his niece. "Make the most of this glorious spring weather. And what about you, Gerald? What are you doing to-day?"

"I haven't made up my mind yet, sir," the boy replied.

Mr. Fentolin sighed.

"Always that lack of initiative," he remarked. "A lack of initiative is one of your worst faults, I am afraid, dear Gerald."

The boy looked up quickly. For a moment it seemed as though he were about to make a fierce reply. He met Mr. Fentolin's steady gaze, however, and the words died away upon his lips.

"I rather thought," he said, "of going into Norwich, if you could spare me. Captain Holt has asked me to lunch at the Barracks."

Mr. Fentolin shook his head gently.

"It is most unfortunate," he declared. "I have a commission for you later in the day."

Gerald continued his breakfast in silence. He bent over his plate so that his face was almost invisible. Mr. Fentolin was peeling a peach. A servant entered the room.

"Lieutenant Godfrey, sir," he announced.

They all looked up. A trim, clean-shaven, hard-featured young man in naval uniform was standing upon the threshold. He bowed to Esther.

"Very sorry to intrude, sir, at this hour of the morning," he said briskly. "Lieutenant Godfrey, my name. I am flag lieutenant of the Britannia. You can't see her, but she's not fifty miles off at this minute. I landed at Sheringham this morning, hired a car and made the best of my way here. Message from the Admiral, sir."

Mr. Fentolin smiled genially.

"We are delighted to see you, Lieutenant Godfrey," he said. "Have some breakfast."

"You are very good, sir," the officer answered. "Business first. I'll breakfast afterwards, with pleasure, if I may. The Admiral's compliments, and he would take it as a favour if you would haul down your wireless for a few days."

"Haul down my wireless," Mr. Fentolin repeated slowly.

"We are doing a lot of manoeuvring within range of you, and likely to do a bit more," the young man explained. "You are catching up our messages all the time. Of course, we know they're quite safe with you, but things get about. As yours is only a private installation, we'd like you, if you don't mind, sir, to shut up shop for a few days."

Mr. Fentolin seemed puzzled.

"But, my dear sir," he protested, "we are not at war, are we?"

"Not yet," the young officer replied, "but God knows when we shall be! We are under sealed orders, anyway, and we don't want any risk of our plans leaking out. That's why we want your wireless disconnected."

"You need say no more," Mr. Fentolin assured him. "The matter is already arranged. Esther, let me present Lieutenant Godfrey - my niece, Miss Fentolin; Mr. Gerald Fentolin, my nephew; Mr. Hamel, a guest. See that Lieutenant Godfrey has some breakfast, Gerald. I will go myself and see my Marconi operator."

"Awfully good of you, sir," the young man declared, "and I am sure we are very sorry to trouble you. In a week or two's time you can go into business again as much as you like. It's only while we are fiddling around here that the Admiral's jumpy about things. May my man have a cup of coffee, sir? I'd like to be on the way back in a quarter of an hour."

Mr. Fentolin halted his chair by the side of the bell, and rang it.

"Pray make use of my house as your own, sir," he said gravely. "From what you leave unsaid, I gather that things are more serious than the papers would have us believe. Under those circumstances, I need not assure you that any help we can render is entirely yours."

Mr. Fentolin left the room. Lieutenant Godfrey was already attacking his breakfast. Gerald leaned towards him eagerly.

"Is there really going to be war?" he demanded.

"Ask those chaps at The Hague," Lieutenant Godfrey answered. "Doing their best to freeze us out, or something. All I know is, if there's going to be fighting, we are ready for them. By-the-by, what have you got wireless telegraphy for here, anyway?"

"It's a fad of my uncle's," Gerald replied. "Since his accident he amuses himself in all sorts of queer ways."

Lieutenant Godfrey nodded.

"Poor fellow!" he said. "I heard he was a cripple, or something of the sort. Forgive my asking, but - you people are English, aren't you?"

"Rather!" Gerald answered. "The Fentolins have lived here for hundreds of years. Why do you ask that?"

Lieutenant Godfrey hesitated. He looked, for the moment, scarcely at his ease.

"Oh, I don't know," he replied. "The old man was very anxious I should find out. You see, a lot of information seems to have got over on the other side, and we couldn't think where it had leaked out, except through your wireless. However, that isn't likely, of course, unless you've got one of these beastly Germans in your receiving-room. Now if I can borrow a cigarette, a cigar, or a pipe of tobacco - any mortal thing to smoke - I'll be off, if I may. The old man turned me out at an unearthly hour this morning, and in Sheringham all the shops were closed. Steady on, young fellow," he laughed, as Gerald filled his pockets with cigarettes. "Well, here's good morning to you, Miss Fentolin. Good morning, sir. How long ought it to take me to get to Sheringham?"

"About forty minutes," Gerald told him, "if your car's any good at all."

"It isn't much," was the somewhat dubious reply. "However, we'll shove along. You in the Service?" he enquired, as they walked down the hall together.

"Hope I shall be before long," Gerald answered. "I'm going into the army, though."

"Have to hurry up, won't you?"

Gerald sighed.

"It's a little difficult for me. Here's your car. Good luck to you!"

"My excuses to Mr. Fentolin," Lieutenant Godfrey shouted, "and many thanks."

He jumped into the automobile and was soon on his way back. Gerald watched him until he was nearly out of sight. On the knoll, two of the wireless operators were already at work. Mr. Fentolin sat in his chair below, watching. The blue sparks were flashing. A message was just being delivered. Presently Mr. Fentolin turned his chair, and with Meekins by his side, made his way back to the house. He passed along the hall and into his study. Gerald, who was on his way to the dining-room, heard the ring of the telephone bell and the call for the trunk special line. He hesitated for a moment. Then he made his way slowly down towards the study and stood outside the door, listening. In a moment he heard Mr. Fentolin's clear voice, very low yet very penetrating.

"The Mediterranean Fleet will be forty-seven hours before it comes together," was the message he heard. "The Channel Fleet will manoeuvre off Sheerness, waiting for it. The North Sea Fleet is seventeen units under nominal strength."

Gerald turned the handle of the door slowly and entered. Mr. Fentolin was just replacing the receiver on its stand. He looked up at his nephew, and his eyebrows came together.

"What do you mean by this?" he demanded. "Don't you know that I allow no one in here when I am telephoning on the private wire?"

Gerald closed the door behind him and summoned up all his courage.

"It is because I have heard what you were saying over the telephone that I am here," he declared. "I want to know to whom you were sending that message which you have intercepted outside."

CHAPTER XXII

Mr. Fentolin sat for a moment in his chair with immovable face. Then he pointed to the door, which Gerald had left open behind him.

"Close that door, Gerald."

The boy obeyed. Mr. Fentolin waited until he had turned around again.

"Come and stand over here by the side of the table," he directed.

Gerald came without hesitation. He stood before his uncle with folded arms. There was something else besides sullenness in his face this morning, something which Mr. Fentolin was quick to recognise.

"I do not quite understand the nature of your question, Gerald," Mr. Fentolin began. "It is unlike you. You do not seem yourself. Is there anything in particular the matter?"

"Only this," Gerald answered firmly. "I don't understand why this naval fellow should come here and ask you to close up your wireless because secrets have been leaking out, and a few moments afterwards you should be picking up a message and telephoning to

London information which was surely meant to be private. That's all. I've come to ask you about it."

"You heard the message, then?"

"I did."

"You listened - at the keyhole?"

"I listened outside," Gerald assented doggedly. "I am glad I listened. Do you mind answering my question?"

"Do I mind!" Mr. Fentolin repeated softly. "Really, Gerald, your politeness, your consideration, your good manners, astound me. I am positively deprived of the power of speech."

"I'll wait here till it comes to you again, then," the boy declared bluntly. "I've waited on you hand and foot, done dirty work for you, put up with your ill-humours and your tyranny, and never grumbled. But there is a limit! You've made a poor sort of creature of me, but even the worm turns, you know. When it comes to giving away secrets about the movements of our navy at a time when we are almost at war, I strike."

"Melodramatic, almost dramatic, but, alas! so inaccurate," Mr. Fentolin sighed. "Is this a fit of the heroics, boy, or what has come over you? Have you by any chance - forgotten?"

Mr. Fentolin's voice seemed suddenly to have grown in volume. His eyes dilated, he himself seemed to have grown in size. Gerald stepped a little back. He was trembling, but his expression had not changed.

"No, I haven't forgotten. There's a great debt we are doing our best to pay, but there's such a thing as asking top much, there's such a thing as drawing the cords to snapping point. I'm speaking for Esther and mother as well as myself. We have been your slaves; in a way I suppose we are willing to go on being your slaves. It's the burden that Fate has placed around our necks, and we'll go through with it. All I want to point out is that there are limits, and it seems to me that we are up against them now."

Mr. Fentolin nodded. He had the air of a man who wishes to be reasonable.

"You are very young, my boy," he said, "very young indeed. Perhaps that is my fault for not having let you see more of the world. You have got some very queer ideas into your head. A little too much novel reading lately, eh? I might treat you differently. I might laugh at you and send you out of the room. I won't. I'll tell you what you ask. I'll explain what you find so mysterious. The person to whom I have been speaking is my stockbroker."

"Your stockbroker!" Gerald exclaimed.

Mr. Fentolin nodded.

"Mr. Bayliss," he continued, "of the firm of Bayliss, Hundercombe & Dunn, Throgmorton Court. Mr. Bayliss is a man of keen perceptions. He understands exactly the effect of certain classes of news upon the market. The message which I have just sent to him is practically common property. It will be in the Daily Mail to-morrow morning. The only thing is that I have sent it to him just a few minutes sooner than any one

E. Phillips Oppenheim

else can get it. There is a good deal of value in that, Gerald. I do not mind telling you that I have made a large fortune through studying the political situation and securing advance information upon matters of this sort. That fortune some day will probably be yours. It will be you who will benefit. Meanwhile, I am enriching myself and doing no one any harm."

"But how do you know," Gerald persisted, "that this message would ever have found its way to the Press? It was simply a message from one battleship to another. It was not intended to be picked up on land. There is no other installation but ours that could have picked it up. Besides, it was in code. I know that you have the code, but the others haven't."

Mr. Fentolin yawned slightly.

"Ingenious, my dear Gerald, but inaccurate. You do not know that the message was in code, and in any case it was liable to be picked up by any steamer within the circle. You really do treat me, my boy, rather as though I were a weird, mischief-making person with a talent for intrigue and crime of every sort. Look at your suspicions last night. I believe that you and Mr. Hamel had quite made up your minds that I meant evil things for Mr. John P. Dunster. Well, I had my chance. You saw him depart."

"What about his papers?"

"I will admit," Mr. Fentolin replied, "that I read his papers. They were of no great consequence, however, and he has taken them away with him. Mr. Dunster, as a matter of fact, turned out to be rather a mare's-nest. Now, come, since you are here, finish everything you have to say to me. I am not angry. I am willing to listen quite reasonably."

Gerald shook his head.

"Oh, I can't!" he declared bitterly. "You always get the best of it. I'll only ask you one more question. Are you having the wireless hauled down?"

Mr. Fentolin pointed out of the window. Gerald followed his finger. Three men were at work upon the towering spars.

"You see," Mr. Fentolin continued tolerantly, "that I am keeping my word to Lieutenant Godfrey. You are suffering from a little too much imagination, I am afraid. It is really quite a good fault. By-the-by, how do you get on with our friend Mr. Hamel?"

"Very well," the boy replied. "I haven't seen much of him."

"He and Esther are together a great deal, eh?" Mr. Fentolin asked quickly.

"They seem to be quite friendly."

"It isn't Mr. Hamel, by any chance, who has been putting these ideas into your head?"

"No one has been putting any ideas into my head," Gerald answered hotly. "It's simply what I've seen and overheard. It's simply what I feel around, the whole atmosphere of the place, the whole atmosphere you seem to create around you with these brutes Sarson and Meekins; and those white-faced, smooth-tongued

Marconi men of yours, who can't talk decent English; and the post-office man, who can't look you in the face; and Miss Price, who looks as though she were one of the creatures, too, of your torture chamber. That's all."

Mr. Fentolin waited until he had finished. Then he waved him away.

"Go and take a long walk, Gerald," he advised. "Fresh air is what you need, fresh air and a little vigorous exercise. Run along now and send Miss Price to me."

Gerald overtook Hamel upon the stairs.

"By this time," the latter remarked, "I suppose that our friend Mr. Dunster is upon the sea."

Gerald nodded silently. They passed along the corridor. The door of the room which Mr. Dunster had occupied was ajar. As though by common consent, they both stopped and looked in. The windows were all wide open, the bed freshly made. The nurse was busy collecting some medicine bottles and fragments of lint. She looked at them in surprise.

"Mr. Dunster has left, sir," she told them.

"We saw him go," Gerald replied.

"Rather a quick recovery, wasn't it, nurse?" Hamel asked.

"It wasn't a recovery at all, sir," the woman declared sharply. "He'd no right to have been taken away. It's my opinion Doctor Sarson ought to be ashamed of himself to have permitted it."

"They couldn't exactly make a prison of the place, could they?" Hamel pointed out. "The man, after all, was only a guest."

"That's as it may be, sir," the nurse replied. "All the same, those that won't obey their doctors aren't fit to be allowed about alone. That's the way I look at it."

Mrs. Fentolin was passing along the corridor as they issued from the room. She started a little as she saw them.

"What have you two been doing in there?" she asked quickly.

"We were just passing," Hamel explained. "We stopped for a moment to speak to the nurse."

"Mr. Dunster has gone," she said. "You saw him go, Gerald. You saw him, too, didn't you, Mr. Hamel?"

"I certainly did," Hamel admitted.

Mrs. Fentolin pointed to the great north window near which they were standing, through which the clear sunlight streamed a little pitilessly upon her worn face and mass of dyed hair.

"You ought neither of you to be indoors for a minute on a morning like this," she declared. "Esther is waiting for you in the car, I think, Mr. Hamel."

Gerald passed on up the stairs to his room, but Hamel lingered. A curious impulse of pity towards his hostess stirred him. The morning sunlight seemed to have suddenly revealed the tragedy of her life. She stood there, a tired, worn woman, with the burden heavy upon her shoulders.

"Why not come out with Miss Fentolin and me?" he suggested. "We could lunch at the Golf Club, out on the balcony. I wish you would. Can't you manage it?"

She shook her head.

"Thank you very much," she said. "Mr. Fentolin does not like to be left."

Something in the finality of her words seemed to him curiously eloquent of her state of mind. She did not move on. She seemed, indeed, to have the air of one anxious to say more. In that ruthless light, the advantages of her elegant clothes and graceful carriage were suddenly stripped away from her. She was the abject wreck of a beautiful woman, wizened, prematurely aged. Nothing remained but the eyes, which seemed somehow to have their message for him.

"Mr. Fentolin is a little peculiar, you know," she went on, her voice shaking slightly with the effort she was making to keep it low. "He allows Esther so little liberty, she sees so few young people of her own age. I do not know why he allows you to be with her so much. Be careful, Mr. Hamel."

Her voice seemed suddenly to vibrate with a curious note of suppressed fear. Almost as she finished her speech, she passed on. Her little gesture bade him remain silent. As she went up the stairs, she began to hum scraps of a little French air.

CHAPTER XXIII

Hamel sliced his ball at the ninth, and after waiting for a few minutes patiently, Esther came to help him look for it. He was standing down on the sands, a little apart from the two caddies who were beating out various tufts of long grass.

"Where did it go?" she asked.

"I have no idea," he admitted.

"Why don't you help look for it?"

"Searching for balls," he insisted, "is a caddy's occupation. Both the caddies are now busy. Let us sit down here. These sand hummocks are delightful. It is perfectly sheltered, and the sun is in our faces. Golf is an overrated pastime. Let us sit and watch that little streak of blue find its way up between the white posts."

She hesitated for a moment.

"We shall lose our place."

"There is no one behind."

She sank on to the little knoll of sand to which he had pointed, with a resigned sigh.

E. Phillips Oppenheim

"You really are a queer person," she declared. "You have been playing golf this morning as though your very life depended upon it. You have scarcely missed a shot or spoken a word. And now, all of a sudden, you want to sit on a sand hummock and watch the tide."

"I have been silent," he told her, "because I have been thinking."

"That may be truthful," she remarked, "but you wouldn't call it polite, would you?"

"The subject of my thoughts is my excuse. I have been thinking of you."

For a single moment her eyes seemed to have caught something of that sympathetic light with which he was regarding her. Then she looked away.

"Was it my mashie shots you were worrying about?" she asked.

"It was not," he replied simply. "It was you - you yourself."

She laughed, not altogether naturally.

"How flattering!" she murmured. "By-the-by, you are rather a downright person, aren't you, Mr. Hamel?"

"So much so," he admitted, "that I am going to tell you one or two things now. I am going to be very frank indeed."

She sat suddenly quite still. Her face was turned from him, but for the first time since he had known her there was a slight undertone of colour in her cheeks.

"A week ago," he said, "I hadn't the faintest idea of coming into Norfolk. I knew about this little shanty of my father's, but I had forgotten all about it. I came as the result of a conversation I had with a friend who is in the Foreign Office."

She looked at him with startled eyes.

"What do you mean?" she asked quickly. "You are Mr. Hamel, aren't you?"

"Certainly," he replied. "Not only am I Richard Hamel, mining engineer, but I really have all that reading to do I have spoken about, and I really was looking for a quiet spot to do it in. It is true that I had this part of the world in my mind, but I do not think that I should ever have really decided to come here if it had not been for my friend in London. He was very interested indeed directly I mentioned St. David's Tower. Would you like to know what he told me?"

"Yes! Go on, please."

"He told me a little of the history of your uncle, Mr. Fentolin, and what he did not tell me at the time, he has since supplemented. I suppose," he added, hesitatingly, "that you yourself -"

"Please go on. Please speak as though I knew nothing."

"Well, then," Hamel continued, "he told me that your uncle was at one time in the Foreign Office himself. He seemed to have a most brilliant career before him when suddenly there was a terrible scandal. A political secret - I don't know what it was - had leaked out. There were rumours that it had been acquired for a large sum of money by a foreign Power. Mr. Fentolin retired to Norfolk, pending an investigation. It was just as that time that he met with his terrible accident, and the matter was dropped."

"Go on, please," she murmured.

"My friend went on to say that during the last few years Mr. Fentolin has once again become an object of some suspicion to the head of our Secret Service Department. For a long time they have known that he was employing agents abroad, and that he was showing the liveliest interest in underground politics. They believed that it was a mere hobby, born of his useless condition, a taste ministered to, without doubt, by the occupation of his earlier life. Once or twice lately they have had reason to change their minds. You know, I dare say, in what a terribly disturbed state European affairs are just now. Well, my friend had an idea that Mr. Fentolin was showing an extraordinary amount of interest in a certain conference which we understand is to take place at The Hague. He begged me to come down, and to watch your uncle while I was down here, and report to him anything that seemed to me noteworthy. Since then I have had a message from him concerning the American whom you entertained - Mr. John P. Dunster. It appears that he was the bearer of very important dispatches for the Continent."

"But he has gone," she said quickly. "Nothing happened to him, after all. He went away without a word of complaint. We all saw him."

"That is quite true," Hamel admitted. "Mr. Dunster has

certainly gone. It is rather a coincidence, however, that he should have taken his departure just as the enquiries concerning his whereabouts had reached such a stage that it had become quite impossible to keep him concealed any longer."

She turned a little in her place and looked at him steadfastly.

"Mr. Hamel," she said, "tell me - what of your mission? You have had an opportunity of studying my uncle. You have even lived under his roof. Tell me what you think."

His face was troubled.

"Miss Fentolin," he said, "I will tell you frankly that up to now I have not succeeded in solving the problem of your uncle's character. To me personally he has been most courteous. He lives apparently a studious and an unselfish life. I have heard him even spoken of as a philanthropist. And yet you three - you, your mother, and your brother, who are nearest to him, who live in his house and under his protection, have the air of passing your days in mortal fear of him."

"Mr. Hamel," she exclaimed nervously, "you don't believe that! He is always very kind."

"Apparently," Hamel observed drily. "And yet you must remember that you, too, are afraid of him. I need not remind you of our conversations, but there the truth is. You praise his virtues and his charities, you pity him, and yet you go about with a load of fear, and - forgive me - of secret terror in your heart, you and Gerald, too. As for your mother -"

"Don't!" she interrupted suddenly. "Why do you bring me here to talk like this? You cannot alter things. Nothing can be altered."

"Can't it!" he replied. "Well, I will tell you the real reason of my having brought you here and of my having made this confession. I brought you here because I could not bear to go on living, if not under your roof, at any rate in the neighbourhood, without telling you the truth. Now you know it. I am here to watch Mr. Fentolin. I am going on watching him. You can put him on his guard, if you like; I shan't complain. Or you can -"

He paused so long that she looked at him. He moved a little closer to her, his fingers suddenly gripped her hand.

"Or you can marry me and come away from it all," he concluded quietly. "Forgive me, please - I mean it."

For a moment the startled light in her eyes was followed by a delicious softness. Her lips were parted, she leaned a little towards him. Then suddenly she seemed to remember. She rose with swift alertness to her feet.

"I think," she said, "that we had better play golf."

"But I have asked you to marry me," he protested, as he scrambled up.

"Your caddy has found your ball a long time ago," she pointed out, walking swiftly on ahead.

He played his shot and caught her up.

"Miss Fentolin - Esther," he pleaded eagerly, "do you think that I am not in earnest? Because I am. I mean it. Even if I have only known you for a few days, it has been enough. I think that I knew it was coming from the moment that you stepped into my railway carriage."

"You knew that what was coming?" she asked, raising her eyes suddenly.

"That I should care for you."

"It's the first time you've told me," she reminded him, with a queer little smile. "Oh, forgive me, please! I didn't mean to say that. I don't want to have you tell me so. It's all too ridiculous and impossible."

"Is it? And why?"

"I have only known you for three days."

"We can make up for that."

"But I don't - care about you. I have never thought of any one in that way. It is absurd," she went on.

"You'll have to, sometime or other," he declared. "I'll take you travelling with me, show you the world, new worlds, unnamed rivers, untrodden mountains. Or do you want to go and see where the little brown people live among the mimosa and the cherry blossoms? I'll take you so far away that this place and this life will seem like a dream."

Her breath caught a little.

"Don't, please," she begged. "You know very well - or rather you don't know, perhaps, but I must tell you - that I couldn't. I am here, tied and bound, and I can't escape."

"Ah! dear, don't believe it," he went on earnestly. "There isn't any bond so strong that I won't break it for you, no knot I won't untie, if you give me the right."

They were climbing slowly on to the tee. He stepped forward and pulled her up. Her hand was cold. Her eyes were raised to his, very softly yet almost pleadingly.

"Please don't say anything more," she begged. "I can't - quite bear it just now. You know, you must remember - there is my mother. Do you think that I could leave her to struggle alone?"

His caddy, who had teed the ball, and who had regarded the proceedings with a moderately tolerant air, felt called upon at last to interfere.

"We'd best get on," he remarked, pointing to two figures in the distance, "or they'll say we've cut in."

Hamel smote his ball far and true. On a more moderate scale she followed his example. They descended the steps together.

"Love-making isn't going to spoil our golf," he whispered, smiling, as he touched her fingers once more.

She looked at him almost shyly.

"Is this love-making?" she asked.

They walked together from the eighteenth green towards the club-house. A curious silence seemed suddenly to have enveloped them. Hamel was conscious of a strange exhilaration, a queer upheaval of ideas, an excitement which nothing in his previous life had yet been able to yield him. The wonder of it amazed him, kept him silent. It was not until they reached the steps, indeed, that he spoke.

"On our way home -" he began.

She seemed suddenly to have stiffened. He looked at her, surprised. She was standing quite still, her hand gripping the post, her eyes fixed upon the waiting motor-car. The delicate softness had gone from her face. Once more that look of partly veiled suffering was there, suffering mingled with fear.

"Look!" she whispered, under her breath. "Look! It is Mr. Fentolin! He has come for us himself; he is there in the car."

Mr. Fentolin, a strange little figure lying back among the cushions of the great Daimler, raised his hat and waved it to them.

"Come along, children," he cried. "You see, I am here to fetch you myself. The sunshine has tempted me. What a heavenly morning! Come and sit by my side, Esther, and fight your battle all over again. That is one of the joys of golf, isn't it?" he asked, turning to Hamel. "You need not be afraid of boring me. To-day is one of my bright days. I suppose that it is the sunshine and the warm wind. On the way here we passed some fields. I could swear that I smelt violets. Where are you going, Esther?"

"To take my clubs to my locker and pay my caddy," she replied.

"Mr. Hamel will do that for you," Mr. Fentolin declared. "Come and take your seat by my side, and let us wait for him. I am tired of being alone."

She gave up her clubs reluctantly. All the life seemed to have gone from her face.

"Why didn't mother come with you?" she asked simply.

"To tell you the truth, dear Esther," he answered, "when I started, I had a fancy to be alone. I think - in fact I am sure - that your mother wanted to come. The sunshine, too, was tempting her. Perhaps it was selfish of me not to bring her, but then, there is a great deal to be forgiven me, isn't there, Esther?"

"A great deal," she echoed, looking steadily ahead of her.

"I came," he went on, "because it occurred to me that, after all, I had my duties as your guardian, dear Esther. I am not sure that we can permit flirtations, you know. Let me see, how old are you?"

"Twenty-one," she replied.

"In a magazine I was reading the other day," he continued, "I was interested to observe that the modern idea as regards marriage is a changed one. A woman, they say, should not marry until she is twenty-seven or twenty-eight - a very excellent idea. I think we agree, do we not, on that, Esther?"

"I don't know," she replied. "I have never thought about the matter."

"Then," he went on, "we will make up our minds to agree. Twenty-seven or twenty-eight, let us say. A very excellent age! A girl should know her own mind by then. And meanwhile, dear Esther, would it be wise, I wonder, to see a little less of our friend Mr. Hamel? He leaves us to-day, I think. He is very obstinate about that. If he were staying still in the house, well, it might be different. But if he persists in leaving us, you will not forget, dear, that association with a guest is one thing; association with a young man living out of the house is another. A great deal less of Mr. Hamel I think that we must see."

She made no reply whatever. Hamel was coming now towards them.

"Really a very personable young man," Mr. Fentolin remarked, studying him through his eyeglass. "Is it my fancy, I wonder, as an observant person, or is he just a little - just a little taken with you, Esther? A pity if it is so - a great pity."

She said nothing, but her hand which rested upon the rug was trembling a little.

"If you have an opportunity," Mr. Fentolin suggested, dropping his voice, "you might very delicately, you know - girls are so clever at that sort of thing-convey my views to Mr. Hamel as regards his leaving us and its effect upon your companionship. You understand me, I am sure?"

For the first time she turned her head towards him.

"I understand," she said, "that you have some particular reason for not wishing Mr. Hamel to leave St. David's Hall."

He smiled benignly.

"You do my hospitable impulses full justice, dear Esther," he declared. "Sometimes I think that you understand me almost as well as your dear mother. If, by any chance, Mr. Hamel should change his mind as to taking up his residence at the Tower, I think you would not find me in any sense of the word an obdurate or exacting guardian. Come along, Mr. Hamel. That seat opposite to us is quite comfortable. You see, I resign myself to the inevitable. I have come to fetch golfers home to luncheon, and I compose myself to listen. Which of you will begin the epic of missed putts and brassey shots which failed by a foot to carry?"

CHAPTER XXIV

Hamel sat alone upon the terrace, his afternoon coffee on a small table in front of him. His eyes were fixed upon a black speck at the end of the level roadway which led to the Tower. Only a few minutes before, Mr. Fentolin, in his little carriage, had shot out from the passage beneath the terrace, on his way to the Tower. Behind him came Meekins, bending over his bicycle. Hamel watched them both with thoughtful eyes. There were several little incidents in connection with their expedition which he scarcely understood.

Then there came at last the sound for which he had been listening, the rustle of a skirt along the terraced way. Hamel turned quickly around, half rising to his feet, and concealing his disappointment with difficulty. It was Mrs. Seymour Fentolin who stood there, a little dog under each arm; a large hat, gay with flowers, upon her head. She wore patent shoes with high heels, and white silk stockings. She had, indeed, the air of being dressed for luncheon at a fashionable restaurant. As she stooped to set the dogs down, a strong waft of perfume was shaken from her clothes.

"Are you entirely deserted, Mr. Hamel?" she asked.

"I am," he replied. "Miss Esther went, I think, to look for you. My host," he added, pointing to the black speck in the distance, "begged me to defer my occupation of the Tower for an hour or so, and has gone down there to collect some of his trifles."

Her eyes followed his outstretched hand. She seemed to him to shiver for a moment.

"You really mean, then, that you are going to leave us?" she asked, accepting the chair which he had drawn up close to his.

He smiled.

"Well, I scarcely came on a visit to St. David's Hall, did I?" he reminded her. "It has been delightfully hospitable of Mr. Fentolin to have insisted upon my staying on here for these few days, but I could not possibly inflict myself upon you all for an unlimited period."

Mrs. Fentolin sat quite still for a time. In absolute repose, if one could forget her mass of unnaturally golden hair, the forced and constant smile, the too liberal use of rouge and powder, the nervous motions of her head, it was easily to be realised that there were still neglected attractions about her face and figure. Only, in these moments of repose, an intense and ageing weariness seemed to have crept into her eyes and face. It was as though she had dropped the mask of incessant gaiety and permitted a glimpse of her real self to steal to the surface.

"Mr. Hamel," she said quietly, "I dare say that even during these few days you have realised that Mr. Fentolin is a very peculiar man."

"I have certainly observed - eccentricities," Hamel assented.

"My life, and the lives of my two children," she went on, "is devoted to the task of ministering to his happiness."

"Isn't that rather a heavy sacrifice?" he asked. Mrs. Seymour Fentolin looked down the long, narrow way along which Mr. Fentolin had passed. He was out of sight now, inside the Tower. Somehow or other, the thought seemed to give her courage and dignity. She spoke differently, without nervousness or hurry.

"To you, Mr. Hamel," she said, "it may seem so. We who make it know of its necessity."

He bowed his head. It was not a subject for him to discuss with her.

"Mr. Fentolin has whims," she went on, "violent whims. We all try to humour him. He has his own ideas about Gerald's bringing up. I do not agree with them, but we submit. Esther, too, suffers, perhaps to a less extent. As for me," - her voice broke a little - "Mr. Fentolin likes people around him who are always cheerful. He prefers even a certain style - of dress. I, too, have to do my little share."

Hamel's face grew darker.

"Has it ever occurred to you," he demanded, "that Mr. Fentolin is a tyrant?"

She closed her eyes for a moment.

"There are reasons," she declared, "why I cannot discuss that with you. He has these strong fancies, and it is our task in life to humour them. He has one now with regard to the Tower, with regard to you. You are, of course, your own master. You can do as you choose, and you will do as you choose. Neither I nor my children have any claim upon your consideration. But, Mr. Hamel, you have been so kind that I feel moved to tell you this. It would make it very much easier for all of us if you would give up this scheme of yours, if you would stay on here instead of going to reside at the Tower."

Hamel threw away his cigarette. He was deeply interested.

"Mrs. Fentolin," he said, "I am glad to have you speak so plainly. Let me answer you in the same spirit. I am leaving this house mainly because I have conceived certain suspicions with regard to Mr. Fentolin. I do not like him, I do not trust him, I do not believe in him. Therefore, I mean to remove myself from the burden of his hospitality. There are reasons," he went on, "why I do not wish to leave the neighbourhood altogether. There are certain investigations which I wish to make. That is why I have decided to go to the Tower."

"Miles was right, then!" she cried suddenly. "You are here to spy upon him!"

He turned towards her swiftly.

"To spy upon him, Mrs. Fentolin? For what reason? Why? Is he a criminal, then?"

She opened her lips and closed them again. There was

a slight frown upon her forehead. It was obvious that the word had unintentionally escaped her.

"I only know what it is that he called you, what he suspects you of being," she explained. "Mr. Fentolin is very clever, and he is generally at work upon something. We do not enquire into the purpose of his labours. The only thing I know is that he suspects you of wanting to steal one of his secrets."

"Secrets? But what secrets has he?" Hamel demanded. "Is he an inventor?"

"You ask me idle questions," she sighed. "We have gone, perhaps, a little further than I intended. I came to plead with you for all our sakes, if I could, to make things more comfortable by remaining here instead of insisting upon your claim to the Tower."

"Mrs. Fentolin," Hamel said firmly. "I like to do what I can to please and benefit my friends, especially those who have been kind to me. I will be quite frank with you. There is nothing you could ask me which I would not do for your daughter's sake - if I were convinced that it was for her good."

Mrs. Seymour Fentolin seemed to be trembling a little. Her hands were crossed upon her bosom.

"You have known her for so short a time," she murmured.

Hamel smiled confidently.

"I will not weary you," he said, "with the usual trite remarks. I will simply tell you that the time has been long enough. I love your daughter."

Mrs. Fentolin sat quite still. Only in her eyes, fixed steadily seawards, there was the light of something new, as though some new thought was stirring in her brain. Her lips moved, although the sound which came was almost inaudible.

"Why not?" she murmured, as though arguing with some unseen critic of her thoughts. "Why not?"

"I am not a rich man," Hamel went on, "but I am fairly well off. I could afford to be married at once, and I should like -"

She turned suddenly upon him and gripped his wrist.

"Listen," she interrupted, "you are a traveller, are you not? You have been to distant countries, where white people go seldom; inaccessible countries, where even the arm of the law seldom reaches. Couldn't you take her away there, take her right away, travel so fast that nothing could catch you, and hide - hide for a little time?"

Hamel stared at his companion, for a moment, blankly. Her attitude was so unexpected, her questioning so fierce.

"My dear Mrs. Fentolin," he began - .

She suddenly relaxed her grip of his arm. Something of the old hopelessness was settling down upon her face. Her hands fell into her lap.

"No," she interrupted, "I forgot! I mustn't talk like that.

She, too, is part of the sacrifice."

"Part of the sacrifice," Hamel repeated, frowning. "Is she, indeed! I don't know what sacrifice you mean, but Esther is the girl whom sooner or later, somehow or other, I am going to make my wife, and when she is my wife, I shall see to it that she isn't afraid of Miles Fentolin or of any other man breathing."

A gleam of hopefulness shone through the stony misery of the woman's face.

"Does Esther care?" she asked softly.

"How can I tell? I can only hope so. If she doesn't yet, she shall some day. I suppose," he added, with a sigh, "it is rather too soon yet to expect that she should. If it is necessary, I can wait."

Mrs. Fentolin's eyes were once more fixed upon the Tower. The sun had caught the top of the telephone wire and played around it till it seemed like a long, thin shaft of silver.

"If you go down there," she said, "Esther will not be allowed to see you at all. Mr. Fentolin has decided to take it as a personal affront. You will be ostracised from here."

"Shall I?" he answered. "Well, it won't be for long, at any rate. And as to not seeing Esther, you must remember that I come from outside this little domain, and I see nothing more in Mr. Fentolin than a bad-tempered, mischievous, tyrannical old invalid, who is fortunately prevented by his infirmities from doing as much mischief as he might. I am not afraid of your brother-in-law, or of the bully he takes about with him, and I am going to see your daughter somehow or other, and I am going to marry her before very long."

She thrust out her hand suddenly and grasped his. The fingers were very thin, almost bony, and covered with rings. Their grip was feverish and he felt them tremble.

"You are a brave man, Mr. Hamel," she declared speaking in a low, quick undertone. "Perhaps you are right. The shadow isn't over your head. You haven't lived in the terror of it. You may find a way. God grant it!"

She wrung his fingers and rose to her feet. Her voice suddenly changed into another key. Hamel knew instinctively that she wished him to understand that their conversation was over.

"Chow-Chow," she cried, "come along, dear, we must have our walk. Come along, Koto; come along, little dogs."

Hamel strolled down the terrace steps and wandered for a time in the gardens behind the house. Here, in the shelter of the great building, he found himself suddenly in an atmosphere of springtime. There were beds of crocuses and hyacinths, fragrant clumps of violets, borders of snowdrops, masses of primroses and early anemones. He slowly climbed one or two steep paths until he reached a sort of plateau, level with the top of the house. The flowers here grew more sparsely, the track of the salt wind lay like a withering band across the flower-beds. The garden below was like a little oasis of colour and perfume. Arrived at the bordering red brick wall, he turned around and looked along the narrow road which led to the sea. There was no sign of Mr. Fentolin's return. Then to his left he saw a gate open and heard the clamour of dogs. Esther appeared, walking swiftly towards the little stretch of road which led to the village. He hurried after her.

"Unsociable person!" he exclaimed, as he caught her up. "Didn't you know that I was longing for a walk?"

"How should I read your thoughts?" she answered. "Besides, a few minutes ago I saw you on the terrace, talking to mother. I am only going as far as the village."

"May I come?" he asked. "I have business there myself."

She laughed.

"There are nine cottages, three farmhouses, and a general shop in St. David's," she remarked. "Also about fifteen fishermen's cottages dotted about the marsh. Your business, I presume, is with the general shop?"

He shook his head, falling into step with her.

"What I want," he explained, "is to find a woman to come in and look after me at the Tower. Your servant who valets me has given me two names."

Something of the lightness faded from her face.

"So you have quite made up your mind to leave us?" she asked slowly. "Mother wasn't able to persuade you to stay?"

He shook his head.

"She was very kind," he said, "but there are really grave reasons why I feel that I must not accept Mr. Fentolin's hospitality any longer. I had," he went on, "a very interesting talk with your mother."

She turned quickly towards him. The slightest possible tinge of additional colour was in her cheeks. She was walking on the top of a green bank, with the wind blowing her skirts around her. The turn of her head was a little diffident, almost shy. Her eyes were asking him questions. At that moment she seemed to him, with her slim body, her gently parted lips and soft, tremulous eyes, almost like a child. He drew a little nearer to her.

"I told your mother," he continued, "all that I have told you, and more. I told her, dear, that I cared for you, that I wanted you to be my wife."

She was caught in a little gust of wind. Both her hands went up to her hat; her face was hidden. She stepped down from the bank.

"You shouldn't have done that," she said quietly.

"Why not?" he demanded. "It was the truth."

He stooped forward, intent upon looking into her face. The mystic softness was still in her eyes, but her general expression was inscrutable. It seemed to him that there was fear there.

"What did mother say?" she whispered.

"Nothing discouraging," he replied. "I don't think she minded at all. I have decided, if you give me permission, to go and talk to Mr. Fentolin this evening."

She shook her head very emphatically.

"Don't!" she implored. "Don't! Don't give him another whip to lash us with. Keep silent. Let me just have the memory for a few days all to myself."

Her words came to him like numb things. There was little expression in them, and yet he felt that somehow they meant so much.

"Esther dear," he said, "I shall do just as you ask me. At the same time, please listen. I think that you are all absurdly frightened of Mr. Fentolin. Living here alone with him, you have all grown under his dominance to an unreasonable extent. Because of his horrible infirmity, you have let yourselves become his slaves. There are limits to this sort of thing, Esther. I come here as a stranger, and I see nothing more in Mr. Fentolin than a very selfish, irritable, domineering, and capricious old man. Humour him, by all means. I am willing to do the same myself. But when it comes to the great things in life, neither he nor any living person is going to keep from me the woman I love."

She walked by his side in silence. Her breath was coming a little quicker, her fingers lay passive in his. Then for a moment he felt the grip of them almost burn into his flesh. Still she said nothing.

"I want your permission, dear," he went on, "to go to him. I suppose he calls himself your guardian. If he says no, you are of age. I just want you to believe that I am strong enough to put my arms, around you and to carry you away to my own world and keep you there, although an army of Mr. Fentolin's creatures followed us."

She turned, and he saw the great transformation. Her face was brilliant, her eyes shone with wonderful things.

"Please," she begged, "will you say or do nothing at all for a little time, until I tell you when? I want just a few days' peace. You have said such beautiful things to me that I want them to lie there in my thoughts, in my heart, undisturbed, for just a little time. You see, we are at the village now. I am going to call at this third cottage. While I am inside, you can go and make what enquiries you like. Come and knock at the door for me when you are ready."

"And we will walk back together?"

"We will walk back together," she promised him.

"I will take you home another way. I will take you over what they call the Common, and come down behind the Hall into the gardens."

She dismissed him with a little smile. He strolled along the village street and plunged into the mysterious recesses of the one tiny shop.

CHAPTER XXV

Hamel met Kinsley shortly before one o'clock the following afternoon, in the lounge of the Royal Hotel at Norwich.

"You got my wire, then?" the latter asked, as he held out his hand. "I had it sent by special messenger from Wells."

"It arrived directly after breakfast," Hamel replied. "It wasn't the easiest matter to get here, even then, for there are only about two trains a day, and I didn't want to borrow a car from Mr. Fentolin."

"Quite right," Kinsley agreed. "I wanted you to come absolutely on your own. Let's get into the coffee-room and have some lunch now. I want to catch the afternoon train hack to town."

"Do you mean to say that you've come all the way down here to talk to me for half an hour or so?" Hamel demanded, as they took their places at a table.

"All the way from town," Kinsley assented, "and up to the eyes in work we are, too. Dick, what do you think of Miles Fentolin?"

"Hanged if I know!" Hamel answered, with a sigh.

E. Phillips Oppenheim

"Nothing definite to tell us, then?"

"Nothing!"

"What about Mr. John P. Dunster?"

"He left yesterday morning," Hamel said. "I saw him go. He looked very shaky. I understood that Mr. Fentolin sent him to Yarmouth."

"Did Mr. Fentolin know that there was an enquiry on foot about this man's disappearance?" Kinsley asked.

"Certainly. I heard Lord Saxthorpe tell him that the police had received orders to scour the country for him, and that they were coming to St. David's Hall."

Kinsley, for a moment, was singularly and eloquently profane.

"That's why Mr. Fentolin let him go, then. If Saxthorpe had only held his tongue, or if those infernal police hadn't got chattering with the magistrates, we might have made a coup. As it is, the game's up. Mr. Dunster left for Yarmouth, you say, yesterday morning?"

"I saw him go myself. He looked very shaky and ill, but he was able to smoke a big cigar and walk down-stairs leaning on the doctor's arm."

"I don't doubt," Kinsley remarked, "but that you saw what you say you saw. At the same time, you may be surprised to hear that Mr. Dunster has disappeared again."

"Disappeared again?" Hamel muttered.

"It looks very much," Kinsley continued, "as though your friend Miles Fentolin has been playing with him like a cat with a mouse. He has been obliged to turn him out of one hiding-place, and he has simply transferred him to another."

Hamel looked doubtful.

"Mr. Dunster left quite alone in the car," he said. "He was on his guard too, for Mr. Fentolin and he had had words. I really can't see how it was possible for him to have got into any more trouble."

"Where is he, then?" Kinsley demanded. "Come, I will let you a little further into our confidence. We have reason to believe that he carries with him a written message which is practically the only chance we have of avoiding disaster during the next few days. That written message is addressed to the delegates at The Hague, who are now sitting. Nothing had been heard of Dunster or the document he carries. No word has come from him of any sort since he left St. David's Hall."

"Have you tried to trace him from there?" Hamel asked.

"Trace him?" Kinsley repeated. "By heavens, you don't seem to understand, Dick, the immense, the extraordinary importance of this man to us! The cleverest detective in England spent yesterday under your nose at St. David's Hall. There are a dozen others working upon the job as hard as they can. All the reports confirm what you say - that Dunster left St. David's Hall at half-past nine yesterday morning, and he certainly arrived in Yarmouth at a little before twelve. From there he seems, however, to have completely disappeared. The car went back to St. David's Hall empty; the man only stayed long enough in Yarmouth, in fact, to have his dinner. We cannot find a single smack owner who was approached in any way for the hire of a boat. Yarmouth has been ransacked in vain. He certainly has not arrived at The Hague or we should have heard news at once. As a last resource, I ran down here to see you on the chance of your having picked up any information."

Hamel shook his head.

"You seem to know a good deal more than I do, already," he said.

"What do you think of Mr. Fentolin? You have stayed in his house. You have had an opportunity of studying him."

"So far as my impressions go," Hamel replied, "everything which you have suggested might very well be true. I think that either out of sheer love of mischief, or from some subtler motive, he is capable of anything. Every one in the place, except one poor woman, seems to look upon him as a sort of supernatural being. He gives money away to worthless people with both hands. Yet I share your opinion of him. I believe that he is a creature without conscience or morals. I have sat at his table and shivered when he has smiled."

"Are you staying at St. David's Hall now?"

"I left yesterday."

"Where are you now, then?"

"I am at St. David's Tower - the little place I told you of that belonged to my father - but I don't know whether I shall be able to stop there. Mr. Fentolin, for some reason or other, very much resented my leaving the Hall and was very annoyed at my insisting upon claiming the Tower. When I went down to the village to get some one to come up and look after me, there wasn't a woman there who would come. It didn't matter what I offered, they were all the same. They all muttered some excuse or other, and seemed only anxious to show me out. At the village shop they seemed to hate to serve me with anything. It was all I could do to get a packet of tobacco yesterday afternoon. You would really think that I was the most unpopular person who ever lived, and it can only be because of Mr. Fentolin's influence."

"Mr. Fentolin evidently doesn't like to have you in the locality," Kinsley remarked thoughtfully.

"He was all right so long as I was at St. David's Hall," Hamel observed.

"What's this little place like - St. David's Tower, you call it?" Kinsley asked.

"Just a little stone building actually on the beach," Hamel explained. "There is a large shed which Mr. Fentolin keeps locked up, and the habitable portion consists just of a bedroom and sitting-room. From what I can see, Mr. Fentolin has been making a sort of hobby of the place. There is telephonic communication with the house, and he seems to have used the sitting-room as a sort of studio. He paints sea pictures and really paints them very well."

A man came into the coffee-room, made some enquiry of the waiter and went out again. Hamel stared at him in a puzzled manner. For the moment he could only remember that the face was familiar. Then he suddenly gave vent to a little exclamation.

"Any one would think that I had been followed," he remarked. "The man who has just looked into the room is one of Mr. Fentolin's parasites or bodyguards, or whatever you call them."

"You probably have," Kinsley agreed. "What post does he hold in the household?"

"I have no idea," Hamel replied. "I saw him the first day I arrived and not since. Sort of secretary, I should think."

"He is a queer-looking fellow, anyway," Kinsley muttered. "Look out, Dick. Here he comes back again."

Mr. Ryan approached the table a little diffidently.

"I hope you will forgive the liberty, sir," he said to Hamel. "You remember me, I trust - Mr. Ryan. I am the librarian at St. David's Hall."

Hamel nodded.

"I thought I'd seen you there."

"I was wondering," the man continued, "whether you had a car of Mr. Fentolin's in Norwich to-day, and if so, whether I might beg a seat back in case you were returning before the five o'clock train? I came in early this morning to go through some manuscripts at a second-hand bookseller's here, and I have unfortunately missed the train back."

Hamel shook his head.

"I came in by train myself, or I would have given you a lift back, with pleasure," he said.

Mr. Ryan expressed his thanks briefly and left the room. Kinsley watched him from over the top of a newspaper.

"So that is one of Mr. Fentolin's creatures, too," he remarked. "Keeping his eye on you in Norwich, eh? Tell me, Dick, by-the-by, how do you get on with the rest of Mr. Fentolin's household, and exactly of whom does it consist?"

"There is his sister-in-law," Hamel replied, "Mrs. Seymour Fentolin. She is a strange, tired-looking woman who seems to stand in mortal fear of Mr. Fentolin. She is always overdressed and never natural, but it seems to me that nearly everything she does is done to suit his whims, or at his instigation."

Kinsley nodded thoughtfully.

"I remember Seymour Fentolin," he said; "a really fine fellow he was. Well, who else?"

"Just the nephew and niece. The boy is half sullen, half discontented, yet he, too, seems to obey his uncle blindly. The three of them seem to be his slaves. It's a thing you can't live in the house without noticing."

"It seems to be a cheerful sort of household," Kinsley

observed. "You read the papers, I suppose, Dick?" he asked, after a moment's pause.

"On and off, the last few days. I seem to have been busy doing all sorts of things."

"Well, I'll tell you something," Kinsley continued. "The whole of our available fleet is engaged in carrying out what they call a demonstration in the North Sea. They have patrol boats out in every direction, and only the short distance wireless signals are being used. Everything, of course, is in code, yet we know this for a fact: a good deal of private information passing between the Admiral and his commanders was known in Germany three hours after the signals themselves had been given. It is suspected - more than suspected, in fact - that these messages were picked up by Mr. Fentolin's wireless installation."

"I don't suppose he could help receiving them," Hamel remarked.

"He could help decoding them and sending them through to Germany, though," Kinsley retorted grimly. "The worst of it is, he has a private telephone wire in his house to London. If he isn't up to mischief, what does he need all these things for - private telegraph line, private telephone, private wireless? We have given the postmaster a hint to have the telegraph office moved down into the village, but I don't know that that will help us much."

"So far as regards the wireless," Hamel said, "I rather believe that it is temporarily dismantled. We had a sailor-man over, the morning before yesterday, to complain of his messages having been picked up. Mr.

Fentolin promised at once to put his installation out of work for a time."

"He has done plenty of mischief with it already," Kinsley groaned. "However, it was Dunster I came down to make enquiries about. I couldn't help hoping that you might have been able to put us on the right track."

Hamel sighed.

"I know nothing beyond what I have told you."

"How did he look when he went away?"

"Very ill indeed," Hamel declared. "I afterwards saw the nurse who had been attending him, and she admitted that he was not fit to travel. I should say the probabilities are that he is laid up again somewhere."

"Did you actually speak to him?"

"Just a word or two."

"And you saw him go off in the car?"

"Gerald Fentolin and I both saw him and wished him good-by."

Kinsley glanced at the clock and rose to his feet. "Walk down to the station with me," he suggested. "I needn't tell you, I am sure," he went on, as they left the hotel a few minutes later, "that if anything does turn up, or if you get the glimmering of an idea, you'll let me know? We've a small army looking for the fellow, but it does seem as though he had disappeared off the face of the earth. If he doesn't turn up before the end of the Conference, we are done."

"Tell me," Hamel asked, after they had walked for some distance in silence, "exactly why is our fleet demonstrating to such an extent?"

"That Conference I have spoken of," Kinsley replied, "which is being held at The Hague, is being held, we know, purposely to discuss certain matters in which we are interested. It is meeting for their discussion without any invitation having been sent to this country. There is only one reply possible to such a course. It is there in the North Sea. But unfortunately -"

Kinsley paused. His tone and his expression had alike become gloomier.

"Go on," Hamel begged.

"Our reply, after all, is a miserable affair," Kinsley concluded. "You remember the outcry over the withdrawal of our Mediterranean Fleet? Now you see its sequel. We haven't a ship worth a snap of the fingers from Gibraltar to Suez. If France deserts us, it's good-by to Malta, good-by to Egypt, good-by to India. It's the disruption of the British Empire. And all this," he wound up, as he paused before taking his seat in the railway carriage, "all this might even now be avoided if only we could lay our hands upon the message which that man Dunster was bringing from New York!"

CHAPTER XXVI

Once more Hamel descended from the little train, and, turning away from St. David's Hall, made his way across the marshes, seawards. The sunshine of the last few days had departed. The twilight was made gloomy by a floating veil of white mist, which hung about in wet patches. Hamel turned up his coat collar as he walked and shivered a little. The thought of his solitary night and uncomfortable surroundings, after all the luxury of St. David's Hall, was scarcely inspiring. Yet, on the whole, he was splendidly cheerful. The glamour of a host of new sensations was upon him. There was a new love of living in his heart. He forgot the cold east wind which blew in his face, bringing with it little puffs of damp grey mist. He forgot the cheerlessness which he was about to face, the lonely night before him. For the first time in his life a woman reigned in his thoughts.

It was not until he actually reached the very side of the Tower that he came back to earth. As he opened the door, he found a surprise in store for him. A fire was burning in the sitting-room, smoke was ascending from the kitchen chimney. The little round table was laid with a white cloth. There was a faint odour of cooking from the back premises. His lamp was lit, there were logs hissing and crackling upon the fire. As he stood there looking wonderingly about him, the door from the back was opened. Hannah Cox came quietly into the room.

"What time would you like your dinner, sir?" she enquired.

Hamel stared at her.

"Why, are you going to keep house for me, Mrs. Cox?" he asked.

"If you please, sir. I heard that you had been in the village, looking for some one. I am sorry that I was away. There is no one else who would come to you."

"So I discovered," he remarked, a little grimly.

"No one else," she went on, "would come to you because of Mr. Fentolin. He does not wish to have you here. They love him so much in the village that he had only to breathe the word. It was enough."

"Yet you are here," he reminded her.

"I do not count," she answered. "I am outside all these things."

Hamel gave a little sigh of satisfaction.

"Well, I am glad you could come, anyhow. If you have something for dinner, I should like it in about half an hour."

He climbed the narrow stairs which led to his bedroom. To his surprise, there were many things there for his comfort which he had forgotten to order - clean bed-linen, towels, even a curtain upon the window.

"Where did you get all the linen up-stairs from, Mrs. Cox?" he asked her, when he descended. "The room was almost empty yesterday, and I forgot nearly all the things I meant to bring home from Norwich."

"Mrs. Seymore Fentolin sent down a hamper for you," the woman replied, "with a message from Mr. Fentolin. He said that nothing among the oddments left by your father had been preserved, but that you were welcome to anything you desired, if you would let them know at the Hall."

"It is very kind of both of them," Hamel said thoughtfully.

The woman stood still for a moment, looking at him. Then she drew a step nearer.

"Has Mr. Fentolin given you the key of the shed?" she asked, very quietly.

Hamel shook his head.

"We don't need the place, do we?"

"He did not give you the key?" she persisted.

"Mr. Fentolin said that he had some things in there which he wished to keep locked up," he explained.

She remained thoughtful for several moments. Then she turned away.

"No," she said, "it was not likely he would not give

you that key!"

Hamel dined simply but comfortably. Mrs. Cox cleared away the things, brought him his coffee, and appeared a few minutes later, her shawl wrapped around her, ready for departure.

"I shall be here at seven o'clock in the morning, sir," she announced.

Hamel was a little startled. He withdrew the pip from his mouth and looked at her.

"Why, of course," he remarked. "I'd forgotten. There is no place for you to stay here."

"I shall go back to my brother's." she said.

Hamel put some money upon the table.

"Please get anything that is necessary," he directed. "I shall leave you to do the housekeeping for a few days."

"Shall you be staying here long, sir?" she asked.

"I am not sure," he replied.

"I do not suppose," she said, "that you will stay for very long. I shall get only the things that you require from day to day. Good night, sir."

She left the room. Hamel looked after her for a moment with a frown. In some indescribable way, the woman half impressed, half irritated him. She had always the air of keeping something in the background. He followed her out on to the little ridge of beach, a few minutes after she had left. The mist was still drifting about. Only a few yards away the sea rolled in, filling the air with dull thunder. The marshland was half obscured. St. David's Hall was invisible, but like strangely-hung lanterns in an empty space he saw the line of lights from the great house gleam through the obscurity. There was no sound save the sound of the sea. He shivered slightly. It was like an empty land, this.

Then, moved by some instinct of curiosity, he made his way round to the closed door of the boat-house, only to find it, as he had expected, locked. He shook it slightly, without result. Then he strolled round to the back, entered his own little abode by the kitchen, and tried the other door which led into the boat-house. It was not only locked, but a staple had been put in, and it was fastened with a padlock of curious design which he did not remember to have seen there before. Again, half unconsciously, he listened, and again he found the silence oppressive. He went back to his room, brought out some of the books which it had been his intention to study, and sat and read over the fire.

At ten o'clock he went to bed. As he threw open his window before undressing, it seemed to him that he could catch the sound of voices from the sea. He listened intently. A grey pall hung everywhere. To the left, with strange indistinctness, almost like something human struggling to assert itself, came the fitful flash from the light at the entrance to the tidal way. Once more he strained his ears. This time there was no doubt about it. He heard the sound of fishermen's voices. He heard one of them say distinctly:

"Hard aport, Dave lad! That's Fentolin's light. Keep her

out a bit. Steady, lad!"

Through a rift in the mist, he caught a glimpse of the brown sail of a fishing-boat, dangerously near the land. He watched it alter its course slightly and pass on. Then again there was silence. He undressed slowly and went to bed.

Later on he woke with a start and sat up in bed, listening intently, listening for he knew not what. Except for the backward scream of the pebbles, dragged down every few seconds by the receding waves, an unbroken silence seemed to prevail. He struck a match and looked at his watch. It was exactly three o'clock. He got out of bed. He was a man in perfect health, ignorant of the meaning of nerves, a man of proved courage. Yet he was conscious that his pulses were beating with absurd rapidity. A new feeling seemed to possess him. He could almost have declared that he was afraid. What sound had awakened him? He had no idea, yet he seemed to have a distinct and absolute conviction that it had been a real sound and no dream. He drew aside the curtains and looked out of the window. The mist now seemed to have become almost a fog, to have closed in upon sea and land. There was nothing whatever to be seen. As he stood there for a moment, listening, his face became moist with the drifting vapour. Suddenly upon the beach he saw what at first he imagined must be an optical illusion - a long shaft of light, invisible in itself except that it seemed to slightly change the density of the mist. He threw on an overcoat over his pyjamas, thrust on his slippers, and taking up his own electric torch, hastily descended the stairs. He opened the front door and stepped out on to the beach. He stood in the very place where the light had seemed to be, and looked inland. There was no sign of any human person, not a sound except the falling of the sea upon the pebbly beach. He raised his voice and called out. Somehow or other, speech seemed to be a relief.

"Hullo!"

There was no response. He tried again.

"Is any one there?"

Still no answer. He watched the veiled light from the harbour appear and disappear. It threw no shadow of illumination upon the spot to which he had gazed from his window. One window at St. David's Hall was illuminated. The rest of the place was wrapped now in darkness. He walked up to the boat-house. The door was still locked. There was no sign that any one had been there. Reluctantly at last he re-entered the Tower and made his way up-stairs.

"Confound that fellow Kinsley!" he muttered, as he threw off his overcoat. "All his silly suggestions and melodramatic ideas have given me a fit of nerves. I am going to bed, and I am going to sleep. That couldn't have been a light I saw at all. I couldn't have heard anything. I am going to sleep."

CHAPTER XXVII

Hamel awoke to find his room filled with sunshine and a soft wind blowing in through the open window. There was a pleasant odour of coffee floating up from the kitchen. He looked at his watch - it was past eight o'clock. The sea was glittering and bespangled with sunlight. He found among his scanty belongings a bathing suit, and, wrapped in his overcoat, hurried down-stairs.

"Breakfast in half an hour, Mrs. Cox," he called out.

She stood at the door, watching him as he stepped across the pebbles and plunged in. For a few moments he swam. Then he turned over on his back. The sunlight was gleaming from every window of St. David's Hall. He even fancied that upon the terrace he could see a white-clad figure looking towards him. He turned over and swam once more. From her place in the doorway Mrs. Cox called out to him.

"Mind the Dagger Rocks, sir!"

He waved his hand. The splendid exhilaration of the salt water seemed to give him unlimited courage. He dived, but the woman's cry of fear soon recalled him. Presently he swam to shore and hurried up the beach. Mrs. Cox, with a sigh of relief, disappeared into the kitchen.

"Those rocks on your nerves again, Mrs. Cox?" he asked, good-humouredly, as he took his place at the breakfast table a quarter of an hour later.

"It's only us who live here, sir," she answered, "who know how terrible they are. There's one - it comes up like my hand - a long spike. A boat once struck upon that, and it's as though it'd been sawn through the middle."

"I must have a look at them some day," he declared. "I am going to work this morning, Mrs. Cox. Lunch at one o'clock."

He took rugs and established himself with a pile of books at the back of a grassy knoll, sheltered from the wind, with the sea almost at his feet. He sharpened his pencil and numbered the page of his notebook. Then he looked up towards the Hall garden and found himself dreaming. The sunshine was delicious, and a gentle optimism seemed to steal over him.

"I am a fool!" he murmured to himself. "I am catching some part of these people's folly. Mr. Fentolin is only an ordinary, crotchety invalid with queer tastes. On the big things he is probably like other men. I shall go to him this morning."

A sea-gull screamed over his head. Little, brown sailed fishing-boats came gliding down the harbourway. A pleasant, sensuous joyfulness seemed part of the spirit of the day. Hamel stretched himself out upon the dry sand.

"Work be hanged!" he exclaimed.

A soft voice answered him almost in his ear, a voice which was becoming very familiar.

"A most admirable sentiment, my young friend, which you seem to be doing your best to live up to. Not a line written, I see."

He sat up upon his rug. Mr. Fentolin, in his little carriage, was there by his side. Behind was the faithful Meekins, with an easel under his arm.

"I trust that your first night in your new abode has been a pleasant one?" Mr. Fentolin asked.

"I slept quite well, thanks," Hamel replied. "Glad to see you're going to paint."

Mr. Fentolin shook his head gloomily.

"It is, alas!" he declared, "one of my weaknesses. I can work only in solitude. I came down on the chance that the fine weather might have tempted you over to the Golf Club. As it is, I shall return."

"I am awfully sorry," Hamel said. "Can't I go out of sight somewhere?"

Mr. Fentolin sighed.

"I will not ask your pardon for my absurd humours," he continued, a little sadly. "Their existence, however, I cannot deny. I will wait."

"It seems a pity for you to do that," Hamel remarked.

"You see, I might stay here for some time."

Mr. Fentolin's face darkened. He looked at the young man with a sort of pensive wrath.

"If," the latter went on, "you say 'yes' to something I am going to ask you, I might even stay - in the neighbourhood - for longer still."

Mr. Fentolin sat quite motionless in his chair; his eyes were fixed upon Hamel.

"What is it that you are going to ask me?" he demanded.

"I want to marry your niece."

Mr. Fentolin looked at the young man in mild surprise.

"A sudden decision on your part, Mr. Hamel?" he murmured.

"Not at all," Hamel assured him. "I have been ten years looking for her."

"And the young lady?" Mr. Fentolin enquired. "What does she say?"

"I believe, sir," Hamel replied, "that she would be willing."

Mr. Fentolin sighed.

"One is forced sometimes," he remarked regretfully, "to realise the selfishness of our young people. For many years one devotes oneself to providing them with all the comforts and luxuries of life. Then, in a single day, they turn around and give everything they have to give to a stranger. So you want to marry Esther?"

"If you please."

"She has a very moderate fortune."

"She need have none at all," Hamel replied; "I have enough."

Mr. Fentolin glanced towards the house.

"Then," he said, "I think you had better go and tell her so; in which case, I shall be able to paint."

"I have your permission, then?" Hamel asked, rising to his feet eagerly.

"Negatively," Mr. Fentolin agreed, "you have. I cannot refuse. Esther is of age; the thing is reasonable. I do not know whether she will be happy with you or not. A young man of your disposition who declines to study the whims of an unfortunate creature like myself is scarcely likely to be possessed of much sensibility. However, perhaps your views as to a solitary residence here will change with your engagement to my niece."

Hamel did not reply for a moment. He was trying to ask himself why, even in the midst of this rush of anticipatory happiness, he should be conscious of a certain reluctance to leave the Tower - and Mr. Fentolin. He was looking longingly towards the Hall. Mr. Fentolin waved him away.

"Go and make love," he ordered, "and leave me alone.

We are both in pursuit of beauty - only our methods differ."

Hamel hesitated no longer but walked up the narrow path with swift, buoyant footsteps. Everywhere he seemed to be surrounded by the glorious spring sunshine. It glittered in the little pools and creeks by his side. It drew a new colour from the dun-coloured marshes, the masses of emerald seaweed, the shimmering sands. It flashed in the long row of windows of the Hall. As he drew nearer, he could see the banks of yellow crocuses in the sloping gardens behind. There were odours of spring in the air. He ran lightly up the terrace steps. There was an easy-chair drawn into her favourite corner, and a book upon the table, but no sign of Esther. He hesitated for a moment, and then, retracing his steps along the terrace, entered the house by the front door, which stood wide open. There was no one in the hall, scarcely a sound about the place. A great clock ticked solemnly from the foot of the stairs. There was not even a servant in sight. Hamel wandered around, a a loss what to do. He opened the door of the drawing-room and looked in. It was empty. He turned away, meaning to ring a bell. On his way across the hall he paused. A curiously suggestive sound reached him faintly from the end of one of the passages. It was the click of a typewriter.

Hamel stood for a moment perfectly still. He had hurried up to the Hall, filled with the one selfish joy common to all mankind. He had had no thought save the thought of seeing Esther. The click of that machine brought him hack to the stern realities of life. He remembered his talk to Kinsley, his promise. On the hall table he could see from where he was standing the great headlines which announced the nation's anxiety.

He was in the house of a suspected spy. The click of the typewriter was an accompaniment to his thought. He looked around once more and listened. Then he made his way quietly across the hail and down the long passage, at the end of which the room which Mr. Fentolin called his workroom was situated. He turned the handle of the door and entered, closing it immediately behind him. The woman who was typing paused with her fingers upon the keys. Her eyes met his coldly, without curiosity. She had paused in her work, but she took no other notice of his coming.

"Has Mr. Fentolin sent you here?" she asked at last.

He came over to the typewriter.

"Mr. Fentolin has not sent me," he said slowly. "I am here on my own account. I dare say you will think that I am a lunatic to come to you like this. Nevertheless, please listen to me."

Her fingers left the keys. She laid her hands upon the table in front of her. He drew a little nearer. She covered over the sheets of paper with which she was surrounded with a pad of blotting-paper. He pointed suddenly to them.

"Why do you do that?" he demanded. "What is there in your work that you are afraid I might see?"

She answered him without hesitation.

"These are private papers of Mr. Fentolin's. No one has any business to see them. No one has any business to enter this room. Why are you here?"

"I came to the Hall to find Miss Fentolin," he replied. "I heard the click of your typewriter. I came to you, I suppose I should say, on impulse."

Her eyes rested upon his, filled with a cold and questioning light.

"There's an impression up in London," Hamel went on, "that Mr. Fentolin has been interfering by means of his wireless in affairs which don't concern him, and giving away valuable information. This man Dunster's disappearance is as yet unexplained. I feel myself justified in making certain investigations, and among the first of them I should like you to tell me exactly the nature of the work for which Mr. Fentolin finds a secretary necessary?"

She glanced towards the bell. He moved to the edge of the table as though to intercept her.

"In any ordinary case," he continued, "I would not ask you to betray your employer's confidence. As things are, I think I am justified. You are English, are you not? You realise, I suppose, that the country is on the brink of war?"

She looked at him from the depths of her still, lusterless eyes.

"You must be a very foolish person," she remarked, "if you expect to obtain information in this manner."

"Perhaps I am," he confessed, "but my folly has brought me to you, and you can give me the information if you will."

"Where is Mr. Fentolin?" she asked.

"Down at the Tower," he replied. "I left him there. He sent me up to see Miss Fentolin. I was looking for her when the click of your typewriter reminded me of other things."

She turned composedly back to her work.

"I think," she said, "that you had better go and find Miss Fentolin."

"Don't talk nonsense! You can't think I have risked giving myself away to you for nothing? I mean to search this room, to read the papers which you are typing."

She glanced around her a little contemptuously.

"You are welcome," she assured him. "Pray proceed."

They exchanged the glances of duelists. Her plain black frock was buttoned up to her throat. Her colourless face seemed set in exact and expressionless lines. Her eyes were like windows of glass. He felt only their scrutiny; nothing of the reason for it, or of the thoughts which stirred behind in her brain. There was nothing about her attitude which seemed in any way threatening, yet he had the feeling that in this interview it was she who possessed the upper hand.

"You are a foolish person," she said calmly. "You are so foolish that you are not, in all probability, in the slightest degree dangerous. Believe me, ours is an unequal duel. There is a bell upon this table which has apparently escaped your notice. I sit with my finger upon the button - so. I have only to press it, and the servants will be here. I do not wish to press it. I do not desire that you should be, as you certainly would be, banished from this house."

He was immensely puzzled. She had not resented his strange intrusion. She had accepted it, indeed, with curious equanimity. Her forefinger lingered still over the little ivory knob of the bell attached to her desk. He shrugged his shoulders.

"You have the advantage of me," he admitted, a little curtly. "All the same, I think I could possess myself of those sheets of paper, you know, before the bell was answered."

"Would it be wise, I wonder, then, to ensure their safety?" she asked coolly.

Her finger pressed the bell. He took a quick step forward. She held out her hand.

"Stop!" she ordered. "These sheets will tell you nothing which you do not know already unless you are a fool. Never mind the bell. That is my affair. I am sending you away."

He leaned a little towards her.

"It wouldn't be possible to bribe you, I suppose?"

She shook her head.

"I wonder you haven't tried that before. No, it would not - not with money, that is to say."

"You'll tell Mr. Fentolin, I presume?" he asked quickly.

"I have nothing to tell him," she replied. "Nothing has happened. Richards," she went on, as a servant entered the room, "Mr. Hamel is looking for Miss Fentolin. Will you see if you can find her?"

The man's expression was full of polite regret.

"Miss Fentolin went over to Legh Woods early this morning, sir," he announced. "She is staying to lunch with Lady Saxthorpe."

Hamel stood quite still for a moment. Then he turned to the window. In the far distance he could catch a glimpse of the Tower. Mr. Fentolin's chair had disappeared from the walk.

"I am sorry," he said. "I must have made a mistake. I will hurry back."

There were more questions which he was longing to ask, but the cold negativeness of her manner chilled him. She sat with her fingers poised over the keys, waiting for his departure. He turned and left the room.

CHAPTER XXVIII

Mr. Fentolin, his carriage drawn up close to the beach, was painting steadily when Hamel stood once more by his side. His eyes moved only from the sea to the canvas. He never turned his head.

"So your wooing has not prospered, my young friend," he remarked gently. "I am sorry. Is there anything I can do?"

"Your niece has gone out to lunch," Hamel replied shortly.

Mr. Fentolin stopped painting. His face was full of concern as he looked up at Hamel.

"My dear sir," he exclaimed, "how can I apologise! Of course she has gone out to lunch. She has gone out to Lady Saxthorpe's. I remember the subject being discussed. I myself, in fact, was the instigator of her going. I owe you a thousand apologies, Mr. Hamel. Let me make what amends are possible for your useless journey. Dine with us to-night."

"You are very kind."

"A poor amends," Mr. Fentolin continued. "A morning like this was made for lovers. Sunshine and blue sky, a

E. Phillips Oppenheim

salt breeze flavoured just a little with that lavender, and a stroll through my spring gardens, where my hyacinths are like a field of purple and gold, a mantle of jewels upon the brown earth. Ah, well! One's thoughts will wander to the beautiful things of life. There were once women who loved me, Mr. Hamel."

Hamel looked doubtfully at the strange little figure in the chair. Was this genuine, he wondered, a voluntary outburst, or was it some subtle attempt to incite sympathy? Mr. Fentolin seemed almost to have read his thought.

"It is not for the sake of your pity that I say this," he continued. "Mine is only the passing across the line which age as well as infirmity makes inevitable. No one in the world who lives to grow old, and who has loved and felt the fire of it in his veins, can pass that line without sorrow, or look back without a pang. I am among a great army. Well, well, I shall paint no more to-day," he concluded abruptly.

"Where is your servant?" Hamel asked.

Mr. Fentolin glanced around him carelessly.

"He has wandered away out of sight. He knows well how necessary solitude is to me if once I take the brush between my fingers - solitude natural and entire, I mean. If any one is within a dozen yards of me I know it, even though I cannot see them. Meekins is wandering somewhere the other side of the Tower."

"Shall I call him?"

"On no account, " Mr. Fentolin begged. "Presently he

will appear, in plenty of time. There is the morning to be passed - barely eleven o'clock, I think, now. I shall sit in my chair, and sink a little down, and dream of these beautiful lights, these rolling, foam-flecked waves, these patches of blue and shifting green. I can form them in my brain. I can make a picture there, even though my fingers refuse to move. You are not an aesthete, I think, Mr. Hamel? The study of beauty does not mean to you what it did to your father, and my father, and, in a smaller way to me."

"Perhaps not," Hamel confessed. "I believe I feel these things somewhere, because they bring a queer sense of content with them. I am afraid, though, that my artistic perceptions are not so keen as some men's."

Mr. Fentolin looked at him thoughtfully.

"It is the physical life in your veins - too splendid to permit you abstract pleasures. Compensations again, you see - compensations. I wonder what the law is that governs these things. I have forgotten sometimes," he went on, "forgotten my own infirmities in the soft intoxication of a wonderful seascape. Only," he went on, his face a little grey, "it is the physical in life which triumphs. There are the hungry hours which nothing will satisfy."

His head sank, his chin rested upon his chest. He had all the appearance now of a man who talks in bitter earnest. Yet Hamel wondered. He looked towards the Tower; there was no sign of Meekins. The sea-gulls went screaming above their heads. Mr. Fentolin never moved. His eyes seemed half closed. It was only when Hamel rose to his feet that he looked swiftly up.

E. Phillips Oppenheim

"Stay with me, I beg you, Mr. Hamel," he said. "I am in one of the moods when solitude, even for a moment, is dangerous. Do you know what I have sometimes thought to myself?"

He pointed to the planked way which led down the steep, pebbly beach to the sea.

"I have sometimes thought," he went on, "that it would be glorious to find a friend to stand by my side at the top of the planks, just there, when the tide was high, and to bid him loose my chair and to steer it myself, to steer it down the narrow path into the arms of the sea. The first touch of the salt waves, the last touch of life. Why not? One sleeps without fear."

He lifted his head suddenly. Meekins had appeared, coming round from the back of the Tower. Instantly Mr. Fentolin's whole manner changed. He sat up in his chair.

"It is arranged, then," he said. "You dine with us to-night. For the other matters of which you have spoken, well, let them rest in the hands of the gods. You are not very kind to me. I am not sure whether you would make Esther a good husband. I am not sure, even, that I like you. You take no pains to make yourself agreeable. Considering that your father was an artist, you seem to me rather a dull and uninspired young man. But who can tell? There may be things stirring beneath that torpid brain of yours of which no other person knows save yourself."

The concentrated gaze of Mr. Fentolin's keen eyes was hard to meet, but Hamel came out of the ordeal without flinching.

"At eight o'clock, Mr. Fentolin," he answered. "I can see that I must try to earn your better opinion."

Hamel read steadily for the remainder of the morning. It was past one o'clock when he rose stiffly from his seat among the sand knolls and, strolling back to the Tower, opened the door and entered. The cloth was laid for luncheon in the little sitting-room, but there were no signs of Hannah Cox. He passed on into the kitchen and came to a sudden standstill. Once more the memory of his own work passed away from him. Once more he was back again among that queer, clouded tangle of strange suspicions, of thrilling, half-formed fears, which had assailed him at times ever since his arrival at St, David's. He stopped quite short. The words which rose to his lips died away. He felt the breathless, compelling need for silence and grew tense in the effort to make no sound.

Hannah Cox was kneeling on the stone floor. Her ear was close to the crack of the door which led into the boat-house. Her face, half turned from it, was set in a strange, concentrated passion of listening; her lips were parted, her eyes half closed. She took no more notice of Hamel or his arrival than if he had been some useless piece of furniture. Every faculty seemed to be absorbed in that one intense effort of listening. There was no need of her out-stretched finger. Hamel fell in at once with a mood so mesmeric. He, too, listened. The small clock which she had brought with her from the village ticked away upon the mantelpiece. The full sea fell with placid softness upon the high beach outside. Some slight noise of cooking came from the stove. Save for these things there was silence. Yet, for a space of time which Hamel could never have measured, they both listened. When at last the woman

E. Phillips Oppenheim

rose to her feet, Hamel, finding words at last, was surprised to find that his throat was dry.

"What is it, Mrs. Cox?" he asked. "Why were you listening there?"

Her face was absolutely expressionless. She was busying herself now with a small saucepan, and her back was turned towards him.

"I spend my life, sir," she said, "listening and waiting. One never knows when the end may come."

"But the boat-house," Hamel objected. "No one has been in there his morning, have they?"

"Who can tell?" she answered. "He could go anywhere when he chose, or how he chose - through the keyhole, if he wanted."

"But why listen?" Hamel persisted. "There is nothing in there now but some odds and ends of machinery."

She turned from the fire and looked at him for a moment. Her eyes were colourless, her tone unemotional.

"Maybe! There's no harm in listening."

"Did you hear anything which made you want to listen?"

"Who can tell?" she answered. "A woman who lives well-nigh alone, as I live, in a quiet place, hears things so often that other folk never listen to. There's always something in my ears, night or day. Sometimes I am not sure whether it's in this world or the other. It was like that with me just then. It was for that reason I listened. Your luncheon's ready, sir."

Hamel walked thoughtfully back into his sitting-room. He seated himself before a spotless cloth and watched Hannah Cox spread out his well-cooked, cleanly-served meal.

"If there's anything you want, sir," she said, "I shall hear you at a word. The kitchen door is open."

"One moment, Mrs. Cox."

She lingered there patiently, with the tray in her hand.

"There was some sound," Hamel continued, "perhaps a real sound, perhaps a fancy, which made you go down on your knees in the kitchen. Tell me what it was."

"The sound I always hear, sir," she answered quietly. "I hear it in the night, and I hear it when I stand by the sea and look out. I have heard it for so many years that who can tell whether it comes from this world or the other - the cry of men who die!"

She passed out. Hamel looked after her, for a moment, like a man in a dream. In his fancy he could see her back again once more in the kitchen, kneeling on the stone floor, - listening!

CHAPTER XXIX

A cold twilight had fallen upon the land when Hamel left the Tower that evening and walked briskly along the foot-way to the Hall. Little patches of mist hung over the creeks, the sky was almost frosty. The lights from St. David's Hall shone like cheerful beacons before him. He hastened up the stone steps, crossed the terrace, and passed into the hall. A servant conducted him at once to the drawing-room. Mrs. Fentolin, in a pink evening dress, with a pink ornament in her hair, held out both her hands. In the background, Mr. Fentolin, in his queerly-cut evening clothes, sat with folded arms, leaning back in his carriage. He listened grimly to his sister-in-law as she stood with Hamel's hands in hers.

"My dear Mr. Hamel!" she exclaimed. "How perfectly charming of you to come up and relieve a little our sad loneliness! Delightful, I call it, of you. I was just saying so to Miles."

Hamel looked around the room. Already his heart was beginning to sink.

"Miss Fentolin is well, I hope?" he asked.

"Well, but a very naughty girl," her mother declared. "I let her go to Lady Saxthorpe's to lunch, and now we have had simply the firmest letter from Lady Saxthorpe. They insist upon keeping Esther to dine and sleep. I have had to send her evening clothes, but you can't tell, Mr. Hamel, how I miss her."

Hamel's disappointment was a little too obvious to pass unnoticed. There was a shade of annoyance, too, in his face. Mr. Fentolin smoothly intervened.

"Let us be quite candid with Mr. Hamel, dear Florence," he begged. "I have spoken to my sister-in-law and told her the substance of our conversation this morning," he proceeded, wheeling his chair nearer to Hamel. "She is thunderstruck. She wishes to reflect, to consider. Esther chanced to be away. We have encouraged her absence for a few more hours."

"I hope, Mrs. Fentolin," Hamel said simply, "that you will give her to me. I am not a rich man, but I am fairly well off. I should be willing to live exactly where Esther wishes, and I would do my best to make her happy."

Mrs. Fentolin opened her lips once and closed them again. She laughed a little - a high-pitched, semi-hysterical laugh. The hand which gripped her fan was straining so that the blue veins stood out almost like whipcord.

"Esther is very young, Mr. Hamel. We must talk this over. You have known her for such a very short time."

A servant announced dinner, and Hamel offered his arm to his hostess.

"Is Gerald away, too?" he asked.

"We do indeed owe you our apologies," Mr. Fentolin declared. "Gerald is spending a couple of days at the Dormy House at Brancaster - a golf arrangement made some time back."

"He promised to play with me to-morrow," Hamel remarked thoughtfully. "He said nothing about going away."

"I fear that like most young men of his age he has little memory," Mr. Fentolin sighed. "However, he will be back to-morrow or the next day. I owe you my apologies, Mr. Hamel, for our lack of young people. We must do our best to entertain our guest, Florence. You must be at your best, dear. You must tell him some of those capital stories of yours."

Mrs. Fentolin shivered for a moment. Hamel, as he handed her to her place, was struck by a strange look which she threw upon him, half furtive, full of pain. Her hand almost clung to his. She slipped a little, and he held her tightly. Then he was suddenly conscious that something hard was being pressed into his palm. He drew his hand away at once.

"You seem a little unsteady this evening, my dear Florence," Mr. Fentolin remarked, peering across the round table.

She eyed him nonchalantly enough.

"The floor is slippery," she said. "I was glad, for a moment, of Mr. Hamel's strong hand. Where are those dear puppies? Chow-Chow," she went on, "come and sit by your mistress at once."

Hamel's fingers inside his waistcoat pocket were smoothing out the crumpled piece of paper which she had passed to him. Soon he had it quite flat. Mrs. Fentolin, as though freed from some anxiety, chattered away gaily.

"I don't know that I shall apologise to Mr. Hamel at all for the young people being away," she declared. "Just fancy what we have saved him from - a solitary meal served by Hannah Cox! Do you know that they say she is half-witted, Mr. Hamel?"

"So far, she has looked after me very well," Hamel observed.

"Her intellect is defective," Mr. Fentolin remarked, "on one point only. The good woman is obsessed by the idea that her husband and sons are still calling to her from the Dagger Rocks. It is almost pitiful to meet her wandering about there on a stormy night. The seacoasts are full of these little village tragedies - real tragedies, too, however insignificant they may seem to us."

Mr. Fentolin's tone was gently sympathetic. He changed the subject a moment or two later, however.

"Nero fiddles to-night," he said, "while Rome burns. There are hundreds in our position, yet it certainly seems queer that we should be sitting here so quietly when the whole country is in such a state of excitement. I see the press this morning is preaching an immediate declaration of war."

"Against whom?" Mrs. Fentolin asked.

Mr. Fentolin smiled.

"That does seem to be rather the trouble," he admitted. "Russia, Austria, Germany, Italy, and France are all assisting at a Conference to which no English representative has been bidden. In a sense, of course, that is equivalent to an act of hostility from all these countries towards England. The question is whether we have or have not a secret understanding with France, and if so, how far she will be bound by it. There is a rumour that when Monsieur Deschelles was asked formally whom he represented, that he replied - 'France and Great Britain.' There may be something in it. It is hard to see how any English statesman could have left unguarded the Mediterranean, with all that it means, trusting simply to the faith of a country with whom we have no binding agreement. On the other hand, there is the mobilisation of the fleet. If France is really faithful, one wonders if there was need for such an extreme step."

"I am out of touch with political affairs," Hamel declared. "I have been away from England for so long."

"I, on the other hand," Mr. Fentolin continued, his eyes glittering a little, "have made the study of the political situation in Europe my hobby for years. I have sent to me the leading newspapers of Berlin, Rome, Paris, St. Petersburg, and Vienna. For two hours every day I read them, side by side. It is curious sometimes to note the common understanding which seems to exist between the Powers not bound by any formal alliance. For years war seemed a very unlikely thing, and now," he added, leaning forward in his chair, "I pronounce it almost a certainty."

Hamel looked at his host a little curiously. Mr. Fentolin's gentleness of expression seemed to have departed. His face was hard, his eyes agleam. He had almost the look of a bird of prey. For some reason, the thought of war seemed to be a joy to him. Perhaps he read something of Hamel's wonder in his expression, for with a shrug of the shoulders he dismissed the subject.

"Well," he concluded, "all these things lie on the knees of the gods. I dare say you wonder, Mr. Hamel, why a poor useless creature like myself should take the slightest interest in passing events? It is just the fascination of the looker-on. I want your opinion about that champagne. Florence dear, you must join us. We will drink to Mr. Hamel's health. We will perhaps couple that toast in our minds with the sentiment which I am sure is not very far from your thoughts, Florence."

Hamel raised his glass and bowed to his host and hostess. He was not wholly at his ease. It seemed to him that he was being watched with a queer persistence by both of them. Mrs. Fentolin continued to talk and laugh with a gaiety which was too obviously forced. Mr. Fentolin posed for a while as the benevolent listener. He mildly applauded his sister-in-law's stories, and encouraged Hamel in the recital of some of his reminiscences. Suddenly the door was opened. Miss Price appeared. She walked smoothly across the room and stood by Mr. Fentolin's side. Stooping down, she whispered in his ear. He pushed his chair back a little from the table. His face was dark with anger.

"I said not before ten to-night," he muttered.

Again she spoke in his ear, so softly that the sound of her voice itself scarcely travelled even as far as where Hamel was sitting. Mr. Fentolin looked steadfastly for a moment at his sister-in-law and from her to Hamel. Then he backed his chair away front the table.

"I shall have to ask to be excused for three minutes," he said. "I must speak upon the telephone. It is a call from some one who declares that they have important news."

He turned the steering-wheel of his chair, and with Miss Price by his side passed across the dining-room, out of the Oasis of rose-shaded lights into the shadows, and through the open door. From there he turned his head before he disappeared, as though to watch his guest. Mrs. Fentolin was busy fondling one of her dogs, which she had raised to her lap, and Hamel was watching her with a tolerant smile.

"Koto, you little idiot, why can't you sit up like your sister? Was its tail in the way, then! Mr. Hamel," she whispered under her breath, so softly that he barely caught the words, although he was only a few feet away, "don't look at me. I feel as though we were being watched all the time. You can destroy that piece of paper in your pocket. All that it says is 'Leave here immediately after dinner.'"

Hamel sipped his wine in a nonchalant fashion. His fingers had strayed over the silky coat of the little dog, which she had held out as though for his inspection.

"How can I?" he asked. "What excuse can I make?"

"Invent one," she insisted swiftly. "Leave here before

ten o'clock. Don't let anything keep you. And destroy that piece of paper in your pocket, if you can - now."

"But, Mrs. Fentolin -" he began.

She caught up one of her absurd little pets and held it to her mouth.

"Meekins is in the doorway," she whispered.

"Don't argue with me, please. You are in danger you know nothing about. Pass me the cigarettes."

She leaned back in her chair, smoking quickly. She held one of the dogs on her knee and talked rubbish to it. Hamel watched her, leaning back in his carved oak chair, and he found it hard to keep the pity from his eyes. The woman was playing a part, playing it with desperate and pitiful earnestness, a part which seemed the more tragical because of the soft splendour of their surroundings. From the shadowy walls, huge, dimly-seen pictures hung about them, a strange and yet impressive background. Their small round dining-table, with its rare cut glass, its perfect appointments, its bowls of pink roses, was like a spot of wonderful colour in the great room. Two men servants stood at the sideboard a few yards away, a triumph of negativeness. The butler, who had been absent for a moment, stood now silently waiting behind his master's place. Hamel was oppressed, during those few minutes of waiting, by a curious sense of unreality, as though he were taking part in some strange tableau. There was something unreal about his surroundings and his own presence there; something unreal in the atmosphere, charged as it seemed to be with some omen of impending happenings; something unreal in

E. Phillips Oppenheim

that whispered warning, those few hoarsely uttered words which had stolen to his hearing across the clusters of drooping roses; the absurd babble of the woman, who sat there with tragic things under the powder with which her face was daubed.

"Koto must learn to sit upon his tail - like that. No, not another grape till he sits up. There, then!"

She was leaning forward with a grape between her teeth, towards the tiny animal who was trying in vain to balance his absurdly shaped little body upon the tablecloth. Hamel, without looking around, knew quite well what was happening. Soon he heard the click of the chair. Mr. Fentolin was back in his place. His skin seemed paler and more parchment-like than ever. His eyes glittered.

"It seems," he announced quietly, as he raised his wine-glass to his lips with the air of one needing support, "that we entertained an angel unawares here. This Mr. Dunster is lost for the second time. A very important personage he turns out to be."

"You mean the American whom Gerald brought home after the accident?" Mrs. Fentolin asked carelessly.

Mr. Fentolin replied. "He insisted upon continuing his journey before he was strong enough. I warned him of what might happen. He has evidently been take ill somewhere. It seems that he was on his way to The Hague."

"Do you mean that he has disappeared altogether this time?" Hamel asked.

Mr. Fentolin shook his head.

"No, he has found his way to The Hague safely enough. He is lying there at a hotel in the city, but he is unconscious. There is some talk about his having been robbed on the way. At any rate, they are tracing his movements backwards. We are to be honoured with a visit from one of Scotland Yard's detectives, to reconstruct his journey from here. Our quiet little corner of the world is becoming quite notorious. Florence dear, you are tired. I can see it in your eyes. Your headache continues, I am sure. We will not be selfish. Mr. Hamel and I are going to have a long evening in the library. Let me recommend a phenacetin and bed."

She rose at once to her feet, with a dog under either arm.

"I'll take the phenacetin," she promised, "but I hate going to bed early. Shall I see you again, I wonder, Mr. Hamel?"

"Not this evening, I fear," he answered. "I am going to ask Mr. Fentolin to excuse me early."

She passed out of the room. Hamel escorted her as far as the door and then returned. Mr. Fentolin was sitting quite still in his chair. His eyes were fixed upon the tablecloth. He looked up quickly as Hamel resumed his seat.

"You are not in earnest, I hope, Mr. Hamel," he said, "when you tell me that you must leave early? I have been anticipating a long evening. My library is filled with books on South America which I want to discuss with you."

"Another evening, if you don't mind," Hamel begged. "To-night I must ask you to excuse my hurrying away."

Mr. Fentolin looked up from underneath his eyelids. His glance was quick and penetrating.

"Why this haste?"

Hamel shrugged his shoulders.

"To tell you the truth," he admitted, "I had an idea while I was reading an article on cantilever bridges this morning. I want to work it out."

Mr. Fentolin glanced behind him. The door of the dining-room was closed. The servants had disappeared. Meekins alone, looking more like a prize fighter than ever in his somber evening clothes, had taken the place of the butler behind his master's chair.

"We shall see," Mr. Fentolin said quietly.

CHAPTER XXX

Mr. Fentolin pointed to the little pile of books upon the table, the deep easy-chair, the green-shaded lamps, the decanter of wine. He had insisted upon a visit, however brief, to the library.

"It is a student's appeal which I make to you, Mr. Hamel," he said, with a whimsical smile. "Here we are in my study, with the door closed, secure against interruption, a bright fire in the grate, a bowling and ever-increasing wind outside. Let us go together over the ground of your last wonderful expedition over the Andes. You will find that I am not altogether ignorant of your profession, or of those very interesting geological problems which you spoke of in connection with that marvellous railway scheme. We will discuss them side by side as sybarites, hang ourselves around with cigarette smoke, drink wine, and presently coffee. It is necessary, is it not, for many reasons, that we become better acquainted? You realise that, I am sure, and you will not persist in returning to your selfish solitude."

Hamel's eyes were fixed a little longingly upon some of the volumes with which the table was covered.

"You must not think me ungrateful or churlish, Mr. Fentolin," he begged. "I have a habit of keeping

E. Phillips Oppenheim

promises which I make to myself, and to-night I have made myself a promise that I will be back at the Tower by ten o'clock."

"You are obdurate?" Mr. Fentolin asked softly.

"I am afraid I am."

Mr. Fentolin busied himself with the handle of his chair.

"Tell me," he insisted, "is there any other person save yourself to whom you have given this mysterious promise?"

"No one," Hamel replied promptly.

"I am a person very sensitive to atmosphere," Mr. Fentolin continued slowly. "Since the unfortunate visit of this man Dunster, I seem to have been conscious of a certain suspicion, a little cloud of suspicion under which I seem to live and move, even among the members of my own household. My sister-in-law is nervous and hysterical; Gerald has been sullen and disobedient; Esther has avoided me. And now - well, I find even your attitude a little difficult to understand. What does it mean, Mr. Hamel?"

Hamel shook his head.

"I am not in the confidence of the different members of your family," he answered. "So far as I, personally, am concerned -"

"It pleases me sometimes," Mr. Fentolin interrupted, "to interfere to some extent in the affairs of the outside world. If I do so, that is my business. I do it for my own amusement. It is at no time a serious position which I take up. Have I by any chance, Mr. Hamel, become an object of suspicion to you?"

"There are matters in which you are concerned," Hamel admitted, "which I do not understand, but I see no purpose in discussing them."

Mr. Fentolin wheeled his chair round in a semicircle. He was now between the door and Hamel.

"Weaker mortals than I, Mr. Hamel," he said calmly, "have wielded before now the powers of life and death. From my chair I can make the lightnings bite. Science has done away with the triumph of muscularity. Even as we are here together at this moment, Mr. Hamel, if we should disagree, it is I who am the preordained victor."

Hamel saw the glitter in his hand. This was the end, then, of all doubt! He remained silent.

"Suspicions which are, in a sense, absurd," Mr. Fentolin continued, "have grown until I find them obtrusive and obnoxious. What have I to do with Mr. John P. Dunster? I sent him out from my house. If he is lost or ill, the affair is not mine. Yet one by one those around me are falling away. I told you an hour ago that Gerald was at Brancaster. It is a lie. He has left this house, but no soul in it knows his destination."

Hamel started.

"You mean that he has run away?"

E. Phillips Oppenheim

Mr. Fentolin nodded.

"All that I can surmise is that he has followed Dunster," he proceeded. "He has an idea that in some way I robbed or injured the man. He has broken the bond of relationship between us. He has broken his solemn vow. He has run a grave and terrible risk."

"What of Miss Esther?" Hamel asked quickly.

"I have sent her away," Mr. Fentolin replied, "until we come to a clear understanding, you and I. You seem to be a harmless enough person, Mr. Hamel but appearances are sometimes deceptive. It has been suggested to me that you are a spy."

"By whom?" Hamel demanded.

"By those in whom I trust," Mr. Fentolin told him sternly. "You are a friend of Reginald Kinsley. You met him in Norwich the other day - secretly. Kinsley's chief is a member of the Government. He is one of those who will find eternal obloquy if The Hague Conference comes to a successful termination. For some strange reason, I am supposed to have robbed or harmed the one man in the world whose message might bring to nought that Conference. Are you here to watch me, Mr. Hamel? Are you one of those who believe that I am either in the pay of a foreign country, or that my harmless efforts to interest myself in great things are efforts inimical to this country; that I am, in short, a traitor?"

"You must admit that many of your actions are incomprehensible," Hamel replied slowly. "There are things here which I do not understand - which certainly require explanation."

"Still, why do you make them your business?" Mr. Fentolin persisted. "If indeed the course which I steer is a harmless one," he continued, with a strange new glitter in his eyes, "then you are an impertinent stranger to whom my doors cannot any longer be open. If you have taken advantage of my hospitality to spy upon me and my actions, if indeed you have a mission here, then you can carry it with you down into hell!"

"I understand that you are threatening me?" Hamel murmured.

Mr. Fentolin smiled.

"Scarcely that, my young friend. I am not quite the obvious sort of villain who flourishes revolvers and lures his victims into secret chambers. These words to you are simply words of warning. I am not like other men, neither am I used to being crossed. When I am crossed, I am dangerous. Leave here, if you will, in safety, and mind your own affairs; but if you show one particle of curiosity as to mine, if you interfere in matters which concern me and me only, remember that you are encircled by powers which are entirely ruthless, absolutely omnipotent. You can walk back to the Tower to-night and remember that there isn't a step you take which might not be your last if I willed it, and never a soul the wiser. There's a very hungry little mother here who takes her victims and holds them tight. You can hear her calling to you now. Listen!"

He held up his finger. The tide had turned, and through the half-open window came the low thunder of the waves.

E. Phillips Oppenheim

"You decline to share my evening," Mr. Fentolin concluded. "Let it be so. Go your own way, Hamel, only take care that your way does not cross mine."

He backed his chair slowly and pressed the bell. Hamel felt himself dismissed. He passed out into the hall. The door of the drawing-room stood open, and he heard the sound of Mrs. Fentolin's thin voice singing some little French song. He hesitated and then stepped in. With one hand she beckoned him to her, continuing to play all the time. He stepped over to her side.

"I come to make my adieux," he whispered, with a glance towards the door.

"You are leaving, then?" she asked quickly.

He nodded.

"Mr. Fentolin is in a strange humour," she went on, a moment later, after she had struck the final chords of her song. "There are things going on around us which no one can understand. I think that one of his schemes has miscarried; he has gone too far. He suspects you; I cannot tell you why or how. If only you would go away!"

"What about Esther?" he asked quietly.

"You must leave her," she cried, with a little catch in her throat. "Gerald has broken away. Esther and I must carry still the burden."

She motioned him to go. He touched her fingers for a moment.

"Mrs. Fentolin," he said, "I have been a good many years making up my mind. Now that I have done so, I do not think that any one will keep Esther from me."

She looked at him a little pitifully, a little wistfully. Then, with a shrug of the shoulders, she turned round to the piano and recommenced to play. Hamel took his coat and hat from a servant who was waiting in the hail and passed out into the night.

He walked briskly until he reached the Tower. The wind had risen, but there was still enough light to help him on his way. The little building was in complete darkness. He opened the door and stepped into the sitting-room, lit the lamp, and, holding it over his head, went down the passage and into the kitchen. Then he gave a start. The lamp nearly slipped from his fingers. Kneeling on the stone floor, in very much the same attitude as he had found her earlier in the day, Hannah Cox was crouching patiently by the door which led into the boat-house, her face expressionless, her ear turned towards the crack. She was still listening.

CHAPTER XXXI

Hamel set down the lamp upon the table. He glanced at the little clock upon the dresser; it was a quarter past ten. The woman had observed his entrance, although it seemed in no way to have discomposed her.

"Do you know the time, Mrs. Cox?" he asked. "You ought to have been home hours ago. What are you doing there?"

She rose to her feet. Her expression was one of dogged but patient humility.

"I started for home before nine o'clock, sir," she told him, "but it was worse than ever to-night. All the way along by the sea I seemed to hear their voices, so I came back. I came back to listen. I have been listening for an hour."

Hamel looked at her with a frown upon his forehead.

"Mrs. Cox," he said, "I wish I could understand what it is that you have in your mind. Those are not real voices that you hear; you cannot believe that?"

"Not real voices," she repeated, without the slightest expression in her tone.

"Of course not! And tell me what connection you find between these fancies of yours and that room? Why do you come and listen here?"

"I do not know," she answered patiently.

"You must have some reason," he persisted.

"I have no reason," she assured him, "only some day I shall see behind these doors. Afterwards, I shall hear the voices no more."

She was busy tying a shawl around her head. Hamel watched her, still puzzled. He could not get rid of the idea that there was some method behind her madness.

"Tell me - I have found you listening here before. Have you ever heard anything suspicious?"

"I have heard nothing yet," she admitted, "nothing that counts."

"Come," he continued, "couldn't we clear this matter up sensibly? Do you believe that there is anybody in there? Do you believe the place is being used in any way for a wrong purpose? If so, we will insist upon having the keys from Mr. Fentolin. He cannot refuse. The place is mine."

"Mr. Fentolin would not give you the keys, sir," she replied. "If he did, it would be useless."

"Would you like me to break the door in?" Hamel asked.

"You could not do it, sir," she told him, "not you nor

E. Phillips Oppenheim

anybody else. The door is thicker than my fist, of solid oak. It was a mechanic from New York who fitted the locks. I have heard it said in the village - Bill Hamas, the carpenter, declares that there are double doors. The workmen who were employed here were housed in a tent upon the beach and sent home the day they finished their job. They were never allowed in the village. They were foreigners, most of them. They came from nobody knows where, and when they had finished they disappeared. Why was that, sir? What is there inside which Mr. Fentolin needs to guard so carefully?"

"Mr. Fentolin has invented something," Hamel explained. "He keeps the model in there. Inventors are very jealous of their work."

She looked down upon the floor for a moment.

"I shall be here at seven o'clock in the morning, sir. I will give you your breakfast at the usual time."

Hamel opened the door for her.

"Good night, Mrs. Cox," he said. "Would you like me to walk a little way with you? It's a lonely path to the village, and the dikes are full."

"Thank you, no, sir," she replied. "It's a lonely way, right enough, but it isn't loneliness that frightens me. I am less afraid out with the winds and the darkness than under this roof. If I lose my way and wander all night upon the marsh, I'll be safer out there than you, sir."

She passed away, and Hamel watched her disappear into the darkness. Then he dragged out a bowl of tobacco and filled a pipe. Although he was half ashamed of himself, he strolled back once more into the kitchen, and, drawing up a stool, he sat down just where he had discovered Hannah Cox, sat still and listened. No sound of any sort reached him. He sat there for ten minutes. Then he scrambled to his feet.

"She is mad, of course!" he muttered.

He mixed himself a whisky and soda, relit his pipe, which had gone out, and drew up an easy-chair to the fire which she had left him in the sitting-room. The wind had increased in violence, and the panes of his window rattled continually. He yawned and tried to fancy that he was sleepy. It was useless. He was compelled to admit the truth - that his nerves were all on edge. In a sense he was afraid. The thought of bed repelled him. He had not a single impulse towards repose. Outside, the wind all the time was gathering force. More than once his window was splashed with the spray carried on by the wind which followed the tide. He sat quite still and tried to think calmly, tried to piece together in his mind the sequence of events which had brought him to this part of the world and which had led to his remaining where he was, an undesired hanger-on at the threshold of Miles Fentolin. He had the feeling that to-night he had burned his boats. There was no longer any pretence of friendliness possible between him and this strange creature. Mr. Fentolin suspected him, realised that he himself was suspected. But of what? Hamel moved in his chair restlessly. Sometimes that gathering cloud of suspicion seemed to him grotesque. Of what real harm could he be capable, this little autocrat who from his chair seemed to exercise such a malign influence upon every one with whom he was brought into contact? Hamel sighed. The riddle was insoluble. With a sudden rush of warmer and more joyous feelings, he let the subject slip away from him. He closed his eyes and dreamed for a while. There was a new world before him, joys which only so short a time ago he had fancied had passed him by.

He sat up in his chair with a start. The fire had become merely a handful of grey ashes, his limbs were numb and stiff. The lamp was flickering out. He had been dozing, how long he had no idea. Something had awakened him abruptly. There was a cold draught blowing through the room. He turned his head, his hands still gripping the sides of his chair. His heart gave a leap. The outer door was a few inches open, was being held open by some invisible force. There was some one there, some one on the point of entering stealthily. Even as he watched, the crack became a little wider. He sat with his eyes riveted upon that opening space. The unseen hand was still at work. Every instant he expected to see a face thrust forward. The sensation of absolute physical fear by which he was oppressed was a revelation to him. He found himself wishing almost feverishly that he was armed. The physical strength in which he had trusted seemed to him at that instant a valueless and impotent thing. There was a splash of spray or raindrops against the window and through the crack in the door. The lamp chimney hissed and spluttered and finally the light went out. The room was in sudden darkness. Hamel sprang then to his feet. Silence had become an intolerable thing. He felt the close presence of another human being creeping in upon him.

"Who's there?" he cried. "Who's there, I say?"

There was no direct answer, only the door was pushed a little further open. He had stepped close to it now. The sweep of the wind was upon his face, although in the black darkness he could see nothing. And then a sudden recollection flashed in upon him. From his trousers pocket he snatched a little electric torch. In an instant his thumb had pressed the button. He turned it upon the door. The shivering white hand which held it open was plainly in view. It was the hand of a woman! He stepped swiftly forward. A dark figure almost fell into his arms.

"Mrs. Fentolin!" he exclaimed, aghast.

An hysterical cry, choked and subdued, broke from her lips. He half carried, half led her to his easy-chair. Suddenly steadied by the presence of this unlooked-for emergency, he closed the outside door and relit the lamp with firm fingers. Then he turned to face her, and his amazement at this strange visit became consternation.

She was still in her dinner-gown of black satin, but it was soaked through with the rain and hung about her like a black shroud. She had lost one shoe, and there was a great hole in her silk stocking. Her hair was all disarranged; one of its numerous switches was hanging down over her ear. The rouge upon her cheeks had run down on to her neck. She sat there, looking at him out of her hollow eyes like some trapped animal. She was shaking with fear. It was fear, not faintness, which kept her silent.

"Tell me, please, what is the matter?" he insisted, speaking as indifferently as he could. "Tell me at once what has happened?"

She pointed to the door.

"Lock it!" she implored.

He turned down the latch and drew the bolt. The sound seemed to give her a little courage. Her fingers went to her throat for a moment.

"Give me some water."

He poured out some soda-water. She drank only a sip and put it down again. He began to be alarmed. She had the appearance of one who has suddenly lost her senses.

"Please tell me just what has happened?" he begged. "If I can help in any way, you know I will. But you must tell me. Do you realise that it is three o'clock? I should have been in bed, only I went to sleep over the fire here."

"I know," she answered. "It is just the wind that has taken away my breath. It was a hard struggle to get here. Listen - you are our friend, Mr. Hamel - Esther's and mine? Swear that you are our friend?"

"Upon my honour, I am," he assured her. "You should know that."

"For eight years," she went on, her voice clear enough now, although it seemed charged with a curious metallic vibration, "for eight years we've borne it, all three of us, slaves, bound hand and foot, lashed with his tongue, driven along the path of his desires. We have seen evil things. We have been on the point of rebellion, and he's come a little nearer and he's pointed back. He has taken me by the hand, and I have walked by the side of his chair, loathing it, loathing myself, out on to the terrace and down below, just where it happened. You know what happened there, Mr. Hamel?"

"You mean where Mr. Fentolin met with his accident."

"It was no accident!" she cried, glancing for a moment around her. "It was no accident! It was my husband who took him up and threw him over the terrace, down below; my husband who tried to kill him; Esther's father - Gerald's father! Miles was in the Foreign Office then, and he did something disgraceful. He sold a secret to Austria. He was always a great gambler, and he was in debt. Seymour found out about it. He followed him down here. They met upon the terrace. I - I saw it!"

He was silent for a moment.

"No one has known the truth," he murmured.

"No one has ever known," she assented, "and our broken lives have been the price. It was Miles himself who made the bargain. We - we can't go on, Mr. Hamel."

"I begin to understand," Hamel said softly. "You suffer everything from Miles Fentolin because he kept the secret. Very well, that belongs to the past. Something has happened, something to-night, which has brought you here. Tell me about it?"

Once more her voice began to shake.

"We've seen - terrible things - horrible things," she faltered. "We've held our peace. Perhaps it's been nearly as bad before, but we've closed our eyes; we haven't wanted to know. Now - we can't help it. Mr. Hamel, Esther isn't at Lord Saxthorpe's. She never went there. They didn't ask her. And Dunster - the man Dunster -"

"Where is Esther?" Hamel interrupted suddenly.

"Locked up away from you, locked up because she rebelled!"

"And Dunster?"

She shook her head. Her eyes were filled with horror.

"But he left the Hall - I saw him!"

She shook her head.

"It wasn't Dunster. It was the man Miles makes use of - Ryan, the librarian. He was once an actor."

"Where is Dunster, then?" Hamel asked quickly. "What has become of him?"

She opened her lips and closed them again, struggled to speak and failed. She sat there, breathing quickly, but silent. The power of speech had gone.

CHAPTER XXXII

Hamel, for the next few minutes, forgot everything else in his efforts to restore to consciousness his unexpected visitor. He rebuilt the fire, heated some water upon his spirit lamp, and forced some hot drink between the lips of the woman who was now almost in a state of collapse. Then he wrapped her round in his own ulster and drew her closer to the fire. He tried during those few moments to put away the memory of all that she had told him. Gradually she began to recover. She opened her eyes and drew a little sigh. She made no effort at speech, however. She simply lay and looked at him like some wounded animal. He came over to her side and chafed one of her cold hands.

"Come," he said at last, "you begin to look more like yourself now. You are quite safe in here, and, for Esther's sake as well as your own, you know that I am your friend."

She nodded, and her fingers gently pressed his.

"I am sure of it," she murmured.

"Now let us see where we are," he continued. "Tell me exactly why you risked so much by leaving St. David's Hall to-night and coming down here. Isn't there any chance that he might find out?"

"I don't know," she answered. "It was Lucy Price who sent me. She came to my room just as I was undressing."

"Lucy Price," he repeated. "The secretary?"

"Yes! She told me that she had meant to come to you herself. She sent me instead. She thought it best. This man Dunster is being kept alive because there is something Miles wants him to tell him, and he won't. But to-night, if he is still alive, if he won't tell, they mean to make away with him. They are afraid."

"Miss Price told you this?" Hamel asked gravely.

Mrs. Fentolin nodded.

"Yes! She said so. She knows - she knows everything. She has been like the rest of us. She, too, has suffered. She, too, has reached the breaking point. She loved him before the accident. She has been his slave ever since. Listen!"

She suddenly clutched his arm. They were both silent. There was nothing to be heard but the wind. She leaned a little closer to him.

"Lucy Price sent me here to-night because she was afraid that it was to-night they meant to take him from his hiding-place and kill him. The police have left off searching for Mr. Dunster in Yarmouth and at The Hague. There is a detective in the neighbourhood and another one on his way here. They are afraid to keep him alive any longer."

"Where was Mr. Fentolin when you left?" Hamel asked.

"I asked Lucy Price that," she replied. "When she came to my room, there were no signs of his leaving. She told me to come and tell you everything. Do you know where Mr. Dunster is?"

Hamel shook his head.

"Within a few yards of here," she went on. "He is in the boat-house, the place where Miles told you he kept a model of his invention. They brought him here the night before they put his clothes on Ryan and sent him off disguised as Mr. Dunster, in the car to Yarmouth."

Hamel started up, but she clutched at his arm and pulled him back. "No," she cried, "you can't break in! There are double doors and a wonderful lock. The boat-house is yours; the building is yours. In the morning you must demand the keys - if he does not come to-night!"

"And how are we to know," Hamel asked, "if he comes to-night?"

"Go outside," she whispered. "Look towards St. David's Hall and tell me how many lights you can see."

He drew back the bolt, unlatched the door, and stepped out into the darkness. The wind and the driving rain beat against his face. A cloud of spray enveloped and soaked him. Like lamps hung in the sky, the lights of St. David's Hall shone out through the black gulf. He counted them carefully; then he stepped back.

"There are seven," he told her, closing the door with an effort.

She counted upon her fingers.

"I must come and see," she muttered. "I must be sure. Help me."

He lifted her to her feet, and they staggered out together.

"Look!" she went on, gripping his arm. "You see that row of lights? If anything happens, if Mr. Fentolin leaves the Hall to-night to come down here, a light will appear on the left in the far corner. We must watch for that light. We must watch -"

The words, whispered hoarsely into his ear, suddenly died away. Even as they stood there, far away from the other lights, another one shone suddenly out in the spot towards which she had pointed, and continued to burn steadily. He felt the woman who was clinging to his arm become suddenly a dead weight.

"She was right!" Mrs. Fentolin moaned. "He is coming down to-night! He is preparing to leave now; perhaps he has already started! What shall we do? What shall we do?"

Hamel was conscious of a gathering sense of excitement. He, too, looked at the signal which was flashing out its message towards them. Then he gripped his companion's arm and almost carried her back into the sitting-room.

"Look here, " he said firmly, "you can do nothing

further. You have done your part and done it well. Stay where you are and wait. The rest belongs to me."

"But what can you do?" she demanded, her voice shaking with fear. "Meekins will come with him, and Doctor Sarson, unless he is here already. What can you do against them? Meekins can break any ordinary man's back, and Mr. Fentolin will have a revolver."

Hamel threw another log on to the fire and drew her chair closer to it.

"Never mind about," he declared cheerfully. "Mr. Fentolin is too clever to attempt violence, except as a last resource. He knows that I have friends in London who would need some explanation of my disappearance. Stay here and wait."

She recognised the note of authority in his tone, and she bowed her head. Then she looked up at him; she was a changed woman.

"Perhaps I have done ill to drag you into our troubles, Mr. Hamel," she said, "and yet, I believe in you. I believe that you really care for Esther. If you can help us now, it will be for your happiness, too. You are a man. God bless you!"

Hamel groped his way round the side of the Tower and took up a position at the extreme corner of the landward side of the building, within a yard of the closed doors. The light far out upon the left was still gleaming brightly, but two of the others in a line with it had disappeared. He flattened himself against the wall and waited, listening intently, his eyes straining through the darkness. Yet they were almost upon him before he had the slightest indication of their presence. A single gleam of light in the path, come and gone like a flash, the gleam of an electric torch directed momentarily towards the road, was his first indication that they were near. A moment or two later he heard the strange click, click of the little engine attached to Mr. Fentolin's chair. Hamel set his teeth and stepped a few inches further back. The darkness was so intense that they were actually within a yard or so of him before he could even dimly discern their shapes. There were three of them - Mr. Fentolin in his chair, Doctor Sarson, and Meekins. They paused for a moment while the latter produced a key. Hamel distinctly heard a slow, soft whisper from Doctor Sarson.

"Shall I go round to the front and see that he is in bed?"

"No need," Mr. Fentolin replied calmly. "It is nearly four o'clock. Better not to risk the sound of your footsteps upon the pebbles. Now!"

The door swung noiselessly open. The darkness was so complete that even though Hamel could have touched them with an outstretched hand, their shapes were invisible. Hamel, who had formed no definite plans, had no time to hesitate. As the last one disappeared through the door, he, too, slipped in. He turned abruptly to the left and, holding his breath, stood against the wall. The door closed behind them. The gleam of the electric light flashed across the stone floor and rested for a moment upon a trap-door, which Meekins had already stooped to lift. It fell back noiselessly upon rubber studs, and Meekins immediately slipped through it a ladder, on either side of which was a grooved stretch of board, evidently fashioned to allow Mr. Fentolin's carriage to pass down. Hamel held his breath. The moment for him was critical. If the light flashed once in his direction, he must be discovered. Both Meekins and Doctor Sarson, however, were intent upon the task of steering Mr. Fentolin's little carriage down below. They placed the wheels in the two grooves, and Meekins secured the carriage with a rope which he let run through his fingers. As soon as the little vehicle had apparently reached the bottom, he turned, thrust the electric torch in his pocket, and stepped lightly down the ladder. Doctor Sarson followed his example. They disappeared in perfect silence and left the door open. Presently a gleam of light came travelling up, from which Hamel knew that they had lit a lamp below. Very softly he crept across the floor, threw himself upon his stomach and peered down. Below him was a room, or rather a cellar, parts of which seemed to have been cut out of the solid rock. Immediately underneath was a plain iron bedstead, on which was lying stretched the figure of a man. In those first few moments Hamel failed altogether to recognise Mr. Dunster. He was thin and white, and he seemed to have shrunken; his face, with its coarse growth of beard, seemed like the face of an old man. Yet the eyes were open, eyes dull and heavy as though with pain. So far no word had been spoken, but at that moment Mr. Fentolin broke the silence.

"My dear guest," he said, "I bring you our most sincere apologies. It has gone very much against the grain, I can assure you, to have neglected you for so long a time. It is entirely the fault of the very troublesome young man who occupies the other portion of this building. In the daytime his presence makes it exceedingly difficult for us to offer you those little attentions which you might naturally expect."

The man upon the bed neither moved nor changed his position in any way. Nor did he speak. All power of initiative seemed to have deserted him. He lay quite still, his eyes fixed upon Mr. Fentolin.

"There comes a time," the latter continued, "when every one of us is confronted with what might be described as the crisis of our lives. Yours has come, my guest, at precisely this moment. It is, if my watch tells me the truth, five and twenty minutes to four. It is the last day of April. The year you know. You have exactly one minute to decide whether you will live a short time longer, or whether you will on this last day of April, and before - say, a quarter to four, make that little journey the nature of which you and I have discussed more than once."

Still the man upon the bed made no movement nor any reply. Mr. Fentolin sighed and beckoned to Doctor Sarson.

"I am afraid," he whispered, "that that wonderful drug of yours, Doctor, has been even a little too far-reaching in its results. It has kept our friend so quiet that he has lost even the power of speech, perhaps even the desire to speak. A little restorative, I think - just a few drops."

Doctor Sarson nodded silently. He drew from his pocket a little phial and poured into a wine-glass which stood on a table by the side of the bed, half a dozen drops of some ruby-coloured liquid, to which he added a tablespoonful of water. Then he leaned once more over the bed and poured the contents of the glass between the lips of the semi-conscious man.

"Give him two minutes," he said calmly. "He will be

able to speak then."

Mr. Fentolin nodded and leaned back in his chair. He glanced around the room a little critically. There was a thick carpet upon the floor, a sofa piled with cushions in one corner, and several other articles of furniture. The walls, however, were uncovered and were stained with damp. A great pink fungus stood out within a few inches of the bed, a grim mixture of exquisite colouring and loathsome imperfections. The atmosphere was fetid. Meekins suddenly struck a match and lit some grains of powder in a saucer. A curious odour of incense stole through the place. Mr. Fentolin nodded appreciatively.

"That is better," he declared. "Really, the atmosphere here is positively unpleasant. I am ashamed to think that our guest has had to put up with it so long. And yet," he went on, "I think we must call it his own fault. I trust that he will no longer be obstinate."

The effect of the restorative began to show itself. The man on the bed moved restlessly. His eyes were no longer altogether expressionless. He was staring at Mr. Fentolin as one looks at some horrible vision. Mr. Fentolin smiled pleasantly.

"Now you are looking more like your old self, my dear Mr. Dunster," he remarked. "I don't think that I need repeat what I said when I first came, need I? You have just to utter that one word, and your little visit to us will be at an end."

The man looked around at all of them. He raised himself a little on his elbow. For the first time, Hamel, crouching above, recognised any likeness to Mr. John

P. Dunster.

"I'll see you in hell first!"

Mr. Fentolin's face momentarily darkened. He moved a little nearer to the man upon the bed.

"Dunster," he said, "I am in grim earnest. Never mind arguments. Never mind why I am on the other side. They are restless about you in America. Unless I can cable that word to-morrow morning, they'll communicate direct with The Hague, and I shall have had my trouble for nothing. It is not my custom to put up with failure. Therefore, let me tell you that no single one of my threats has been exaggerated. My patience has reached its breaking point. Give me that word, or before four o'clock strikes, you will find yourself in a new chamber, among the corpses of those misguided fishermen, mariners of ancient days, and a few others. It's only a matter of fifty yards out to the great sea pit below the Dagger Rocks - I've spoken to you about it before, haven't I? So surely as I speak to you of it at this moment."

Mr. Fentolin's speech came to an abrupt termination. A convulsive movement of Meekins', an expression of blank amazement on the part of Doctor Sarson, had suddenly checked the words upon his lips. He turned his head quickly in the direction towards which they had been gazing, towards which in fact, at that moment, Meekins, with a low cry, had made a fruitless spring. The ladder down which they had descended was slowly disappearing. Meekins, with a jump, missed the last rung by only a few inches. Some unseen hand was drawing it up. Already the last few feet were vanishing in mid-air. Mr. Fentolin sat quite quiet and still. He looked through the trap-door and saw Hamel.

"Most ingenious and, I must confess, most successful, my young friend!" he exclaimed pleasantly. "When you have made the ladder quite secure, perhaps you will be so good as to discuss this little matter with us?"

There was no immediate reply. The eyes of all four men were turned now upon that empty space through which the ladder had finally disappeared. Mr. Fentolin's fingers disappeared within the pocket of his coat. Something very bright was glistening in his hand when he withdrew it.

"Come and parley with us, Mr. Hamel," he begged. "You will not find us unreasonable."

Hamel's voice came back in reply, but Hamel himself kept well away from the opening.

"The conditions," he said, "are unpropitious. A little time for reflection will do you no harm."

The trap-doors were suddenly closed. Mr. Fentolin's face, as he looked up, became diabolic.

"We are trapped!" he muttered; "caught like rats in a hole!"

CHAPTER XXXIII

A gleam of day was in the sky as Hamel, with Mrs. Fentolin by his side, passed along the path which led from the Tower to St. David's Hall. Lights were still burning from its windows; the outline of the building itself was faintly defined against the sky. Behind him, across the sea, was that one straight line of grey merging into silver. The rain had ceased and the wind had dropped. On either side of them stretched the brimming creeks.

"Can we get into the house without waking any one?" he asked.

"Quite easily," she assured him. "The front door is never barred."

She walked by his side, swiftly and with surprising vigour. In the still, grey light, her face was more ghastly than ever, but there was a new firmness about her mouth, a new decision in her tone. They reached the Hall without further speech, and she led the way to a small door on the eastern side, through which they entered noiselessly and passed along a little passage out into the hall. A couple of lights were still burning. The place seemed full of shadows.

"What are you going to do now?" she whispered.

"I want to ring up London on the telephone," he replied. "I know that there is a detective either in the neighbourhood or on his way here, but I shall tell my friend that he had better come down himself."

She nodded.

"I am going to release Esther," she said. "She is locked in her room. The telephone is in the study. I will come down there to you."

She passed silently up the broad staircase. Hamel groped his way across the hail into the library. He turned on the small electric reading-lamp and drew up a chair to the side of the telephone. Even as he lifted the receiver to his ear, he looked around him half apprehensively. It seemed as though every moment he would hear the click of Mr. Fentolin's chair.

He got the exchange at Norwich without difficulty, and a few minutes later a sleepy reply came from the number he had rung up in London. It was Kinsley's servant who answered.

"I want to speak to Mr. Kinsley at once upon most important business," Hamel announced.

"Very sorry, sir," the man repelled. "Mr. Kinsley left town last night for the country."

"Where has he gone?" Hamel demanded quickly. "You can tell me. You know who I am; I am Mr. Hamel."

"Into Norfolk somewhere, sir. He went with several other gentlemen."

"Is that Bullen?" Hamel asked.

The man admitted the fact.

"Can you tell me if any of the people with whom Mr. Kinsley left London were connected with the police?" he inquired.

The man hesitated.

"I believe so, sir," he admitted. "The gentlemen started in a motor-car and were going to drive all night."

Hamel laid down the receiver. At any rate, he would not be left long with this responsibility upon him. He walked out into the hall. The house was still wrapped in deep silence. Then, from somewhere above him, coming down the stairs, he heard the rustle of a woman's gown. He looked up, and saw Miss Price, fully dressed, coming slowly towards him. She held up her finger and led the way back into the library. She was dressed as neatly as ever, but there was a queer light in her eyes.

"I have seen Mrs. Seymour Fentolin," she said. "She tells me that you have left Mr. Fentolin and the others in the subterranean room of the Tower."

Hamel nodded.

"They have Dunster down there," he told her. "I followed them in; it seemed the best thing to do. I have a friend from London who is on his way down here now with some detective officers, to enquire into the matter of Dunster's disappearance."

"Are you going to leave them where they are until these people arrive?" she asked.

"I think so," he replied, after a moment's hesitation. "I don't seem to have had time to consider even what to do. The opportunity came, and I embraced it. There they are, and they won't dare to do any further harm to Dunster now. Mrs. Fentolin was down in my room, and I thought it best to bring her back first before I even parleyed with them again."

"You must be careful," she advised slowly. "The man Dunster has been drugged, he has lost some of his will; he may have lost some of his mental balance. Mr. Fentolin is clever. He will find a dozen ways to wriggle out of any charge that can be brought against him. You know what he has really done?"

"I can guess."

"He has kept back a document signed by the twelve men in America who control the whole of Wall Street, who control practically the money markets of the world. That document is a warning to Germany that they will have no war against England. Owing to Mr. Fentolin, it has not been delivered, and the Conference is sitting now. War may be declared at any moment."

"But as a matter of common sense," Hamel asked, "why does Mr. Fentolin desire war?"

"You do not understand Mr. Fentolin," she told him quietly. "He is not like other men. There are some who live almost entirely for the sake of making others happy, who find joy in seeing people content and satisfied. Mr. Fentolin is the reverse of this. He has but

E. Phillips Oppenheim

one craving in life: to see pain in others. To see a human being suffer is to him a debauch of happiness. A war which laid this country waste would fill him with a delight which you could never understand. There are no normal human beings like this. It is a disease in the man, a disease which came upon him after his accident."

"Yet you have all been his slaves," Hamel said curiously.

"We have all been his slaves," she admitted, "for different reasons. Before his accident came, Mr. Fentolin was my master and the only man in the world for me. After his accident, I think my feelings for him, if anything, grew stronger. I became his slave. I sold my conscience, my self-respect, everything in life worth having, to bring a smile to his lips, to help him through a single moment of his misery. And just lately the reaction has come. He has played with me just as he would sit and pull the legs out of a spider to watch its agony. I have been one of his favourite amusements. And even now, if he came into this room I think that I should be helpless. I should probably fall at his feet and pray for forgiveness."

Hamel looked at her wonderingly.

"I have come down to warn you," she went on. "It is possible that this is the beginning of the end, that his wonderful fortune will desert him, that his star has gone down. But remember that he has the brains and courage of genius. You think that you have him in a trap. Don't be surprised, when you go back, to find that he has turned the tables upon you."

"Impossible!" Hamel declared. "I looked all round the place. There isn't a window or opening anywhere. The trap-door is in the middle of the ceiling and it is fifteen feet from the floor. It shuts with a spring."

"It may be as you say," she observed. "It may be that he is safe. Remember, though, if you go near him, that he is desperate."

"Do you know where Miss Fentolin is?" he interrupted.

"She is with her mother," the woman replied, impatiently. "She is coming down. Tell me, what are you going to do with Mr. Fentolin? Nothing else matters."

"I have a friend," Hamel answered, "who will see to that."

"If you are relying upon the law," she said, "I think you will find that the law cannot touch him. Mr. Dunster was brought to the house in a perfectly natural manner. He was certainly injured, and injured in a railway accident. Doctor Sarson is a fully qualified surgeon, and he will declare that Mr. Dunster was unfit to travel. If necessary, they will have destroyed the man's intelligence. If you think that you have him broken, let me warn you that you may be disappointed. Let me, if I may, give you one word of advice."

"Please do," Hamel begged.

She looked at him coldly. Her tone was still free from any sort of emotion.

"You have taken up some sort of position here," she

continued, "as a friend of Mrs. Seymour Fentolin, a friend of the family. Don't let them come back under the yoke. You know the secret of their bondage?"

"I know it," he admitted.

"They have been his slaves because their absolute obedience to his will was one of the conditions of his secrecy. He has drawn the cords too tight. Better let the truth be known, if needs be, than have their three lives broken. Don't let them go back under his governance. For me, I cannot tell. If he comes back, as he will come back, I may become his slave again, but let them break away. Listen - that is Mrs. Fentolin."

She left him. Hamel followed her out into the hail. Esther and her mother were already at the foot of the stairs. He drew them into the study. Esther gave him her hands, but she was trembling in every limb.

"I am terrified!" she whispered. "Every moment I think I can hear the click of that awful carriage. He will come back; I am sure he will come back!"

"He may," Hamel answered sturdily, "but never to make you people his slaves again. You have done enough. You have earned your freedom."

"I agree," Mrs. Fentolin said firmly. "We have gone on from sacrifice to sacrifice, until it has become a habit with us to consider him the master of our bodies and our souls. To-day, Esther, we have reached the breaking point. Not even for the sake of that message from the other side of the grave, not even to preserve his honour and his memory, can we do more."

Hamel held up his finger. He opened the French windows, and they followed him out on to the terrace. The grey dawn had broken now over the sea. There were gleams of fitful sunshine on the marshes. Some distance away a large motor-car was coming rapidly along the road.

E. Phillips Oppenheim

CHAPTER XXXIV

Mr. John P. Dunster, lying flat upon his little bed, watched with dilated eyes the disappearance of the ladder. Then he laughed. It was a queer sound - broken, spasmodic, devoid of any of the ordinary elements of humor - and yet it was a laugh. Mr. Fentolin turned his head towards his prisoner and nodded thoughtfully.

"What a constitution, my friend!" he exclaimed, without any trace of disturbance in his voice. "And what a sense of humour! Strange that a trifling circumstance like this should affect it. Meekins, burn some more of the powder. The atmosphere down here may be salubrious, but I am unaccustomed to it."

"Perhaps," Mr. Dunster said in a hollow tone, "you will have some opportunity now of discovering with me what it is like."

"That, too, is just possible," Mr. Fentolin admitted, blowing out a little volume of smoke from a cigarette which he had just lit, "but one never knows. We have friends, and our position, although, I must admit, a little ridiculous, is easily remedied. But how that mischief-making Mr. Hamel could have found his way into the boat-house does, I must confess, perplex me."

"He must have been hanging around and followed us in when we came," Meekins muttered. "Somehow, I fancied I felt some one near."

"Our young friend," Mr. Fentolin continued, "has, without doubt, an obvious turn of mind. He will send for his acquaintance in the Foreign Office; they will haul out Mr. Dunster here, and he will have a belated opportunity of delivering his message at The Hague."

"You aren't going to murder me first, then?" Mr. Dunster grunted.

Mr. Fentolin smiled at him benignly.

"My dear and valued guest," he protested, "why so forbidding an idea? Let me assure you from the bottom of my heart that any bodily harm to you is the most unlikely thing in the world. You see, though you might not think it," he went on, "I love life. That is why I keep a doctor always by my side. That is why I insist upon his making a complete study of my constitution and treating me in every respect as though I were indeed an invalid. I am really only fifty-nine years old. It is my intention to live until I am eighty-nine. An offence against the law of the nature you indicate might interfere materially with my intentions."

Mr. Dunster struggled for a moment for breath.

"Look here," he said, "that's all right, but do you suppose you won't be punished for what you've done to me? You laid a deliberate plot to bring me to St. David's Hall; you've kept me locked up, dosed me with drugs, brought me down here at the dead of night, kept me a prisoner in a dungeon. Do you think you can do

E. Phillips Oppenheim

that for nothing? Do you think you won't have to suffer for it?"

Mr. Fentolin smiled.

"My dear Mr. Dunster," he reminded him, "you were in a railway accident, you know; there is no possible doubt about that. And the wound in your head is still there, in a very dangerous place. Men who have been in railway accidents, and who have a gaping wound very close to their brain, are subject to delusions. I have simply done my best to play the Good Samaritan. Your clothes and papers are all untouched. If my eminent physician had pronounced you ready to travel a week ago, you would certainly have been allowed to depart a week ago. Any interference in your movements has been entirely in the interests of your health."

Mr. Dunster tried to sit up but found himself unable.

"So you think they won't believe my story, eh?" he muttered. "Well, we shall see."

Mr. Fentolin thoughtfully contemplated the burning end of his cigarette for a moment.

"If I believed," he said, "that there was any chance of your statements being accepted, I am afraid I should be compelled, in all our interests, to ask Doctor Sarson to pursue just a step further that experiment into the anatomy of your brain with which he has already trifled."

Mr. Dunster's face was suddenly ghastly. His reserve of strength seemed to ebb away. The memory of some horrible moment seemed to hold him in its clutches.

"For God's sake, leave me alone!" he moaned. "Let me get away, that's all; let me crawl away!"

"Ah!" Mr. Fentolin murmured. "That sounds much more reasonable. When you talk like that, my friend. I feel indeed that there is hope for you. Let us abandon this subject for the present. Have you solved the puzzle yet?" he asked Meekins.

Meekins was standing below the closed trap-door. He had already dragged up a wooden case underneath and was piling it with various articles of furniture.

"Not yet, sir," he replied. "When I have made this steadier, I am just going to see what pressure I can bring to bear on the trap-door."

"I heard the bolts go," Doctor Sarson remarked uneasily.

"In that case," Mr. Fentolin declared, "it will indeed be an interesting test of our friend Meekins' boasted strength. Meekins holds his place - a very desirable place, too - chiefly for two reasons: first his discretion and secondly his muscles. He has never before had a real opportunity of testing the latter. We shall see."

Doctor Sarson came slowly and gravely to the bedside. He looked down upon his patient. Mr. Dunster shivered.

"I am not sure, sir," he said very softly, "that Mr. Dunster, in his present state of mind, is a very safe person to be allowed his freedom. It is true that we have kept him here for his own sake, because of his fits of mental wandering. Our statements, however, may be doubted. An apparent return to sanity on his part may lend colour to his accusations, especially if permanent. Perhaps it would be as well to pursue that investigation a shade further. A touch more to the left and I do not think that Mr. Dunster will remember much in this world likely to affect us."

Mr. Dunster's face was like marble. There were beads of perspiration upon his forehead, his eyes were filled with reminiscent horror. Mr. Fentolin bent over him with genuine interest.

"What a picture he would make!" he murmured. "What a drama! Do you know, I am half inclined to agree with you, Sarson. The only trouble is that you have not your instruments here."

"I could improvise something that would do the trick," the doctor said thoughtfully. "It really isn't a complicated affair. It seems to me that his story may gain credence from the very fact of our being discovered in this extraordinary place. To have moved him here was a mistake, sir."

"Perhaps so," Mr. Fentolin admitted, with a sigh. "It was our young friend Mr. Hamel who was responsible for it. I fancied him arriving with a search warrant at any moment. We will bear in mind your suggestion for a few minutes. Let us watch Meekins. This promises to be interesting."

By dint of piling together all the furniture in the place, the man was now able to reach the trap-door. He pressed upon it vigorously without even bending the wood. Mr. Fentolin smiled pleasantly.

"Meekins," he said, "look at me."

The man turned and faced his master. His aspect of dogged civility had never been more apparent.

"Now listen," Mr. Fentolin went on. "I want to remind you of certain things, Meekins. We are among friends here - no secrecy, you understand, or anything of that sort. You need not be afraid! You know how you came to me? You remember that little affair of Anna Jayes in Hartlepool?"

The face of the man was filled with terror. He began to tremble where he stood. Mr. Fentolin played for a moment with his collar, as though he found it tight.

"Such a chance it was, my dear Meekins," Mr. Fentolin continued cheerfully, "which brought me that little scrap of knowledge concerning you. It has bought me through all these years a good deal of faithful service. I am not ungrateful, believe me. I intend to retain you for my body-servant and to keep my lips sealed, for a great many years to come. Now remember what I have said. When we leave this place, that little episode will steal back into a far corner of my mind. I shall, in short, forget it. If we are caught here and inconvenience follows, well, I cannot say. Do your best, Meekins. Do a little better than your best. You have the reputation of being a strong man. Let us see you justify it."

The man took a long breath and returned to his task. His shoulders and arms were upon the door. He began to strain. He grew red in the face; the veins across his forehead stood out, blue, like tightly-drawn string. His complexion became purple. Through his open mouth his breath came in short pants. With every muscle of his body and neck he strained and strained. The woodwork gave a little, but it never even cracked. With a sob he suddenly almost collapsed. Mr. Fentolin looked at him, frowning.

"Very good - very good, Meekins," he said, "but not quite good enough. You are a trifle out of practice, perhaps. Take your breath, take time. Remember that you have another chance. I am not angry with you, Meekins. I know there are many enterprises upon which one does not succeed the first time. Get your breath; there is no hurry. Next time you try, see that you succeed. It is very important, Meekins, for you as well as for us, that you succeed."

The man turned doggedly back to his task. The eyes of the three men watched him - Mr. Dunster on the bed; Doctor Sarson, pale and gloomy, with something of fear in his dark eyes; and Mr. Fentolin himself, whose expression seemed to be one of purely benevolent and encouraging interest. Once more the face of the man became almost unrecognisable. There was a great crack, the trap-door had shifted. Meekins, with a little cry, reeled and sank backwards. Mr. Fentolin clapped his hands lightly.

"Really, Meekins," he declared, "I do not know when I have enjoyed any performance so much. I feel as if I were back in the days of the Roman gladiators. I can see that you mean to succeed. You will succeed. You do not mean to end your days amid objectionable surroundings."

With the air of a man temporarily mad, Meekins went back to his task. He was sobbing to himself now. His clothes had burst away from him. Suddenly there was a crash, the hinges of the trap-door had parted. With the blood streaming from a wound in his forehead, Meekins staggered back to his feet. Mr. Fentolin nodded.

"Excellent!" he pronounced. "Really excellent. With a little assistance from our friend Meekins, you, I am sure, Sarson, will now be able to climb up and let down the steps."

Doctor Sarson stood by Mr. Fentolin's chair, and together they looked up through the fragments of the trap-door. Meekins was still breathing heavily. Suddenly they heard the sound of a sharp report, as of a door above being slammed.

"Some one was in the boat-house when I broke the trap-door," Meekins muttered. "I heard them moving about."

Mr. Fentolin frowned.

"Then let us hurry," he said. "Sarson, what about your patient?"

Mr. Dunster was lying upon his side, watching them. The doctor went over to the bedside and felt his pulse and head.

"He will do for twelve hours," he pronounced. "If you think that other little operation -"

He broke off and looked at Mr. Fentolin meaningly.

The man on the bed shrank back, his eyes lit with horror. Mr. Fentolin smiled pleasantly.

"I fear," he said, "that we must not stay for that just now. A little later on, perhaps, if it becomes necessary. Let us first attend to the business on hand."

Meekins once more clambered on to the little heap of furniture. The doctor stood by his side for a moment. Then, with an effort, he was hoisted up until he could catch hold of the floor of the outhouse. Meekins gave one push, and he disappeared.

"Any one up there?" Mr. Fentolin enquired, a shade of anxiety in his tone.

"No one," the doctor reported.

"Has anything been disturbed?"

Doctor Sarson was some little time before he replied.

"Yes," he said, "some one seems to have been rummaging about."

"Send down the steps quickly," Mr. Fentolin ordered. "I am beginning to find the atmosphere here unpleasant."

There was a brief silence. Then they heard the sound of the ladder being dragged across the floor, and a moment or two later it was carefully lowered and placed in position. Mr. Fentolin passed the rope through the front of his carriage and was drawn up. From his bed Mr. Dunster watched them go. It was hard to tell whether he was relieved or disappointed.

"Who has been in here?" Mr. Fentolin demanded, as he looked around the place.

There was no reply. A grey twilight was struggling now through the high, dust-covered windows. Meekins, who had gone on towards the door, suddenly called out:

"Some one has taken away the key! The door is locked on the other side!"

Mr. Fentolin's frown was malign even for him.

"Our dear friend, Mr. Hamel, I suppose," he muttered. "Another little debt we shall owe him! Try the other door."

Meekins moved towards the partition. Suddenly he paused. Mr. Fentolin's hand was outstretched; he, too, was listening. Above the low thunder of the sea came another sound, a sound which at that moment they none of them probably understood. There was the steady crashing of feet upon the pebbles, a low murmur of voices. Mr. Fentolin for the first time showed symptoms of fear.

"Try the other door quickly," he directed.

Meekins came back, shaking his head. Outside, the noise seemed to be increasing. The door was suddenly thrown open. Hannah Cox stood outside in her plain black dress, her hair wind-tossed, her eyes aflame. She held the key in her fingers, and she looked in upon them. Her lips seemed to move, but she said nothing.

"My good woman," Mr. Fentolin exclaimed, frowning,

"are you the person who removed that key?"

She laid her hand upon his chair. She took no notice of the other two.

"Come," she said, "there is something here I want you to listen to. Come!"

CHAPTER XXXV

Mr. Fentolin, arrived outside on the stone front of the boat-house, pointed the wheel of his chair towards the Hall. Hannah Cox, who kept by his side, however, drew it gently towards the beach.

"Down here," she directed softly. "Bring your chair down the plank-way, close to the water's edge."

"My good woman," Mr. Fentolin exclaimed furiously, "I am not in the humour for this sort of thing! Lock up, Sarson, at once; I am in a hurry to get back."

"But you will come just this little way," she continued, speaking without any change of tone. "You see, the others are waiting, too. I have been down to the village and fetched them up."

Mr. Fentolin followed her outstretched finger and gave a sudden start. Standing at the edge of the sea were a dozen or twenty fishermen. They were all muttering together and looking at the top of the boat-house. As he realised the direction of their gaze, Mr. Fentolin's face underwent a strange transformation. He seemed to shrink in his chair. He was ghastly pale even to the lips. Slowly he turned his head. From a place in the roof of the boat-house a tall support had appeared. On the top was a swinging globe.

E. Phillips Oppenheim

"What have you to do with that?" he asked in a low tone.

"I found it," she answered. "I felt that it was there. I have brought them up with me to see it. I think that they want to ask you some questions. But first, come and listen."

Mr. Fentolin shook her off. He looked around for Meekins.

"Meekins, stand by my chair," he ordered sharply. "Turn round; I wish to go to the Hall. Drive this woman away."

Meekins came hurrying up, but almost at the same moment half a dozen of the brown jerseyed fishermen detached themselves from the others. They formed a little bodyguard around the bath-chair.

"What is the meaning of this?" Mr. Fentolin demanded, his voice shrill with anger. "Didn't you hear what I said? This woman annoys me. Send her away."

Not one of the fishermen answered a word or made the slightest movement to obey him. One of them, a grey-bearded veteran, drew the chair a little further down the planked way across the pebbles. Hannah Cox kept close to its side. They came to a standstill only a few yards from where the waves were breaking. She lifted her hand.

"Listen!" she cried. "Listen!"

Mr. Fentolin turned helplessly around. The little group of fishermen had closed in upon Sarson and Meekins.

The woman's hand was upon his shoulder; she pointed seaward to where a hissing line of white foam marked the spot where the topmost of the rocks were visible.

"You wondered why I have spent so much of my time out here," she said quietly. "Now you will know. If you listen as I am listening, as I have listened for so many weary hours, so many weary years, you will hear them calling to me, David and John and Stephen. 'The light!' Do you hear what they are crying? 'The light! Fentolin's light!' Look!"

She forced him to look once more at the top of the boat-house.

"They were right!" she proclaimed, her voice gaining in strength and intensity. "They were neither drunk nor reckless. They steered as straight as human hand could guide a tiller, for Fentolin's light! And there they are, calling and calling at the bottom of the sea - my three boys and my man. Do you know for whom they call?"

Mr. Fentolin shrank back in his chair.

"Take this woman away!" he ordered the fishermen. "Do you hear? Take her away; she is mad!"

They looked towards him, but not one of them moved. Mr. Fentolin raised his whistle to his lips, and blew it.

"Meekins!" he cried. "Where are you, Meekins?"

He turned his head and saw at once that Meekins was powerless. Five or six of the fishermen had gathered around him. There were at least thirty of them about, sinewy, powerful men. The only person who moved towards Mr. Fentolin's carriage was Jacob, the coast guardsman.

"Mr. Fentolin, sir," he said, "the lads have got your bully safe. It's a year and more that Hannah Cox has been about the village with some story about two lights on a stormy night. It's true what she says - that her man and boys lie drowned. There's William Green, besides, and a nephew of my own - John Kallender. And Philip Green - he was saved. He swore by all that was holy that he steered straight for the light when his boat struck, and that as he swam for shore, five minutes later, he saw the light reappear in another place. It's a strange story. What have you to say, sir, about that?"

He pointed straight to the wire-encircled globe which towered on its slender support above the boat-house. Mr. Fentolin looked at it and looked back at the coast guardsman. The brain of a Machiavelli could scarcely have invented a plausible reply.

"The light was never lit there," he said. "It was simply to help me in some electrical experiments."

Then, for the first time in their lives, those who were looking on saw Mr. Fentolin apart from his carriage. Without any haste but with amazing strength, Hannah Cox leaned over, and, with her arms around his middle, lifted him sheer up into the air. She carried him, clasped in her arms, a weird, struggling object, to the clumsy boat that lay always at the top of the beach. She dropped him into the bottom, took her seat, and unshipped the oars. For one moment the coast guardsman hesitated; then he obeyed her look. He gave the boat a push which sent it grinding down the pebbles into the sea. The woman began to work at the oars. Every now and then she looked over her shoulder at that thin line of white surf which they were all the time approaching.

"What are you doing, woman?" Mr. Fentolin demanded hoarsely. "Listen! It was an accident that your people were drowned. I'll give you an annuity. I'll make you rich for life - rich! Do you understand what that means?"

"Aye!" she answered, looking down upon him as he lay doubled up at the bottom of the boat. "I know what it means to be rich - better than you, maybe. Not to let the gold and silver pieces fall through your fingers, or to live in a great house and be waited upon by servants who desert you in the hour of need. That isn't being rich. It's rich to feel the touch of the one you love, to see the faces around of those you've given birth to, to move on through the days and nights towards the end, with them around; not to know the chill loneliness of an empty life. I am a poor woman, Mr. Fentolin, and it's your hand that made me so, and not all the miracles that the Bible ever told of can make me rich again."

"You are a fool!" he shrieked. "You can buy forgetfulness! The memory of everything passes."

"I may be a fool," she retorted grimly, "and you the wise man; but this day we'll both know the truth."

There was a little murmur from the shore, where the fishermen stood in a long line.

"Bring him back, missus," Jacob called out. "You've scared him enough. Bring him back. We'll leave him to the law."

E. Phillips Oppenheim

They were close to the line of surf now; they had passed it, indeed, a little on the left, and the boat was drifting. She stood up, straight and stern, and her face, as she looked towards the land, was lit with the fire of the prophetess.

"Aye," she cried, "we'll leave him to the law - to the law of God!"

Then they saw her stoop down, and once more with that almost superhuman strength which seemed to belong to her for those few moments, she lifted the strange object who lay cowering there, high above her head. From the shore they realised what was going to happen, and a great shout arose. She stood on the side of the boat and jumped, holding her burden tightly in her arms. So they went down and disappeared.

Half a dozen of the younger fishermen were in the water even before the grim spectacle was ended; another ran for a boat that was moored a little way down the beach. But from the first the search was useless. Only Jacob, who was a person afflicted with many superstitions, wiped the sweat from his forehead as he leaned over the bow of his boat and looked down into that fathomless space.

"I heard her singing, her or her wraith," he swore afterwards. "I'll never forget the moment I looked down and down, and the water seemed to grow clearer, and I saw her walking there at the bottom among the rocks, with him over her back, singing as she went, looking everywhere for George and the boys!"

But if indeed his eyes were touched with fire at that

moment, no one else in the world saw anything more of Miles Fentolin.

E. Phillips Oppenheim

CHAPTER XXXVI

Mr. John P. Dunster removed the cigar from his teeth and gazed at the long white ash with the air of a connoisseur. He was stretched in a long chair, high up in the terraced gardens behind the Hall. At his feet were golden mats of yellow crocuses; long borders of hyacinths - pink and purple; beds of violets; a great lilac tree, with patches of blossom here and there forcing their way into a sunlit world. The sea was blue; the sheltered air where they sat was warm and perfumed. Mr. Dunster, who was occupying the position of a favoured guest, was feeling very much at home.

"There is one thing," he remarked meditatively, "which I can't help thinking about you Britishers. You may deserve it or you may not, but you do have the most almighty luck."

"Sheer envy," Hamel murmured. "We escape from our tight corners by forethought."

"Not on your life, sir," Mr. Dunster declared vigorously. "A year or less ago you got a North Sea scare, and on the strength of a merely honourable understanding with your neighbour, you risk your country's very existence for the sake of adding half a dozen battleships to your North Sea Squadron. The day the last of those battleships passed through the Straits of Gibraltar, this little Conference was plotted. I tell you they meant to make history there.

"There was enough for everybody - India for Russia, a time-honoured dream, but why not? Alsace-Lorraine and perhaps Egypt, for France; Australia for Japan; China and South Africa for Germany. Why not? You may laugh at it on paper but I say again - why not?"

"It didn't quite come off, sir," Gerald observed.

"It didn't," Mr. Dunster admitted, "partly owing to you. There were only two things needed: France to consider her own big interests and to ignore an entente from which she gains nothing that was not assured to her under the new agreement, and the money. Strange," Mr. Dunster continued, "how people forget that factor, and yet the man who was responsible for The Hague Conference knew it. We in the States are right outside all these little jealousies and wrangles that bring Europe, every now and then, right up to the gates of war, but I'm hanged if there is one of you dare pass through those gates without a hand on our money markets. It's a new word in history, that little document, news of which Mr. Gerald here took to The Hague, the word of the money kings of the world. There is something that almost nips your breath in the idea that a dozen men, descended from the Lord knows whom, stopped a war which would have altered the whole face of history."

"There was never any proof," Hamel remarked, "that France would not have remained staunch to us."

" Very likely not," Mr. Dunster agreed, "but, on the

E. Phillips Oppenheim

other hand, your country had never the right to put such a burden upon her honour. Remember that side by side with those other considerations, a great statesman's first duty is to the people over whom he watches, not to study the interests of other lands. However, it's finished. The Hague Conference is broken up. The official organs of the world allude to it, if at all, as an unimportant gathering called together to discuss certain frontier questions with which England had nothing to do. But the memory of it will live. A good cold douche for you people, I should say, and I hope you'll take warning by it. Whatever the attitude of America as a nation may be to these matters, the American people don't want to see the old country in trouble. Gee whiz! What's that?"

There was a little cry from all of them. Only Hamel stood without sign of surprise, gazing downward with grim, set face. A dull roar, like the booming of a gun, flashes of fire, and a column of smoke - and all that was left of St. David's Tower was one tottering wall and a scattered mass of masonry.

"I had an idea," Hamel said quietly, "that St. David's Tower was going to spoil the landscape for a good many years. My property, you know, and there's the end of it. I am sick of seeing people for the last few days come down and take photographs of it for every little rag that goes to press."

Mr. Dunster pointed out to the line of surf beyond. "If only some hand," he remarked, "could plant dynamite below that streak of white, so that the sea could disgorge its dead! They tell me there's a Spanish galleon there, and a Dutch warship, besides a score or more of fishing-boats."

Mrs. Fentolin shivered a little. She drew her cloak around her. Gerald, who had been watching her, sprang to his feet.

"Come," he exclaimed, "we chose the gardens for our last afternoon here, to be out of the way of these places! We'll go round the hill."

Mrs. Fentolin shook her head once more. Her face had recovered its serenity. She looked downward gravely but with no sign of fear.

"There is nothing to terrify us there, Gerald," she declared. "The sea has gathered, and the sea will hold its own."

Hamel held out his hand to Esther.

"I have destroyed the only house in the world which I possess," he said. "Come and look for violets with me in the spinney, and let us talk of the houses we are going to build, and the dreams we shall dream in them."

Choose from Thousands of 1stWorldLibrary Classics By

Adolphus WilliamWard
Aesop
Agatha Christie
Alexander Aaronsohn
Alexander Kielland
Alexandre Dumas
Alfred Gatty
Alfred Ollivant
Alice Duer Miller
Alice Turner Curtis
Alice Dunbar
Ambrose Bierce
Amelia E. Barr
Andrew Lang
Andrew McFarland Davis
Anna Sewell
Annie Besant
Annie Hamilton Donnell
Annie Payson Call
Anton Chekhov
Arnold Bennett
Arthur Conan Doyle
Arthur Ransome
Atticus
B. M. Bower
Basil King
Bayard Taylor
Ben Macomber
Booth Tarkington
Bram Stoker
C. Collodi
C. E. Orr
C. M. Ingleby
Carolyn Wells
Catherine Parr Traill
Charles A. Eastman
Charles Dickens
Charles Dudley Warner
Charles Farrar Browne
Charles Ives
Charles Kingsley
Charles Lathrop Pack
Charles Whibley
Charles Willing Beale
Charlotte M. Braeme
Charlotte M.Yonge
Clair W. Hayes
Clarence Day Jr.
Clarence E. Mulford

Clemence Housman
Confucius
Cornelis DeWitt Wilcox
Cyril Burleigh
D. H. Lawrence
Daniel Defoe
David Garnett
Don Carlos Janes
Donald Keyhole
Dorothy Kilner
Dougan Clark
E. Nesbit
E.P.Roe
E. Phillips Oppenheim
Edgar Allan Poe
Edgar Rice Burroughs
Edith Wharton
Edward J. O'Biren
John Cournos
Edwin L. Arnold
Eleanor Atkins
Elizabeth Cleghorn
Gaskell
Elizabeth Von Arnim
Ellem Key
Emily Dickinson
Erasmus W. Jones
Ernie Howard Pie
Ethel Turner
Ethel Watts Mumford
Eugenie Foa
Eugene Wood
Evelyn Everett-Green
Everard Cotes
F. J. Cross
Federick Austin Ogg
Ferdinand Ossendowski
Francis Bacon
Francis Darwin
Frances Hodgson Burnett
Frank Gee Patchin
Frank Harris
Frank Jewett Mather
Frank L. Packard
Frederick Trevor Hill
Frederick Winslow Taylor
Friedrich Kerst
Friedrich Nietzsche
Fyodor Dostoyevsky

Gabrielle E. Jackson
Garrett P. Serviss
Gaston Leroux
George Ade
Geroge Bernard Shaw
George Ebers
George Eliot
George MacDonald
George Orwell
George Tucker
George W. Cable
George Wharton James
Gertrude Atherton
Grace E. King
Grant Allen
Guillermo A. Sherwell
Gulielma Zollinger
Gustav Flaubert
H. A. Cody
H. B. Irving
H. G. Wells
H. H. Munro
H. Irving Hancock
H. Rider Haggard
H. W. C. Davis
Hamilton Wright Mabie
Hans Christian Andersen
Harold Avery
Harold McGrath
Harriet Beecher Stowe
Harry Houidini
Helent Hunt Jackson
Helen Nicolay
Hendy David Thoreau
Henrik Ibsen
Henry Adams
Henry Ford
Henry Frost
Henry James
Henry Jones Ford
Henry Seton Merriman
Henry Wadsworth
Longfellow
Henry W Longfellow
Herbert A. Giles
Herbert N. Casson
Herman Hesse
Homer
Honore De Balzac

Horace Walpole
Horatio Alger, Jr.
Howard Pyle
Howard R. Garis
Hugh Lofting
Hugh Walpole
Humphry Ward
Ian Maclaren
Israel Abrahams
J.G.Austin
J. Henri Fabre
J. M. Barrie
J. Macdonald Oxley
J. S. Knowles
J. Storer Clouston
Jack London
Jacob Abbott
James Allen
James Lane Allen
James Andrews
James Baldwin
James DeMille
James Joyce
James Oliver Curwood
James Oppenheim
James Otis
Jane Austen
Jens Peter Jacobsen
Jerome K. Jerome
John Burroughs
John F. Kennedy
John Gay
John Glasworthy
John Habberton
John Joy Bell
John Milton
John Philip Sousa
Jonathan Swift
Joseph Carey
Joseph Conrad
Joseph Jacobs
Julian Hawthrone
Julies Vernes
Justin Huntly McCarthy
Kakuzo Okakura
Kenneth Grahame
Kate Langley Bosher
L. A. Abbot
L. T. Meade
L. Frank Baum
Laura Lee Hope

Laurence Housman
Leo Tolstoy
Leonid Andreyev
Lewis Carroll
Lilian Bell
Lloyd Osbourne
Louis Tracy
Louisa May Alcott
Lucy Fitch Perkins
Lucy Maud Montgomery
Lydia Miller Middleton
Lyndon Orr
M. H. Adams
Margaret E. Sangster
Margaret Vandercook
Maria Edgeworth
Maria Thompson Daviess
Mariano Azuela
Marion Polk Angellotti
Mark Overton
Mark Twain
Mary Austin
Mary Cole
Mary Rowlandson
Mary Wollstonecraft
Shelley
Max Beerbohm
Myra Kelly
Nathaniel Hawthrone
O. F. Walton
Oscar Wilde
Owen Johnson
P.G.Wodehouse
Paul and Mable Thorn
Paul G. Tomlinson
Paul Severing
Peter B. Kyne
Plato
R. Derby Holmes
R. L. Stevenson
Rabindranath Tagore
Rahul Alvares
Ralph Waldo Emmerson
Rene Descartes
Rex E. Beach
Richard Harding Davis
Richard Jefferies
Robert Barr
Robert Frost
Robert Gordon Anderson
Robert L. Drake

Robert Lansing
Robert Michael Ballantyne
Robert W. Chambers
Rosa Nouchette Carey
Ross Kay
Rudyard Kipling
Samuel B. Allison
Samuel Hopkins Adams
Sarah Bernhardt
Selma Lagerlof
Sherwood Anderson
Sigmund Freud
Standish O'Grady
Stanley Weyman
Stella Benson
Stephen Crane
Stewart Edward White
Stijn Streuvels
Swami Abhedananda
Swami Parmananda
T. S. Ackland
The Princess Der Ling
Thomas A. Janvier
Thomas A Kempis
Thomas Anderton
Thomas Bailey Aldrich
Thomas Bulfinch
Thomas De Quincey
Thomas H. Huxley
Thomas Hardy
Thomas More
Thornton W. Burgess
U. S. Grant
Valentine Williams
Victor Appleton
Virginia Woolf
Walter Scott
Washington Irving
Wilbur Lawton
Wilkie Collins
Willa Cather
Willard F. Baker
William Makepeace
Thackeray
William W. Walter
Winston Churchill
Yei Theodora Ozaki
Young E. Allison
Zane Grey